# STRANGE
# VACATION

WUNDERFOOL

W P

PRESS

**Also by Brad Whittington**

**Fred Novels**

Welcome to Fred

Living with Fred

Postcards from Fred

Escape from Fred


**Jake and Berf Novels**

Open Season


Muffin Man

Endless Vacation


**Non-fiction**

What Would Jesus Drink?
What the Bible Really Says About Alcohol

# Brad Whittington

# STRANGE VACATION

## A JAKE AND BERF STORY

ISBN: 978-1-937274-24-5
Published by Wunderfool Press
Austin, Texas

Dewey Decimal Classification: F
Subject Heading: Fiction / Humorous

# What they're saying about Whittington

Whittington spins an enjoyable literary story
and is definitely a novelist to watch.
–Publisher's Weekly

Brad Whittington is an artist with a pen.
–Ethan C. McDonald, DancingWord.com

It is always a joy to find a new writer who knows
what he's doing. –Rick Lewis, Logos Bookstore

Whittington is a welcome new voice in the world of
fiction.
–Cindy Crosby, author of By Willoway Brook

Who can resist a story of someone else's alienated
youth if that someone else is as talented as Brad
Whittington?
–JT Conroe, author of The Blue Hotel

The pacing, humor, honesty, and believable
characters made me turn page after page in rapid
succession until there were none.
–T Leigh

Brad Whittington paints some of the best word
pictures I've seen.
–Cammi Ellis

# Cast of Characters

In Order of Appearance

BERF WIGGINS Bon vivant, man-with-a-Code
KATERINA Beach cabin owner
SPIDER World-weary extreme athlete
JAKE OAKLEY Berf's best fried, engaged to
CHINA WIGGINS Berf's sister
DONNER Sailboat salesman
BLAKE Overripe frat buddy
ROGER WIGGINS Berf's father
MARGE WIGGINS Berf's mother
LONNIE'S BOY Aspiring teenaged YouTuber
HIGGINS Employee of The Lawn Arranger
ESTHER Comptroller for The Lawn Arranger
DUNCAN Bartender par excellence
FRANK SUMMERS Ugly American
CATHERINE Long-suffering flight attendant
DEREK RUNYON Buzz-cut body builder
KATE COLLINS Employee of Strange Vacations
NOAH Contender for bartender par excellence
MICHAEL STRANGE CEO of Strange Vacations
PEARL Hit man with a strong work ethic, aka Weasel
SULLY Fixer for Strange Vacations, aka Hulk
RITA Local beauty who has entranced Berf
FERNANDO Rita's "brother"
GUS WEST Captain of the *Desert Flower*
DYKE HEALD Superannuated millionaire
JACK HEALD Dyke's son
THELMA and LOUISE Vactioneers
DUSTIN Jumpmaster
SEGUNDO Secret admirer of Rita

**For Jackie and Bill**

Who loved it from the beginning,

warts and all

Go placidly amid the noise and haste,
and remember what peace there may be
in silence.
As far as possible without surrender
be on good terms with all persons.

Speak your truth quietly and clearly;
and listen to others,
even the dull and the ignorant;
they too have their story.

—Desiderata, Max Ehrmann

# CHAPTER ONE

Berf knew it was a mistake when he escaped to Mexico, but he went anyway. And that was a mistake.

Down deep he had known better when he left Austin last month, but with the whole wedding thing, well, it was clear that if he stayed in town he would end up saying something he would regret.

He made it all the way to Belize and Katerina's beach cabins before he realized he had to go back to Austin and face it. Better to say something that he would regret later than to regret that he didn't say something sooner. Or something like that. It had made more sense to him last night on a Belize beach under the influence of a full moon and an empty bottle.

So this morning he packed his Jag and walked into the open-air office at the center of the half circle of cabins. Katerina had her back to the counter, attempting to create order from the chaos of paperwork on the desk. Berf slapped the key on the counter.

Katerina spun around and caught sight of the key. "*Señor Berf,*" she said in her Austrian accent. "I thought you were here for the summer."

"Got to see a man about a dog."

She studied him for a moment and then shook her head slowly. "It is the wedding, is not it? China and Jake."

Berf didn't say anything. He didn't have to.

Katerina hung the key on a hook behind the counter and tied a bandana over her wiry blonde hair. "Come on." She slammed the counter open. "It's a long drive. You need some breakfast."

They had fresh fruit and smoked salmon and three pots of coffee, and she told him a disturbing rumor. Even more disturbing than the wedding. So disturbing that when he crossed back into Mexico, instead of heading west on Highway 186 out of the Yucatán, he pointed his Jag north on Highway 307 and waited for the Caribbean to appear out his right window. Five hours later, the Jag was in the parking lot and Berf was on the ferry.

Berford Oswald Wiggins was a man who could take it as it comes, and what's more, he frequently did. And it was coming at full speed here in Cozumel at sunset. Even by the light of tiki torches, anyone could see that the place was oozing scenery of one type or another. Swaying palms, pristine sand, languid waves, and unlanguid women, if he could use that word.

The average drifter would trade a broke-in saddle and a new pair of California-style spurs for a ticket to this party. But Berf wasn't the average drifter. Not by a long shot. And neither was his prey.

He crossed the white sand in front of the reggae band and pushed through the dancing throng, scanning the crowd. He finally found what he sought on a stool at the beachside cabana. He walked up and slapped a hand on a well-tanned shoulder.

"Spider, my man, what brings you to this hotbed of consumer-grade recreation?"

The shaggy-headed extreme athlete on the stool pulled his gaze away from the gyrating crowd. "Berf?"

Spider stood and initiated an elaborate greeting ritual involving elbows and fist bumps and slipping some skin that Berf did his best to follow.

Then Spider resumed his perch, his elbows resting on the bar behind him. He nodded to the next stool. "What are you doing here?"

Berf remained standing. "Raise not that censorious eyebrow at me, pilgrim, or I'll have to read you from the Book." He indicated the party on the beach. "I heard a vicious rumor you were here. Why aren't you snowboarding the Himalayas or body-surfing Jaws or some such?"

"I just got back from Bhutan."

Expecting a detailed explanation was imminent, Berf signaled the bartender. "I'll have two of whatever he's having."

The man looked to Spider, got the nod, and set up two shots from a bottle sitting next to Spider's elbow.

Berf cast an appraising eye at the bottle of tequila. More than four hundred dollars at liquor store prices. When you could find it. No telling how much it was per shot in this tourist trap. "Spidey! Did your rich uncle just get out of the poor house?"

"Bought the bottle. No sense wasting it."

This was a bit rich, even for Spider's impetuous nature, but the purchase price was already sunk costs, so he had a point. "What are we celebrating?"

"The grand masquerade."

Berf raised his glass. "*La masquerade grande.*" He downed a shot and turned back to Spider. "So what adventures befell you in Bhutan?"

Spider roused himself from his reflections, poured himself a shot, and sipped it like scotch. "The true adventure is within."

Berf couldn't argue with that. In fact, he might have said the same thing to Spider sometime in the past. Like in junior high. On the other hand, unlike others he could mention, specifically, reading left to right, one Spider Griffin, Berf hadn't spent the last decade circumnavigating the globe in search of a perpetual adrenaline fix. "If the true adventure is within, you wasted a lot of money on airfare in the past ten years. Not to mention gear."

"Have you heard of the Gross National Happiness index?"

While Berf was a man who lived by a Code, the concept of developing metrics of happiness on a national scale seemed as useful as entering a mule in a horse race. "Does this have anything to do with SpongeBob SquarePants?"

"It's a Bhutan thing. Everybody measures their life somehow. Like the Gross National Product and stuff."

Berf enjoyed a good chat as much as the next man, and maybe more than most, but he had a job to do here and then another back in Austin, so he shucked formality and applied himself to the task at hand. "Spider, my man, what are you doing in Cozumel? You have circled the globe a half dozen times without ever staying in a corporate hotel. And now you're drinking expense-account-level tequila at this quaint cabana bar designed by corporate flunkies on The Island of Patent-Pending Toys and Package Vacations? Tell me it ain't so."

He sat down on the stool next to Spider. "I'm not saying the place should be firebombed. It serves its demographic. But . . ." Berf searched for the right words, the words that would divide joint and marrow. "Men such as you and I, men with the bark on, we leave places like this to the city folk, to those who are content to cluster in herds and take their entertainment in off-the-shelf pre-packaged doses."

Berf took the second shot in hand with a gesture that took in all the frantic vacationeers. "We're more like Tell Sackett. We take the lonely ways, keeping an ear tuned to the siren call of that elusive El Dorado that could be lurking around the next corner."

Then he killed the shot and placed a concerned hand on Spider's arm. "What happened in Bhutan that would drive you here? A man who has lived his life on the fringe?"

Spider shook his head and sipped his pricy shot. "There are no more frontiers, Berfman. The world is one giant corporate logo." Spider framed a marquee in the air. "Dubya dubya dubya dot the world dot com."

Berf had no response. He nodded to the bartender, who poured him another shot.

"There's only one frontier left," Spider said, his voice almost a whisper. "The final frontier."

"Love long and prosper."

"I'm talking the ultimate adventure."

Berf exhaled his relief. "That's more like it. I heard you had sold out and got a job as an Abercrombie and Fitch model."

Spider laughed and slapped Berf on the back. Then he dug into a zippered pocket of his safari pants and extracted a business card. "Far from it, my man." He handed the card to Berf. "When you're ready to transcend the threshold past the point of no return, call these dudes and tell them I sent you. Say the magic word and get ready for the trip of your life."

Berf inspected the business card. "Strange Vacations. Nice." He flipped it over. *Vacation with Dignity* was scrawled on the back. "So you're hooking up with these guys? What kind of deal is it? Ecotourism? Zero-carbon-footprint backpacking?"

"Think of it as the vacation that never ends."

Berf stared at the card. "That's some serious adventuring, Kemosabe."

"No doubt, Brussels sprout. It's the vacation you take when nothing else will do."

"Seems the rumors of your demise were exaggerated. I leave you in good hands." Berf slid the card into his wallet. "How about one more to celebrate?"

They toasted with another shot, and Berf felt the warm glow of universal brotherhood emanate from his heart and spread along the twentieth parallel westward from the bar, past the dancing crowd illuminated by flickering tiki torches, to the gently rolling sea and beyond, circling the globe before sneaking up behind him and warming the back of his head here in Cozumel. He set down his glass, stood, and held his hand out to Spider. "See you tomorrow."

Spider slipped off his stool. "No, you won't." He engulfed Berf in a monstrous man hug.

Berf was startled, but considering he had just downed one hundred bucks of the man's tequila, he went along with the hug. Besides, he had to get on the road early. To get back to Austin and save another life before it was too late.

# CHAPTER TWO

In the twilight on the veranda of the country club, Jake took one bite of the crostini and chewed with a critical palate. He shook his head, set the remainder aside, and took a sip of wine.

China Wiggins held a fork suspended halfway between her plate and mouth, a healthy serving of Crab Louis hanging off the sides. "What?"

He shook his head. It was too late to change catering for the wedding anyway.

"Don't shake your head at me, Jake Oakley." She set down the fork. "It's about the wedding, isn't it? You want to call it off."

Leave it to China to turn a crostino into a crisis. She was priceless, irreplaceable in fact, but she could make a haboob out of a dust devil when she was in the mood. "Dovey, if I wanted to call off the wedding, you wouldn't have to read about it in the paper the next day." He thrust his fork into the Crab Louis. "Besides, I'd hate to spoil the surprise." He took a tentative bite. Not bad. He'd give them that. Perhaps the country club was up to the job after all.

"Oh?" China arched a plucked eyebrow.

Jake's cell phone cut off her question. "Hang on, dovey." He pushed the button. "Jake."

"Donner here. I'm looking at a Pacific Seacraft 27 on a trailer right here in my lot."

Jake checked his watch. "Just in time. What's the next step?"

"All I need is signed papers and a check."

"Excellent. I'll send somebody over in the morning." Jake disconnected and slid the phone into his pocket.

"Who was that?"

Jake dismissed the call with a wave. "One of the franchises. Just taking care of business before we disappear for a month." A hint of a smile escaped before he could contain it. After the wedding tomorrow her head would explode. A month in a sailboat on the Caribbean, alone with your true love. How many people got a chance at something like that?

She eyed Jake with a mixture of suspicion and excitement. "Why are you making this so mysterious?"

"You take care of the wedding. I take care of the honeymoon. That was the deal."

"But I don't know what to pack."

"You just bring your cute little self and an overnight case. I'll take care of everything else." He had picked out her wardrobe months ago. Everything she would need for days of sailing and the occasional night in port.

Although it was a warm evening, China shivered. A less discerning fiancé would have assumed she was overcome with anticipation, but Jake knew better. At least fifty percent of China's shiver was discomfort that something was completely outside of her control. But marriage was a matter of trust and the sooner she learned that lesson, the better. He wondered how things might have been different if his own parents had figured that out.

He took another bite of the Crab Louis and decided to recommend that they substitute the capers with asparagus. "Dovey, I've been thinking maybe it's time."

"Mmm?" China answered through her own bite of salad.

He offered the suggestion casually. "We could open up a little place off West Sixth."

China frowned. "A little place?"

"A bistro. Eclectic but choice menu. A nice selection of wines."

"Sugar, restaurants are high risk. We've been over this." She set her fork down. "That reminds me. What did you do with the bonus?"

"What bonus?"

"From last quarter. The franchise performance multiplier."

He opened his mouth, but instead of answering, he shoved in another bite. He answered through the Romaine and eggs. "I paid off the cards. Remember?"

China reached into her valise, pulled out some papers, and shuffled through them. "I only ask because I checked the balances and they're not paid off."

"You checked my credit card balances? They let you do that?"

"Don't make a scene, Jake. If you rent an apartment, they run a credit check. It's not a big deal."

"But your name's not even on the account. How did you do that?"

"Don't be silly. It's easy." She set the papers aside, dug into her valise, and held a statement out at him like a loaded gun. "They still show a balance."

"Well, I just sent the check. It takes time to show on the account."

"I don't want to start our life together with debt." She picked up her fork. "You don't know what it's like. Just ask Daddy."

Jake had heard the story before. Of all the business ventures Roger had started on a shoestring and a credit line, then going bust, declaring bankruptcy, and starting over, until he finally hit on The Lawn Arranger. But Jake wasn't her dad, and the sooner she understood that, the better. He shrugged and scooped up another bite. "That's the American dream, dovey."

China stopped, fork in mid-air. "Debt is not a joking matter, Jake."

"No, of course not." He offered what he hoped was a disarming smile. "Don't worry. I've got another bonus coming this quarter that will pay off the Bimmer."

"I hope so."

Jake signaled Antonio for a dessert menu. In forty-eight hours China would be too overwhelmed to worry about little things like credit card balances. He'd bet his sailboat on it.

# Chapter Three

When Berf pulled his silver Jag into the garage, he had a mere twenty-four hours to orchestrate a bachelor party that would make Mr. Guinness bring out a special edition of his book. But that was about twenty hours more than required for a man of his talents. He got the ball rolling by calling in a few favors, registered his requisite eight hours of horizontal contemplation on the verities of the universe, and then popped downstairs for a leisurely omelet with a pot of cowboy coffee. Bolivian, strong and black to steel himself for the task at hand.

Sitting in the breakfast nook, elbows on the table, mug at his chin, Berf's eyes came to rest on the framed, 1961 first-edition cover of Louis L'Amour's *Sackett* hanging next to the swinging door. Tell Sackett stands on a mesa, looking out over the valley, probably checking his back trail for sign of the Bigelows.

It was coming on sixteen years since Grandpa Berford had smuggled a time bomb into Berf's life disguised as a Christmas present—a box of paints and a paperback copy of *Sackett*. As Berf devoured the western and a dozen other Sackett novels, he discovered The Code, a way of living, an alternative to the madhouse rollercoaster that was the life of a Wiggins, or this one Wiggins at any rate.

Berf took a deep breath and a sip of the Bolivian. Maybe he would move the print to the foyer where he would see it whenever he left the house, a kind of reminder that a drifter in the old West didn't let down his guard or take anything for granted if he wanted to keep his hair.

And he would need to keep that in mind as he executed the balancing act required to deliver a party that left no stone unturned. After all, Berf had a motto:

You will find art in the middle of party.
And you will find me in the middle of both.

When it came to throwing a party, he had a reputation to consider. He had always done what it took to get the 'coon, but lately the 'coon seemed more ornery and the scratches took longer to heal. Metaphorically, of course. When it came to actual raccoons, Berf's philosophy was more along the lines of a polite nod in passing as they each indulged their nocturnal pursuits.

As Berf lingered over his final cup the day before the wedding, he acknowledged that he had suffered for his art and for his parties. In the context of the Sackett mythos, he realized that in his youth he had leaned toward the Clinch Mountain Sacketts, a solitary rough-and-tumble bunch who turned it up to eleven and let others look to their own concerns.

But as he inched closer to thirty, he began to feel a greater kinship with the Smokey Mountain Sacketts, equally solitary but focused on building a legacy. In the words of Tell Sackett, the consummate Smokey Mountain boy, "We come into life alone, we face our worst troubles alone, and we are alone when we die." But that didn't stop Tell from pulling together a stake to build a future with Ange Kerry. Although that didn't turn out well, so perhaps it was a bad example.

The point was that age had brought a certain level of maturity, and Berf now saw he had an obligation to those he loved. That was why he had returned to Austin, despite his misgivings. In his Clinch Mountain days, he had given no thought to tomorrow when he introduced Jake to his sister. When Jake announced his engagement to China last year and asked Berf to be his best man, Berf's first thought was that he would make the bachelor party the crowning achievement of his career, the mother of all stag parties.

But now in his Smoky Mountain maturity, thoughts of a Jake-China union conjured a vision of Jake standing helplessly in the path of a Kiowa war party intent on counting coups and taking scalps.

Oh, he would still throw Jake the best party he had ever seen.

But more importantly, he would sacrifice himself and their friendship to save Jake from the war party or die trying. Or at least take one for the team. Being the one responsible for this ill-advised union, he owed Jake that much.

Eight hours later, Berf pushed back from the remains of a four-course meal at Dugan's that left little room for discontent and glanced across the private dining room. He was surrounded by dark wood, polished brass, leather, and the warm glow that only a bottle of Bruichladdich 21 can impart. To his left, Jake fired up one of the Cubans that Berf had smuggled in from Mexico. Before them, eleven groomsmen, four ushers, and a smattering of party crashers lined either side of the table.

Berf stood, steadied himself against the chair, and tapped a glass with a spoon.

"Gentlemen, as the noted philosopher Sir Thomas of Lehrer once said, 'Life is like a sewer. What you get out of it depends on what you put into it.'"

Blake, an overgrown, overripe frat boy halfway down the rank of groomsmen and a decade past his prime, held up his glass and responded with a sonorous burp.

Berf let Blake's wordless commentary pass without response. "More to the point, let us consider the words of that great hip-hop artist, Michel de Montaigne: Marriage is like a cage; the birds outside are desperate to get in, and those inside are desperate to get out." He raised his glass. "A toast! To Jake, the man joining the family I have spent my life trying to escape."

There were cheers, clinks, and drinks all around. Berf turned to Jake. "Don't forget. Tomorrow is the yesterday you'll regret the next day."

Jake nodded with deliberate gravitas. "Very true."

Berf resurrected his cigar. "That reminds me of a story."

A collective groan filled the room.

Berf dodged a dinner roll. "When I was a kid, I prayed for a brother. God gave me China instead." He paused for the cheers and jeers, then resumed. "I tried again. I got a dog." A few chuckles. "The third time, I got a raccoon suit."

The room fell into a puzzled silence.

"For the Lawn Arranger commercials. So I quit while I was behind. Then I went to college and met a skinny maniac, my randomly assigned roommate. He didn't have an off switch or a speed control. He did everything all the time at the maximum intensity possible, if not more maximum. By the end of the first week, I decided to smother him in his sleep and put us both out of our misery." Berf appealed to the crowd. "It was the decent thing to do. Any one of you would have done the same under the circumstances."

Jake nodded to the room, acknowledging the authenticity of the story.

"In the dead of night, I sneaked to his bed and flipped on the lamp. Then I saw the scar on his shoulder. Just like my scar from when Blake shot me with a BB gun."

Blake stood and took a solemn bow.

"The light woke him up. I offered him a drink and we talked the sun up. Turned out we had the same birthday."

Berf dropped a hand on Jake's shoulder. Life was a funny thing. It threw things at you and nobody could tell you what they meant at the time. Sometimes it took a few days or weeks on the trail to sort it all out. But on this occasion a decade ago, in a dorm room as the sun rose on the forty acres the Congress of the Republic of Texas set aside in 1839 for a college, Berf had achieved a moment of clarity. Despite the personal nature of this revelation, Berf steeled himself to declare it to the world. Sometimes you just had to say what was and let the chips bury their dead.

"It was then I realized my prayer was answered on my first birthday. It just took me eighteen years to see it."

He took a deep breath. "Unfortunately, I introduced him to my sister and thus sealed his doom." Berf raised his glass again. "To my brother, and tomorrow, my brother-in-law."

The room cheered and took a drink.

Jake stood and raised his glass. "So how about you, Berf? When will you join the birds in the cage?"

Berf warded off this curse with a cross improvised from available silverware. "Any last words on your final night of freedom, J-Bird?"

"I can't say it any better than Socrates: 'By all means, marry. If you get a good wife, you'll become happy; if you get a bad one, you'll become a philosopher.'"

"You already are a philosopher," Blake shouted.

Jake smiled. "Then tomorrow, I'll be a happy philosopher."

The time had come to do the deed and plant the seed. Berf stepped to the podium, picked up the remote like it was a six-shooter, and pushed a button. A screen lowered on the wall behind him. He pushed another button. A projector lowered from the ceiling. He opened a laptop and fiddled with it.

Jake watched, puffing on his cigar in amused silence.

Berf had not forgotten his private vow to save Jake from the war party. If he failed, then he and Jake and the willing and able members of the loyal opposition would repair to a less stately establishment and celebrate as required by tradition, as if to forget, however briefly, that they were destined to lead a dawn attack on Little Big Horn.

The words "Life Outside the Cage" appeared on the screen as the voice of Willie Nelson sang "To All the Girls I've Loved Before" from the speakers in the ceiling.

Berf stood by the screen, remote in hand, like Tyrel Sackett facing down Reed Carney in Abilene. "Until you say those two dreaded words, it's not too late to back out. I'm giving you the gift of a last chance."

Jake nodded. "Do your worst."

Berf hit the remote. First up was Rachel, a saucy Latina in bike shorts and tube top—one of the women Jake had dated during the many breakups China had initiated. The crowd erupted in whistles and catcalls.

Berf turned to Jake. "Change your mind?"

"Nope."

Berf clicked again. Amy, a bouncy blonde in a strapless evening gown appeared. "Now?"

"Nope."

Next, Janice, an African-Asian with long lashes and legs to match. Berf was giving it his best shot. He glanced at Jake.

"Nope."

Berf clicked the remote with a twinge of malice. Desperate times required desperate measures. The screen filled with a tight shot of Gladwys of the British Isles, a blind date early in Jake's college days with an unfortunate similarity to a cassowary. A collective cry emerged from the crowd as they cowered behind upraised arms.

Jake recovered and took a strong belt of the Laddi. "You should warn a guy."

"I rely on the element of surprise to reveal the truth." Berf flipped to the next photo, Ginger of Charleston in a wet t-shirt competition.

Jake shook his head. "You really don't have to do this."

Berf clicked the remote to another beauty. "My motto is life without regret."

"I thought it was minimum effort, maximum pleasure."

"They're interchangeable, really."

Berf clicked again, mercilessly. Sometimes you had to do what it took and make no apologies. The screen filled with a school photo of China at age nine, back before The Lawn Arranger had changed all their fortunes. China smiled at them from the past, snaggletoothed, arrayed in a plaid jumper over a crisp white blouse and adorned with a glorious crown of bed head. It looked like a prime submission for BadSchoolPhotos.com.

Jake smiled and gestured to the screen. "How could you not love this?"

Berf responded. "Remember, you're going to wake up next to that every day for the rest of your life, if not longer."

"Why are you doing this? It's not like it's a shotgun wedding."

"Full disclosure. It's my duty to remind you of the alternatives and warn you about the implications. I'd do the same if you were signing up for an option ARM mortgage."

"I have an option ARM mortgage. On the condo. Interest only."

Berf stared and shivered. The remote slipped from his fingers. "Does China know?"

"No."

"But . . . but . . ."

"I'll refinance it before it explodes. I'm just waiting for the interest rates to bottom out."

Berf was jolted from his temporary paralysis by this wishful thinking. "Ha!"

It wasn't much of a riposte, but it was a nuanced warning delivered as only Berf could manage. If anything could have penetrated Jake's iron-plated resolve, it would have been that single shot, friendly fire from deep within enemy territory.

But Jake never registered the hit. He was looking at the elementary school photo of China and smiling.

# Chapter Four

When Roger thought about it later, he had one consolation. Right up until the moment the sailboat crashed through the entrance to the country club, everybody said it was the nicest wedding they had ever seen. After that, not so much.

Roger had only one chance to throw a wedding for his princess that she would never forget. That was the Wiggins way—go the extra mile. And watching from the back of the nave as the bridesmaids inched down the aisle, he could see that he had nailed it right between the eyes.

A mountain of flowers cascaded across the front of the cathedral. The bishop and Jake stood in the foothills while a chamber orchestra in the middle heights and a full choir in the peaks gushed the "Bridal Chorus" from *Lohengrin* in German. All six minutes of it.

Roger and China waited in an anteroom. Well, it was actually the mother's room, the room where nursing mothers could sit and see the service without being seen. They had a ringside seat as the dozen bridesmaids and groomsmen and flower girls and other whatnot that China had specified made the long trip to the altar.

Roger watched China as she watched the spectacle, her eyes shining. His little princess had never been so beautiful. It was almost painful to look at her, like she was too beautiful for the world.

He stifled a moment of panic, the nagging suspicion that finally he had done too well, that things were too perfect and it would now all be snatched from him, leaving him in the outer darkness, with the weeping and wailing and gnashing of teeth, the rending of raiment and tossing of ashes upon the head.

At the front, Jake stood, expectant and confident. You could take a DNA sample and it wouldn't register even trace amounts of doubt or regret. Berf stood next to him, looking like, well, like Berf always did, a stargazer with the oblivious air of someone genetically endowed with a low body-fat index. Courtesy of his mother.

The feeling that life was too perfect passed.

Roger took China's hand. "Princess, it's not too late. If you have even the slightest doubt, we can shut this thing down."

"Daddy, stop that this instant."

"What?"

"I am not backing out."

"I could probably get fifty percent back on the catering."

"Quit. You wouldn't say that if Mom was in here."

Roger looked to the pew where Marge sat, escorted by Aggie's oldest boy, who was an usher and seemed a lot older than he should be, considering he was just a kid last week. Wasn't he?

The last bridesmaid cleared the door. The sexton popped his head into the mother's room. "It's time."

China took Roger's arm. They stepped up to the door and stopped, waiting for the music to pause and the organ to cue them to begin the walk. It did and they did. It was the final walk China would take as Ms. Wiggins. When she came back down the aisle she would be Mrs. China Oakley and then where would you be? A father-in-law, that's what.

The organ blared and the chamber orchestra blew and the choir gushed and Jake couldn't stop smiling as they approached. China practically glowed as the sunlight splashed through the stained-glass windows and seemed to follow her.

The preacher asked "Who" and Roger said "Me" and China whispered "I, not me" and Roger kissed her and sat down next to Marge and it seemed like he had walked a long way uphill through tall grass carrying a fifty-pound bag of mulch on each shoulder.

The ceremony was perfect, except for the moment when Berf dug through every pocket in his tux searching for the ring. And the part where Roger cried and pretended he didn't and Marge also pretended he didn't, so it was pretty much the same as if he hadn't, which made it okay.

When Jake and China came back down the aisle together, Roger suddenly felt useless, a pitch pine log in a stack of firewood. He wasn't even needed to escort Marge out. Aggie's boy did that and Roger walked out alone.

At the country club, aside from posing in a few of the 600,000 photos the photographer took, Roger continued to be useless, but at least there was alcohol to ease the pangs. He supplied himself with a flute of champagne and stood by as Jake and China fed each other wedding cake with chopsticks.

Finally they led off the celebration with an exhibition salsa dance that Lonnie's youngest boy filmed, promising to make it a hit on his YouTube channel. Everybody cheered the finale and crowded onto the dance floor. The band switched to disco. Several couples tried to impress Lonnie's boy with their moves, maybe hoping to also be a hit on his channel. But the real YouTube hit came later.

Roger wandered, drinking more champagne and trolling for somebody to talk to. The dozen bridesmaids gossiped with each other and flirted with the dozen groomsmen. Lonnie's boy, denied access to the open bar, adapted by finishing off unattended glasses of champagne. Roger admired his resourcefulness. He might be good material for summer work at The Lawn Arranger.

But with all the champagne he was gulping down, the kid was signing up for the morning regrets class in the school of life experience without knowing it. Would he film that for YouTube? Probably not.

By the bar, Roger encountered something he hadn't seen for a decade or more—Berf and China talking and laughing. It was a strange afternoon.

Finding he had neglected his champagne, and now, thanks to Lonnie's boy, it was empty, Roger navigated the crowd, steadying himself on the shoulders of men he passed, but disguising it as a greeting. He grabbed one shoulder and Jake turned around.

"Jake! Just the man I wanted to see. You know what? The first time China brought you home for dinner, I told Marge we finally had a keeper on our hands. I said,

'Marge, we finally have a keeper on our hands.' And you know what she told me?"

Roger peered around the room, looking for Marge to provide confirmation. She was deep in the processes of an aura analysis of Father Mahoney, God help him.

Jake opened his mouth to answer, but Roger didn't wait for him. "She told me she saw it in a dream. 'Roger,' she said, 'I saw it in a dream. Last night. He's the one.'" Roger punctuated "He's the one" with a finger on Jake's tux. Boom, boom, boom.

"Well—"

"And she couldn't be more right. You're tearing it up with the franchises."

Roger spotted Higgins on the dance floor, balding and paunchy, hitting on a bridesmaid. Number eleven, maybe. His wife would be giving him holy heck tonight, and why not, that's what.

"Tearing it up." Roger's finger went into action on the three words. Boom, boom, boom. It paid to hammer home the important points. He inhaled to continue, but Jake turned toward the bar. Roger glanced behind him.

Berf nodded at Jake and left. Jake stepped to the bandstand and commandeered a mike.

"Your attention, please."

The poor fellow didn't make a dent in the crowd noise.

"Hello? Can I have your attention?"

Roger put two fingers in his mouth and emitted a whistle that probably caused a deer on the eleventh green to raise its head. He winked at Jake.

Jake cleared his throat. "Hello. I hope you're all having a good time."

There were deafening cheers, whistles, and catcalls. The open bar must have poured enough to fill a goldfish pond. Roger mentally estimated the tab. Not a pretty calculation.

Jake continued. "If you could follow me, I have a surprise for my lovely new wife."

China's face flushed with excitement. Jake stepped down from the stage and held out his hand. China took it.

Roger followed along with the rest of the crowd to the front entrance of the country club, a grand horseshoe arc that descended from the road down to a brick awning that protected the members during rainstorms. It was lined with cars, overflow from the parking lot.

Under the awning, Roger's new Mercedes, cardboard dealer plates still in the window, was parked in front of Jake's not-quite-as-new BMW, which was decorated in the manner of groomsmen restrained by raging hangovers and the fear of the wrath of China should they color outside the lines. They obviously knew what they were dealing with. Roger was surprised and impressed by their wisdom.

On the road to the country club, a new Dodge RAM with the power to pull a doublewide appeared over the rise. Behind it, a new Pacific Seacraft 27 sparkled in the sun.

Jake slipped his arm around China. "Ready to sail the Caribbean for a month?"

Roger stared at Jake in disbelief. A month on a sailboat? Who did he think he married? But China surprised him. Maybe that's what happened when your princess found her prince.

"Oh, Jake!" China grabbed Jake's face with both hands and kissed him.

Then she pulled back, suspicious. A man with horse sense would have seen her eyes and heard the dark, invisible wings of doom beating the air. For a moment Roger felt the sense of disaster return and he flinched. But he could tell that Jake missed it.

China gave him The Look. "Jake. Tell me how you paid for it."

Roger leaned forward to hear the answer, but at that moment someone stumbled into him.

Higgins held out a cell phone. "Boss, Esther wants to talk to you."

Now was no time for a chat with the company comptroller. "Get a grip, Higgins."

Higgins leaned closer. "I think you're going to want to take this one," he whispered with all the subtlety of a musk ox.

"Fine." Roger grabbed the phone. "What's so important, Esther? I got a wedding going on here."

"Sorry, Mr. Wiggins. Has the wedding started?"

"It's over. The couple is about to sail off into the sunset."

"Oh, dear. Well, you might want to have a chat with Mr. Oakley before they leave for the honeymoon."

"Esther, I don't have time for twenty questions. Cut to the chase."

"I've been going over the franchise advertising account. Well over half of the checks we cut for advertising in the last six months have gone to a company that seems to be owned by Mr. Oakley."

"A company owned by . . ." Roger swiveled his head toward Jake and his princess. "What?"

"I called some of the franchises. They haven't seen a TV spot in their market since—"

Esther's sentence was cut off by Jake yelling. "Berf! Cut it to the left!" He stepped forward. "No, the other left!"

Roger turned to the street where the truck was attempting to back down the hill. The driver leaned out the window for a better view. It was Berf.

Roger dropped the phone. "You let him pull a trailer? Lord love a duck! My car!" He rushed to the Mercedes, twitching like an earthworm on a hot shovel, keeping his eye on the truck.

At the top of the hill, Berf waved and spun the wheel. Then he appeared to erupt into convulsions, his arms flailing about.

The truck had been inching down the drive like an octogenarian pushing a walker, intent on scoring a slice of lean roast beef at the early bird buffet. But now it lurched down the hill, ping-ponging off cars like a bull out of the gate after the flank strap is cinched up. Berf got it back under control, pulled forward slightly to extract the rear bumper of the trailer from a car door, and got out to inspect the damage.

Roger dug into his pocket for the keys, but dropped them on the pavement. The rest of the wedding party, stunned by the sudden violence, stirred to life as cries of dismay marked the individuals speed-dialing their insurance agents. A small contingent rushed up the hill to inspect the damage.

Lonnie, whose boy was now rolling film with glee, reached Berf first. The words weren't audible from this distance, but the sense was clear. Lonnie wished to remove Berf's head and relocate it to a region where it wouldn't get full sun in the morning, midday, or afternoon. At least, that was his opening suggestion. He followed it with other, less appealing, advice.

Roger retrieved his keys and staggered to his car, instructed by long experience that this pause was merely an interlude, not a cessation in the devastation.

Just as Roger reached his Mercedes, the truck and trailer, neglected as Berf attempted to reason with Lonnie, began rolling down the hill toward them. The crowd gasped.

Roger ripped the door of his car open and dove in. He kept an eye on the truck as he tried to shove the key into the ignition.

Lonnie was the first to grasp the situation. He shoved Berf aside as the truck and boat rolled past.

Roger frantically cranked the engine of the Mercedes. It roared to life as the truck/boat/juggernaut careened down the drive. The wedding party sprang in all directions like streams from a water feature.

Just as Roger shifted into drive, the back of the boat split the difference between the rear of his Mercedes and the front of Jake's BMW. It pushed them aside like a saloon door and plunged into the country club entrance in a bloom of glass and aluminum, obliterating the reception desk as the bed of the truck lodged in the gap.

Silence closed on the crowd, broken by the occasional falling shard of glass.

As the weight of the collective repair bill settled on the collective consciousness of Roger and the crowd, the wedding party converged on the entrance and surveyed the damage.

Roger emerged from the Mercedes and zombie-walked to the truck-and-boat embedded in the entrance like a knife in a corpse.

Lonnie's boy dashed forward with his camera still running, no doubt hyperventilating at the thought of the hits his YouTube channel would get by morning.

Berf's reaction wafted down from the hill. "Oh, man."

Roger's foot hit something. Higgins's phone. He picked it up. "Esther, you still there?"

"Yes, sir."

"Bottom line it for me."

"I can't say for sure, but it seems that Mr. Oakley has been siphoning money from the advertising budget."

Roger tossed the phone into the shrubbery. He worked his way through the crowd, pushing friends aside without a word until he arrived next to his soon-to-be ex-son-in-law. He grabbed Jake's arm and spun him around. "Who the heck do you think you are?"

Jake stared at him. "Uh—"

That was as much as he could get out before Roger's finger shot into action, jabbing Jake in the chest. "If my princess wasn't here, I'd break you in two right now and feed you to the goldfish."

"Sir," Jake blurted out. "It was an accident."

Berf appeared in Roger's peripheral vision. "There was a bee."

Roger pushed Jake aside and took China by the arm. "Come on, princess. We're going home."

"But, Daddy—"

"You want to know how he paid for that boat?" Roger gestured to what was left of the sailboat sitting atop the reception desk. "Ask him about the advertising budget."

"What?"

Roger turned to Jake, who stared back like a man who has just seen the ghost of Christmas future and has suddenly lost the Christmas spirit. "Go ahead. Tell her."

"It was the darnedest thing," Berf interjected into the silence. "Just as I reached to shift into drive and pulled forward, there was this bee—"

"Put a sock in it," Roger said without taking his eyes off Jake.

"Uh, right, sir," Berf said. "Just what I was thinking."

"Daddy, what are you . . ." China pulled away from Roger and turned a searching gaze on her new husband. "Jake, what is this all about?"

"Dovey, it was just a short-term thing. To hold us over until we got the wedding squared away."

China drew in a long breath and seemed to grow two feet taller. Roger nodded with approval. He could always count on his princess to do the right thing.

She threw the bouquet at Jake. "Daddy, call for a limo."

Jake caught the bouquet and tossed it aside distractedly. The girls in the crowd scrambled for it. Lonnie's boy zoomed in for a tight shot as they fought for possession.

China wrenched the ring off her finger. "You were right for once. It's a short-term thing." She threw the ring at Jake, stepped around the truck, and disappeared inside the country club.

Roger stepped up, his finger ready for action. "Last night I was telling Marge the jury was still out on you. I said, 'Marge, the jury is still out on that boy.'" Boom, boom, boom. He gave Jake another good hard look, gave one to Berf for good measure, and followed China into the country club. He'd have an annulment in hand before that kid knew what hit him.

# CHAPTER FIVE

Five hours later, after all the insurance adjusters and country club functionaries faded into background noise, Berf took charge.

He hadn't caught the salient points of the final exchange between Jake and China, but when she launched the bouquet at him like a mortar and then gathered her armies and decamped, it was clear to the meanest intelligence that perhaps Jake might want to get his deposit back on whatever arrangements he had made for the honeymoon.

Questions swarmed through Berf's head like Kmart shoppers around a Blue Light Special, but he knew better than to voice them. No matter what mountain he hailed from, any Sackett worth his salt knew there was a time for questions and a time for action. Lucky for Jake, fate had placed Berf square in the center of his wheelhouse.

That old King Solomon feller knew a thing or two when he said, "Give strong drink unto him that is ready to perish, and wine unto those that be of heavy hearts."

And if any man was ready to perish, Jake was on the short list and trending toward the top in the exit polls.

Berf installed the shell-shocked Jake in the passenger seat of the silver Jag, one of the few vehicles still in working order, and ferried him downtown to the Board Room, where muted Telemann, hardwood paneling, and studied indifference allowed for the painful conversation that must be faced. It also had the virtue of proximity to Jake's condo.

They sat at the bar, and for the first hour, Berf directed Duncan to keep them supplied with Irish boilermakers—Jameson shots with a Guinness back. They passed the time in silence, exchanging knowing nods and scanning the subtitles on the various screens within view.

Of all the wickets Berf had ever stuck, this was the stickiest of the lot. During his hour of reflection, he couldn't help but think of Tell Sackett holed up on the Mogollon rim, shot up to doll rags, one man against thirty or forty. Although Tell didn't know it at the time, the whole Sackett clan was about to ride to his rescue. But Berf had no such clan to back him up, only The Code. It would have to do.

Jake was first to break the silence. "She was the only one who really understood me."

Berf glanced at him in the mirror behind the bar. "First, I can't tell you how sorry I am about the boat. And the truck. And the other stuff. But think about it. If China really understood you, would she chuck it all over a glorified fender bender?"

In the silence that followed, Berf turned to face Jake directly. He was a sorry sight, as forlorn as a lost bear cub in a pit mine.

Jake tossed him a sideways glance and took a deep breath. "There's more to it."

Berf held his peace, giving Jake the time to tell it in his own way. To facilitate the process, he signaled to Duncan for another round.

Duncan assessed the line of empties in a slow, meaningful gaze and looked a wordless question back at Berf.

Berf settled the question with a world-weary nod that packed in all the gravity of the situation, and Duncan stepped to the task at hand without comment. Berf had to give it to the beefy bartender, tattoos peeking from the collar and cuffs of his starched white shirt. At first glance, he didn't seem like a good fit for a high-toned establishment, but in such matters Austin was much like the Old West, where a man was judged not by his appearance but by his sand.

And Duncan had more sand than your average bear. If Berf were asked to construct the Platonic ideal of the quintessential bartender, he would simply point to Duncan and declare the job done. Duncan was quick to listen and slow to advise. He could quote poets and philosophers and pop songs with equal facility and settle most any dispute of fact without consulting his smartphone. In a word, Duncan was the man, and Berf had no doubt that a core sample taken from any point on his physique would render empirical evidence to back up this assessment.

Thus supplied with reinforcements, Berf continued. "Cheer up. It could be worse. You could be in the family now."

Jake shrugged. "They're not so bad."

"Sure. Until you get to know them." Berf tossed off the whiskey and took a sip of the Guinness. "You know what you need, J-Bird? A road trip. We could kick it on Route 66."

Jake shook his head like a bull beleaguered by flies. "I can't."

"I'm sure Dad would give you some time off. Considering."

"Oh, he's giving me plenty of time off. All the time a guy could want."

"Perfect. How about Belize? There are few things a month on a Caribbean beach can't cure."

"No. I have to come up with a hundred grand as soon as possible."

Berf frowned. "The insurance will take care of all that."

"No, for something else. If I don't set this straight, I'll lose China forever."

"You say that like it's a bad thing." Berf deflected Jake's seething glare with a sip of Guinness. "I direct your attention to the presentation of last night and then the events of today. There are worse things than a China-free future."

Based on Jake's reaction, it seemed Berf had finally launched the precise combination of words to resurrect Jake from his slough of despond.

Jake turned on his stool to face Berf with all due deliberation. "If you're not careful, you might find yourself with a pulse-free future."

This was more like it. As Berf always said, it's hard to steer a ship caught in the doldrums. If you can just get it moving, then with the slightest of adjustments, you can point it wherever you want. "Touché, my fine feathered friend. I'm not opposed to the happy union of two soul mates. But let's just back up a spell and take a gander at the long view. Where do you see yourself in ten years?"

"That all depends on what I do in the next ten days."

Berf shook his head like a kindly uncle. "No, no, no. Set aside today's little dust-up and cast your mind's eye back on your true passion."

Jake frowned and took a sip of whiskey and Guinness. "Here's the deal. You promise to quit talking out of the back of your neck, and I'll reconsider my instinct to jerk the stool out from under you and knock you into a new time zone."

Duncan stepped forward, but Berf waved him back. The patient was finally showing signs of life. "You remember the night we met? At the Sigma Chi smoker?"

Berf wasn't sure how to interpret the expression on Jake's face, but it was clear this shot over the bow had registered.

"You mean the restaurant?" Jake asked.

"You couldn't be more right if you took three lefts. But once China lassoed you, it was all climbing the ladder. Real estate and then taking on the franchise operation for Dad." Berf picked up the Guinness and held it out it in Jake's general direction. "Sure, you're good at it, but at what cost?" He took a swig of the beer to lubricate the gears. "For what shall it profit a man if he shall gain a positive balance sheet and lose his own dream?"

It was clear from Jake's vacant expression that Berf's dart had hit the fifty pointer. He sat back on the stool to let his words marinate.

"No," Jake said, as if from a place far away. "Too volatile. High risk."

That was China talking. But time and distance would break the spell, and then Jake would see reason. And after what had happened today, Berf owed him that much at least. "You might be right, J-Bird. I say we hit the road, clear our heads, and consider our options."

Jake didn't object, so Berf pressed on. "Should we drive east or west? Maybe spend a week on your home turf in San Francisco. Clear out the cobwebs. The mother of all road trips."

Something teased Berf's mind, an echo of an experience he couldn't place. A vacation to end all vacations.

Then it hit him. "Hey! Remember Spider?" He glanced over, but Jake was lost in his own ruminations. Berf continued. "Last month Spider told me about a good deal. Ultimate Adventures. I think."

Berf pulled out his cell and found Spider in his contacts. He got an automated message.

*You have reached a number that has been disconnected or is no longer in service. If you feel you have reached this message in error—*

As Berf pocketed the phone, he recalled that Spider had given him a card. He dug in his wallet and pulled it out. "Just what you need, J-Bird. A Strange Vacation." He flashed the put-it-on-the-tab signal at Duncan and elbowed Jake. "Time to hang up the spurs and let sleep knit up the raveled sleeve of care."

The night was muggy, the streetlights gleaming wetly from inside a nimbus of humidity. They covered the few blocks to Jake's condo in silence, dodging revelers and pedicabs. Inside the penthouse, Jake dropped onto a couch, turned on the TV, and flipped through a sailing magazine.

Berf invaded the kitchen, where he heated water, ground coffee beans, and combined them in a French press. Then he leaned on the bar, gazed out over the lights of downtown Austin, and called the number on the card he got from Spider.

"Strange Vacations. This is Trina. Where in the world would you like to go today?"

The voice on the line sounded like the love child of Lauren Bacall and Leonard Cohen. Berf tried to imagine her face.

"Hello?" Trina said.

"Ah, yes. Well, Trina, I was thinking Belize might be just the place."

Before Trina could respond, Jake leapt from the couch like a cornered coon spooked by a hound and bayed, "Cancún!"

Berf dropped the phone. It bounced off the bar and onto the tile floor. "A tourist trap is just what we don't want." He picked up the phone. "Sorry, Trina. How about a remote cabin in Belize?"

"When did you want to arrive?"

"Yesterday, if you could fix us up with a time machine."

"Tomorrow then. And the return date?"

Jake rounded the couch, waving a magazine. "Cancún!"

Berf shook his head emphatically. "Can I leave the return date open?"

"You can't get the package price without a return date."

"Oh, I forgot." Berf flipped over the card. "I want the Vacation with Dignity package."

"That package is available only in select locations."

"Cancún," Jake shouted, holding the magazine in front of Berf. A two-page spread announced the Iron Fish Triathlon with a $100,000 prize. In Cancún.

"Cancún is one of the locations," the voice said.

Berf dropped onto a bar stool. "I guess it's Cancún then."

"Thank you for calling Strange Vacations," Trina said. "Hold please."

There was a click and a steel drum came on the line playing "Three Little Birds."

Jake poured the coffee, set a cup in front of Berf, and took his magazine back to the couch.

A few clicks came from the phone, followed by a male voice with a Belgian accent. "You wish to book the Vacation with Dignity package?"

"Arriving tomorrow if possible."

"It requires the reference."

A reference? What kind of vacation . . . Then he remembered what Spider said. "Spider said to tell you he sent me."

There was a pause. "Would that be Maurice Lindsay?"

Berf chuckled. "Not many people know that. He doesn't answer to anything but Spider."

"Name?"

"Maurice Lindsay."

"Your name."

"Ah. Berf Wiggins."

"Burt Wiggins."

"Berf. Like barf, but with an E."

"Berf Wiggins."

"And Jake Oakley."

There was a pause on the other end of the line. "Will Mr. Oakley be accompanying you? Is he a medical professional?"

"No, he's just a guy who really needs this vacation. Worse than I do." There was another pause on the line. Berf sipped the coffee. It was strong enough to grow fur on an egg. He sighed with satisfaction.

"You both want the same package?"

"We hear this is the vacation to end all vacations."

"Yes, it is."

"Then that's what we need. We don't care if we never come back."

"That's the idea."

"Perfectamundo."

"You are aware of the special terms for this package?"

"Of course not."

"The fee covers $500,000 of life insurance payable to Save Our Reefs International to guarantee vacations for others like yourself."

Berf shrugged. "I won't need it if I'm dead."

"Exactly."

Berf sorted out the particulars with the nameless Belgian, hung up the phone, and joined Jake on the couch. "All settled. We leave at noon." He picked up the magazine. "What's this about a fishing triathlon?"

"Winner walks away with $100,000. Exactly what I need to fix this mess."

Berf tossed the magazine on the coffee table. "J-Bird, the point of this trip is decompression, not damage control."

"What about China?"

"She's not invited."

"If I can—"

"If you can what?" Berf sprang up from the couch. "Bend yourself into a pretzel to jump through her hoops?" He paced in front of the TV. "Sure, you can dot all the Ts, cross all the Is, fill in all the squares without going outside the lines. But for what?"

"For China."

Berf pointed his coffee cup at Jake. "Exactly! For China." He took a sip with the finality of a man who has delivered the crushing blow to a straw man. Mission accomplished.

Jake stared at Berf blankly. "Uh. What?"

Did Berf really have to draw a picture? Okay, if that was what it took. "You do all that, and what do you get? Just China. Is that enough?"

"Yes."

"No!" Berf lurched forward, losing a bit of coffee. "Aren't you listening? That's over."

Jake picked up the magazine. "No. It's not over until I give up."

"It was over the minute you didn't fit the plan anymore. Look." Berf grabbed the remote and turned up the TV. If ever there was a time for tough love, this was it.

A Lawn Arranger commercial was on. A much younger and thinner Roger came on the screen with a raccoon mask and barked like a used-car salesman.

"Fountains!"

A kid in a raccoon suit leapt on-screen and conjured a fountain, which magically appeared in a starburst.

"Bird baths!"

The raccoon waved his arms. A bird bath sparkled into place.

"Garden statues!"

Various statues appeared in showers of fireworks as the raccoon pranced around the screen and pointed at them.

Jake stared at the screen in fascinated horror. "Is that you?"

Berf stood, his arms limp at his side. He spoke in a voice mixed with resignation and regret. "That's what they do. Dress you up and pull your strings. If you don't dance the dance, they don't want you. China doesn't want you."

Jake looked at the Iron Fish ad, then at the TV. The commercial ended and Judge Judy came on. "No," he said with fading conviction. "A loser is just a winner who quits too early."

Berf turned off the TV and dropped the remote on the coffee table. Maybe a month in Cancún would get the voice of China out of Jake's head. Or not. But a feller had to try. It was the last arrow in his quiver, and he would let it fly.

# Chapter Six

Berf glanced out the window as the plane banked south. The Formula One racing track seemed like a Hot Wheels kit, too clean and simple to be a real place. He'd spent a few afternoons down there with his Jag, but he preferred a leisurely drive to the frantic competition to stay in front.

He was of two minds about this trip, maybe three for those keeping score at home, but now that they were wheels up, he had to trust Spider's instincts. The hour of shots on the Cozumel beach last week had reassured Berf that the rumors of Spider's fall from grace had been no more than the grapevine talking through its collective hat.

Yes, their destination was Cancún, a meringue of resort hotels on a pie crust of sand six miles long and an inch deep. Yes, there was this Iron Fish competition, hardly an environment conducive to deprogramming a mind seduced by one-percenter dreams of unbridled ambition. But Spider had assured Berf that Strange Vacations could provide the ultimate vacation to end all vacations.

A transcendent experience. And that was what Jake needed. Shoot, Berf could use a few servings of that himself.

About one second after the seatbelt light went off, the guy in front of Jake pushed the flight attendant button. As an old trail hand accustomed to constant vigilance of his surroundings, Berf had noticed him when he boarded. Took five minutes to get his overstuffed carry-on bag into the overhead, oblivious to the increasing hostility of the line forming behind him.

Middle-aged guy with an eroding hairline and a burgeoning paunch. The odometer on his shiny brown suit had rolled over at least twice and the skinny tie had been in and out of style at least three times since he bought it. Berf had him pegged for a retired news-hound. Probably on the police beat.

A woman who looked more like a librarian than a flight attendant came down the aisle. "How can I help you, sir?"

The man held up a twenty. "Hey, there . . . Cathy, how about two bottles of Sauza and a glass of ice? I got cash."

Berf watched the flight attendant's smile harden into stone, and he glanced at her nametag. Catherine. You would think a guy who spent a career getting information from reluctant strangers would know better. People went to the trouble to put their full name on a nametag for a reason.

"We will begin service as soon as we prep the carts." She punched the call button off. "And we don't take cash."

"I got plastic. But I'd like a little something now to prime the pump." The guy flashed the twenty in front of her face. "Think of it as an expedite fee."

Catherine returned to the galley and began stocking the cart. The other flight attendant listened to her while casting a paint-peeling glare at the reporter. Berf let loose a small smile. Good thing for the news-hound that the tequila came in sealed bottles.

Half an hour later, Newsy had his tequila, Berf had his bourbon, Jake had his wine, and everything calmed down a bit. Berf was a man of action, not given to maudlin reflection, but he was human after all, and sometimes the occasional introspective moment wandered into his crosshairs.

In the normal course of things, he would rather be dragged nekkid behind a horse through a field of prickly pear than opt for a month in a glintzy resort destination like the Cancún hotel district. But despite what others might think, Berf didn't live solely for his own gratification.

If you found a stranger afoot in the wilderness, stranded and short on rations, you didn't just tip your hat and say "Howdy" as you passed by. If that was all you were prepared to do, you might as well shoot him. It would be kinder.

More to the point, Jake was no stranger to Berf. They shared a birthday. They shared a scar or two. They were practically brothers. For a few years, it had been clear Jake had lost his way out in the old West, blinded by gold fever, but every man had to chop his own cotton, and Sacketts weren't the interfering sort.

Once Berf had made his final pitch at the bachelor party and Jake declined to exercise the escape clause, Berf closed ranks and presented the united front. A feller had to take the long view in these things. Any man who was married to China would need a listening ear and a comforting word. Sooner rather than later, if Berf was any judge of horseflesh.

But nobody could have predicted how quickly that time would come. Or how fierce and decisive the blow.

That was the one thing that puzzled Berf. When he sprinted to the scene of the disaster, China seemed more stunned than upset. But then Dad said something about advertising, and the next thing anyone knew, China had nullified all treaties and unilaterally declared war. Her exit through the wreckage had the air of Sherman's march from Atlanta to Savannah.

So it wasn't the wreck. The insurance would take care of that anyway. It was something else. But what? And why was Jake so intent on getting his hands on a hundred gees immediately?

Berf poured the second bottle of Woodford Reserve into the plastic cup and dropped in a single ice cube. Despite the unnecessary indignities of air travel these days, and there were many, you had to admire an airline that stocked decent whiskey. It almost made up for the practically criminal lack of legroom. Almost.

He glanced over at Jake, who sipped wine while flipping through a sailing magazine. Maybe the insurance money would be enough to replace the Seacraft.

Jake turned to Berf. "Let's say you win the lottery. The Powerball. Enough cash that you could do whatever you wanted for the rest of your life. What would you do?"

"I'm already—"

"I'd get one of these puppies." Jake nodded at the magazine. "A thirty-seven footer. Ditch the job and disappear off the grid with a good woman."

"So if you win the Iron Fish, that's what you'll do?"

"If?" Jake snorted. "Of course I'll win."

"And if you don't? Hypothetically speaking."

Jake started to answer immediately, but Berf silenced him with two raised eyebrows. Jake stared at him for a few seconds, and his eyes went vacant as he seriously considered the question. "Well, in that case there'd be no point in going home. No prize money, no China, no reason to be there."

Jake had clearly chosen his filly for this race, and if Berf couldn't endorse Jake's obsession with this particular fixture, he could at least have the consideration to refrain from second-guessing him every time the topic came up.

The plane shuddered and the seatbelt light flickered on. The pilot came on the intercom and asked everyone, including the flight attendants, to buckle up.

As Berf complied, the purpose of this trip became clear. It was about something bigger than getting Jake over this rough patch with China. It was about reconnecting Jake with his dreams.

Back in college, Jake seemed to have a vision for a new venture every other week. A gourmet restaurant chain with locations on every continent. A line of designer casual wear. A gallery of fine art photography. Back then it had never been about the money. But not long after Berf introduced him to China, that ambition was redirected to more practical and immediate concerns. He couldn't remember the last time Jake had talked about a goal that wasn't connected to a profit and loss statement.

If he achieved nothing else on this trip, Berf would do his best to help Jake to see that he didn't have to live his life with a dream deferred. "So if you win the Iron Fish, you're going to take China and sail into the sunset?"

"China living on a sailboat? Seriously?" Jake laughed like Berf had suggested a round of umbrella drinks.

Berf frowned. "Hey, you're the one who wants to strike out for the frontier with a woman from good pioneer stock. Why work that hard to hitch your wagon to a woman with no taste for the wilderness?"

Jake took a sip of wine as the plane jolted, leaving him looking like a model in a "Got Merlot?" commercial. "Life is the art of the possible." He wiped his lip with the napkin.

"Dude, anything is possible."

If Jake had one character flaw—not that Berf would suggest such a thing—it was the tendency toward pedantry. He assumed the expression of a man explaining to a three-year-old why you can't wash the cat by closing the toilet lid on it and flushing. "Berf, there are dreams and there is reality."

"No, there is what you want and what you'll settle for."

Their philosophical debate was interrupted. "Hey, cupcake. I need another one."

Newsy held his plastic cup aloft toward Catherine, who was strapped into the jump seat. Her face was a mask, but her eyes communicated a message that would have caused Genghis Khan to cancel the Afghanistan campaign.

"Sir, the seat belt light is on."

The plane bounced like a buckboard racing over a mountain pass.

Newsy waved the twenty again. "How about some hazard pay?"

Catherine shook her head. He sweetened the offer with another twenty.

"Sir, you will have to wait."

"Bzzzt. Thank you for playing." He stood. "Never mind. I got a flask in my bag." He stumbled into the aisle and opened the overhead.

Catherine didn't move from the jump seat. "Sir, you must return to your seat."

"Yeah, yeah, yeah." He fumbled with the bags.

The man across from Jake stepped into the aisle. Berf had noticed him when they boarded. He was a jock, all buff and buzz cut. Probably military. Or maybe ex-military. He seemed more menacing than your average serviceman on a plane. He stepped toward Newsy. "Let me help you with that, sir."

In a single smooth motion, the jock pushed Newsy's head down, grabbed a roll-on bag, and jerked it out, but he lost his grip as it cleared the overhead compartment. "Oops."

Berf reached forward, but the seatbelt vetoed his good intentions. "Watch out!"

The wheel hit the base of Newsy's skull. He dropped like a hog hit with a hammer.

The jock caught the bag and stared down at the inert form sprawled across the seat. "Oh my."

Berf caught the profile of a puppy-dog expression of apology directed at Catherine.

Catherine almost smiled. "Sir, you need to take your seat."

"Right away, ma'am."

As the jock replaced the bag and wrestled Newsy into his seat, the cabin erupted in spontaneous cheers and applause.

Berf exchanged a glance with Jake and settled back into his seat.

"Why didn't you think of that?" Jake whispered.

"You're the one with the aisle seat," Berf whispered back.

The jock glanced over at them as he returned to his seat. Berf nodded. They were fellow travelers in more ways than one. He knew a man with a Code when he saw one. But Berf sensed that the jock was all Clinch Mountain, boys who weren't known for their gentle ways. Like Logan Sackett when he rescued Pennywell from that Siwash bar by giving Spud Tavis a good thumping.

Berf appreciated the sentiment, but couldn't endorse his methods. He glanced past Jake and saw the jock looking back at him. They locked eyes. For ten long seconds they stared at each other, neither blinking.

Then Berf acknowledged him with a raised-chin half-nod and picked up his whiskey. The boy was Clinch Mountain all right. Would fight at the drop of a hat, and would even drop it himself if that's what it took.

Jake regarded Berf with a raised eyebrow. "What was that?"

Berf shrugged and sipped his bourbon. "Just two drifters passing on the trail is all."

"Well, I'd keep on drifting down the trail if I was you. He smells like trouble."

Berf waived aside Jake's concerns. "Once we clear baggage claim, we'll never see him again."

# CHAPTER SEVEN

Kate stood next to baggage claim holding a Strange Vacations sign and a clipboard. Tourists of all shapes, sizes, and colors flowed past in all manner of dress and half-dress, dragging all manner of bags behind them.

Half of her demanded to know what she was doing here. The other half told her to give it a little wait-and-see. After all, it had only been a week. And as crazy as it was, still it made sense. Mr. Heald had come to Strange Vacations for a reason, and there would be others. She could play activity director in between if she had to.

Two guys in their twenties caught sight of her sign. Kate consulted her clipboard as they came to a stop in front of her.

"Mr. Wiggins and Mr. Oakley?"

The thinner one stepped close and smiled warmly. "Please, call me Berf."

"Burt."

"Berf. Like berth, but with an F."

Kate wrote on the clipboard. "B-I-R-"

The guy leaned in over the clipboard. "And an E. An E and an F. And an R between."

Another traveler joined them. Kate glanced up. One more guy in his twenties. His hair and rock-solid physique gave him a slight military air. He dropped a duffel bag and a backpack and held out his hand. "Derek Runyon."

The first guy edged the new guy aside and pointed to the clipboard. "And a B." He smiled at Kate again.

Kate dismissed him with a forced smile, stuck her pen behind her ear, and shook the hand of the new arrival. "Mr. Runyon."

Mr. Runyon held onto her hand a bit longer than customary as he studied her face.

Kate stared back, wondering if she should recognize him. The name wasn't familiar, but she'd been a lot of places in her life and met a lot of people.

Mr. Runyon's eyebrows inched up. "Wait. Are you Kate Collins? Global Health Alliance?"

Kate inspected him more closely but still couldn't place him. "How did you—"

"Cover story, Global Health newsletter, last year."

"Yes, actually." They smiled at each other for a few seconds, and then it started feeling a little weird. She withdrew her hand from his grasp.

Mr. Runyon indicated baggage claim with a nod of his head. "Cancún is a long way from Micronesia."

Kate retrieved the pen, the sense of guilt for taking the job sneaking back up on her. "Financial necessity," she said, not sure if she was trying to justify it to him or to herself.

Mr. Runyon nodded sympathetically.

A voice broke into the awkward silence. "So where to?"

Kate glanced up. It was the guy with the name issues, Burt. She checked the clipboard. "I think we have one more."

A short, dumpy guy staggered up to the group, dragging his luggage behind him like a mule pulling a cart. From the looks of him he could have made the trip from the wrong side of a window seat.

Kate ran her finger down the list of names. "And you are . . ."

"Frank Summers."

"Yes, here you are." She checked off his name. "Rough flight, Mr. Summers?"

Mr. Runyon laughed. It was a noise like pouring water out of a large jug. "He had a luggage malfunction."

"Turbulence," Burt said.

Mr. Oakley coughed. Kate thought she detected the ghost of a smile. But if there was a joke, Mr. Summers didn't seem to be in on it. He narrowed his eyes and glanced from one to the other with a frown.

"I hope you got some aspirin back at the hotel," he said.

Kate led them out. "Oh, we're well supplied with medication, Mr. Summers."

In the limo to the hotel, Kate rode up front. Mr. Runyon had caught her off guard with the comment about Micronesia, and the voices had started up again.

What was she doing here in a Caribbean resort catering to high-dollar tourists when Jim was struggling to keep the clinic running back in the Federated States of Micronesia? On the surface the answer came easily enough. Helping pay off Dad's medical bills. And with the money Mr. Strange was paying, by this time next year she could be back at the clinic. That was the main reason she took the job. That and the other thing. The chance to help people like Mr. Heald.

# CHAPTER EIGHT

Jake stood on the beach, turning China's wedding ring over in his fingers and watching a Pacific Seacraft 44 skim the Nichupte Lagoon. It had been a few hours since the flight, and the fading effects of the in-flight wine party had left him in an introspective mood.

Was he fooling himself? After he repaid the money he had borrowed from the advertising budget, China would come around, right?

He followed the progress of the sailboat and thought about what Berf had said on the plane. Was he settling? Maybe if he got China out on the open water for a week or so, nothing but the sky and the sea and the occasional tropical island port, a real one, not like this tourist trap, she might start to see life differently. A short sail was a lark, but he knew from experience that an extended trip could change your life.

He understood China's reaction. She didn't know. She was hypnotized by the sparkling life that dangled in front of her eyes every day, not even knowing there was something else out there, something that reached down to your core.

To feel the wind on your face, to read its subtle changes and taste the salty spray of a building sea. To cleanse your mind of the mirages of the past and the illusions of the future. To awaken each morning, your senses fully alert, humming to the vibrations of the universe like a tuning fork, not fighting to gain ground but instead flowing forward, with a knowledge that was more revelation than reason.

It wasn't sailing; it was the mystery of life crystallized in the beauty of the moment. But you got there by sailing. That was the true destination, not the X on the chart.

He could hear what she would say. "Jake, you have to face reality." He'd said the same thing just a few hours ago. But maybe, just maybe, he could get her to that place. He had to give it a shot, didn't he? After all, you didn't just throw away five years without even making the effort.

A noise behind him caught his ear. Kate walked up, consulting her clipboard. "Mr. Oakley, the party's over here."

Over her shoulder, tiki torches sputtered in the breeze, fitfully illuminating the nightly beach party. Over the surf, Jake heard the sound of local music, shouts, laughter. Kate held out an umbrella drink. Jake took it absently.

"Thanks."

Kate stepped next to him. "You look like you'd rather be somewhere else."

"To be honest, I'd rather take that sailboat and a good woman and disappear."

She studied him for a few seconds. Her expression didn't fill Jake with confidence.

"So are you down here searching for a woman? Or maybe two?" She nodded toward a couple of partiers, two bustomatically enhanced college girls in rebel flag bikinis, flirting with a waiter.

Jake shook his head. "I'm talking about a hard-headed woman."

"A what?"

"Like in the Cat Stevens song."

Kate frowned. Obviously not a fan. But who was, these days? The guy was too old and his name was on government watch lists.

"A hard-headed woman makes you dream big, change the world just to please her." He could feel her evaluating him again.

"So why are you here instead of on a sailboat with your hard-headed woman?"

Jake drained the umbrella drink in a gulp. It was a typical, weak, massed-produced party cocktail. "I . . . uh . . . I'm down here with my friend. He lost his wife on his wedding day. He just needed to get away."

"Your friend?"

"Yeah. Sad story. Not suitable for a beach party."

The more he thought about it, the sadder it felt. Maybe Berf was right. Maybe it was hopeless. Maybe he was an idiot for entering the Iron Fish, killing himself to win back China. He rattled the ice. "You got any more of these?"

They walked through the party to the bar. The crowd tended toward younger types, college kids. Attractive college kids used to hanging out with lots of drinks and not so many clothes.

Berf appeared. "J-Bird! My main man. Kate! Let me get you a drink." He snagged a couple of glasses from a passing waiter.

Kate studied Berf, then Jake. "Is this your friend?"

Jake nodded. Not much sense in denying it now. Berf set the drinks on a table and pulled out some chairs. They sat down.

Kate checked her clipboard. "Burt."

"Berf," Berf corrected.

"He seems to be taking it well," Kate said to Jake.

Berf held up his drink. "I'll take it any way I can get it."

Jake winced. He'd been flying by the seat of his pants when he pulled out the "for a friend" misdirection, and now that he thought about it, he couldn't have chosen a worse person to play the part of the heartbroken lover.

Kate took a deep breath, clutched the clipboard, and stood. "Well, I'm glad you're enjoying yourself. See you tomorrow."

Berf jumped up. "Kate! Relax! Have a drink!"

"I need to meet all the guests."

"Don't think of us as guests. Think of us as . . ." A shapely local maiden in a sarong caught Berf's attention, and it took him a second to finish the sentence. ". . . available."

Jake downed his drink and picked up the other one. Suddenly it all seemed hopeless. Who was he fooling?

Kate picked up her clipboard. "I think not."

Berf pulled her back to the chair. "We need help in planning our week."

Kate sat with a forced air of professionalism and consulted her clipboard. "Okay, we have—"

"Skydiving," Berf said.

Jake frowned. "What does that cost?"

Berf waved aside his objection. "It's all included in our package."

"You got the Dignity package?" she asked, seeming confused.

"Right," Berf said.

Kate searched Jake's face. "He's right. It's all included."

Jake shrugged. The way things were going, jumping out of a perfectly good airplane almost made sense. "There are worse ways to go. The ultimate adrenaline rush followed by instantaneous, painless death. It's like the perfect exit."

Kate nodded. "That's the Strange Vacations philosophy right there."

Berf held up his drink. "That's why we came, for the ultimate adventure. Let's do it."

Berf and Jake clinked glasses but discovered they were both empty.

Kate waited, pen poised over the calendar. "Two for skydiving. When?"

Berf slammed his glass down on the table. "Tomorrow."

Jake stared off into the distance at everything and nothing. "Tomorrow's the Iron Fish." He spoke as if commenting on the weather or the color of a passing dog. "Or so I hear." He glanced back at Kate.

She smiled. "That's right. Surf fishing at sunrise."

Berf shrugged. "The next day then. We can't have Jake moping about his wedding forever."

"Jake's wedding?"

Jake froze, caught in the headlights of her glare.

At that moment, the shapely local maiden in the sarong walked by again. Berf jumped up.

Kate eyed Jake. "But I thought—"

"Okay. Tomorrow, then," Berf said. "I'll get us some more drinks."

Jake avoided Kate's gaze by watching Berf catch up with the girl. As he turned away, he briefly locked eyes with a guy at the next table. The jerk from the plane. Frank something.

Frank was leaning forward, an open notebook in front of him and a pen in his hand. He closed the notebook, picked up his drink, and leaned back, looking down the beach toward the band.

## CHAPTER NINE

Kate knew Mr. Oakley was lying when he first said the word friend. "So it was your wedding."

"It's a long, sad, boring story."

"Yes, you said that earlier." Something didn't line up here, and not just the lie about his wedding. She checked the clipboard. Dignity was noted in the far right column across from Oakley and Wiggins, something she hadn't noticed until Wiggins pointed it out. But that didn't make sense.

Mr. Strange had said there would be one or two a year, and here she had two in her first week. Both young, both seemingly fit. Both evidently ready to party like it was 2999. This was not what she had signed up for.

"You don't fit the Vacation with Dignity profile."

Mr. Oakley tore his gaze from Berf and the girl. "The what?"

"The package you signed up for."

"Why is that exactly?"

"They tend to be older."

He seemed to reset something in his mind. "You prefer older?"

"It has nothing to do with—" Kate reined in her instinctive response. His reaction was no more than what she expected from a guy like Mr. Oakley, but if there was any place in the world for a judgment-free zone, it was with the Dignity guests of Strange Vacations. She reminded herself that there were many kinds of suffering, and no one could fully appreciate the pain of another.

It was just that he was so young, probably close to her age, and seemingly in excellent health. Surely he had a host of less final alternatives. In Mr. Heald's case . . . well, when you took in the whole picture, it made sense. He was ninety-four and pretty much down for the count. But if life had taught her anything, it was that not everything was what it seemed to be.

She moderated her reaction. "We do have younger guests, but regardless of age, usually the need for an escape is . . . obvious."

The sadness returned, his expression when she approached him on the beach. He had said he lost his wife on their wedding day. It must have been recent.

Mr. Oakley looked away. "The deepest wounds aren't visible to the naked eye."

"No. They're not," Kate said softly. After all, what did she know of his story? The profile she received didn't give the details, only the wishes.

Mr. Oakley stared at the sand like it was the burial ground of everything worth living for. "I had a brand new BMW, a Pacific Seacraft 27 in mint condition, and a brand new Dodge Ram to pull it with, and a brand new wife. I lost them all in one day."

Kate was a little concerned with the laundry list. Surely the last was the only one that mattered. "I'm so sorry, Mr. Oakley. Was it unexpected?"

"What?"

"Your wife. How did she die?"

"China didn't die."

"But . . . but you said you lost her."

"She left me. When Berf wrecked the car, the boat, and the truck." He looked out to the water. "I pretty much lost everything I cared about that day."

Kate struggled to connect the dots. As much as she wanted to understand Mr. Oakley, everything he said seemed to reinforce her initial impressions. Despite her best efforts, an edge crept into her voice as she said, "And that's why you signed up for the Vacation with Dignity package?"

Mr. Oakley grabbed his glass, seemingly surprised it was empty, although he had downed the contents in one go a few minutes back. He looked to the bar. "That and the Iron Fish."

Kate followed his gaze. Mr. Wiggins was at the bar, the promised drinks lined up in front of him. He was talking to the girl, working his way through the drinks as he did so.

She was done with giving him the benefit of the doubt. This pair should come with a government warning stamped on their foreheads. "And what about Mr. Wiggins?"

Mr. Oakley looked back at Kate, a caution light in his eyes. "What about him?"

"Why did he sign up? Ingrown toenail? Terminal hangover?"

"He's got issues with his family. China is his sister. And his dad is a nut job. Ever hear of The Lawn Arranger?"

Kate watched Mr. Wiggins slip his arm around the girl as they disappeared into the gloom outside the torchlight. "He doesn't seem to be feeling the pain too deeply at the moment."

Mr. Oakley bristled like a porcupine with a chip on its shoulder. "His family really jacked him up. But he doesn't whine about it and get depressed like a lot of people would. Berf lives every day like it's his last."

"He's an inspiration to us all." Kate grabbed her clipboard and stood to leave. Mr. Strange would hear about this.

"Are you . . . upset?"

She turned back to him. "Your wife left you and his dad's a jerk? That's it? There are people out there with real issues, real pain. And you come here with this?"

Kate thought back on the five years at the hospice in the Netherlands. There she had made a difference, even if she had to opt for the shoulder instead of the filet when she went to the butcher. Maybe the pay with Strange Vacations was better. Okay, it *was* better. A lot better. But at what cost?

Her outrage evidently sparked an equal and opposite outrage in Mr. Oakley. He brought the full bore of his jet-black eyes to bear on her like a Howitzer. "What are you, the pain fairy? You can judge who has real pain?"

"I know it when I see it."

"What? Do you have some kind of pain gauge?" He blustered up from the table and stood toe-to-toe with her. "Oh, this guy shows a gazillion pity-grams. He's in. But Berf and Jake, they don't register on the pain-o-meter. Who are you to say we don't deserve a Strange Vacation?"

Kate took a few steps away, then spun around. "A Strange Vacation is a sacred passage, not an easy way out."

She stormed past Mr. Summers, who seemed to be watching them closely. Well, a lot of people were watching. Perhaps she had made a bit of a scene. But when she thought of Mr. Heald and how brave he had been, listening to that buffoon just made her want to scream or cry or hit something.

As she strode through the bar, she felt a hand on her shoulder. She pulled away and kept walking.

"Kate, are you all right?"

She whirled around, ready to unleash the collective force of her indignation. Mr. Runyon stood there, concern written on his face. She inhaled deeply and let out a long, shuddering breath. "I will be. It's just—"

"Does that pencil-necked geek need an attitude adjustment?" He cast a malevolent gaze at Mr. Oakley.

"What?"

"Say the word and he'll be fish food."

"Oh. No, thanks." Kate twittered out a brittle laugh hinting of tears and caught her breath. That wasn't like her. It was just that too much had happened in the last few days. She hadn't even been here a week and already her life was turning into a soap opera soaked in tequila.

Mr. Runyon put his arm around her shoulders. It felt solid and reassuring. She relaxed slightly, glad of a sympathetic soul in this tropical circus.

"How about we take a sanity stroll?"

Kate nodded, and they walked out of the light of the tiki torches onto the beach.

# CHAPTER TEN

Frank Summers sat at his table, trying to fade into the background. Not easy for a guy like him, especially since that flight from Austin. He had attempted to file a complaint with the airline, but he hadn't been able to construct a coherent narrative for the form. The last thing he remembered was signaling the stewardess for a refill, and the next thing he knew the plane was empty and she was ordering him off.

Man, they didn't make stewardesses like they used to. Back in the day, they were more accommodating, both on the clock and off, and didn't look like a waitress at a diner in Oklahoma.

He just hoped he didn't get the same crew on the return flight. That led him to thoughts of what he would be returning to, particularly the results of his most recent performance review. All the items that could be marked on a scale were marked on the low end. Hand-written comments provided color commentary, like Frank Gifford or something.

"When he does show initiative, it is completely misguided, often with disastrous results . . . Fails to establish constructive relationships with coworkers . . . Not a team player . . . Ignores important goals to focus on dead ends and distractions."

It was amazing how somebody who couldn't find his own butt with a Geiger counter if he pooped plutonium could have been promoted up the chain to the point of being a boss over actual humans, much less over a veteran like Frank Summers. The man was a regular bozo. All he needed was the orange hair and the nose. And Frank's coworkers? Most of them couldn't get a ride on the clue train with an annual pass and a box lunch.

And then there was the note scrawled on the last page.

"Frank, I'm giving you two weeks off, whether you want it or not. If you come back, I expect you to focus on the remediation plan and quit wasting your time on pointless nonsense."

Pointless nonsense? The guy was an international expert grandmaster world champion guru on pointless nonsense. Just look at the staff meetings. Who gives out a Busy Bee award every week? To adults?

Frank's ruminations were interrupted by activity at the kiddie table. The redhead disappeared with the Charlie Atlas wannabe. The yuppie shuffled through the sand to the bar like a guy who never saw what hit him. Poor sap. Frank abandoned his strategically selected table and followed.

The guy dropped on a stool and signaled the bartender. "Suicide. Absolut."

Frank slid onto the next stool. "Make it two, Noah. On me." He slapped a twenty on the bar like he did it every day. No problem. He'd expense it. Whether his boss liked it or not, Frank was on the clock, baby.

Noah nodded, spun cocktail napkins in front of them, and pulled several bottles from the shelves.

The schmo on the next stool said, "Thanks."

"Frank." He held out his hand.

"Jake."

They shook.

Jake stared at the bar and nodded his head toward the beach. "She says I don't fit the profile."

Frank peered out into the dark at the point of the last known sighting of the redhead. Now that was the thing of which he was speaking. Too bad she wasn't a stewardess. "She's hotter than a two-dollar pistol on Saturday night."

"I don't have enough pain," Jake muttered.

"I'd like to pull her trigger."

"Only people with some indeterminate amount of pain deserve a Strange Vacation."

Noah set the drinks in front of them. "Two vodka suicides."

Jake picked up the glass. "And I don't have it." He downed the drink and signaled for another.

Frank watched him closely but said nothing. He was a pro, after all, and the way this was going, the kid was lubricating himself into a nonstop talking machine.

Jake filled the silence like Frank knew he would. "Like my money's not good enough for her. I have to have pain too."

Frank sipped his drink and asked offhandedly, "Which package did you book?"

"The Dignity package."

Frank frowned. "I didn't see that on the website. How much is it?"

"What? Oh. I don't know. Berf booked it. But he doesn't have enough pain either."

Noah delivered the second suicide.

Jake slurped it and nudged Frank. "Look, tell me what you think. I'm getting married. I borrow a little money from the advertising budget to tide me over, just a short term thing . . ."

# Chapter Eleven

Michael Strange sat in his Cayman office, selecting an aromatherapy scent for his wind-down bath. It was more of a bungalow than an office, designed for comfort and escape, but still equipped with all the high-tech gadgets he needed to run his international interests.

The sounds of an angry person making dinner clattered out of the speakerphone. Pans rattling, drawers slamming. And Kate's voice. "I don't like it, Mr. Strange. It's not right."

Strange sat on the edge of the Jacuzzi tub and pulled a bottle from the rack. Cypress? No. He let it drop back in. "Kate, I don't have to remind you that we don't make that decision for the Dignity guests." He selected another vial. Star anise? Not tonight.

A bang and a sizzle came over the line. Running water or frying bacon?

"He's not a terminal case," Kate said. "Just a clueless jerk."

Strange frowned at the phone. This was not helping with his decompression strategy. "Can you really judge that? There is such a thing as unbearable emotional pain."

It suddenly got quiet on the line. The background noise must have been water.

"This is not what I signed up for, Mr. Strange. You said this was for real people who didn't want to die in a hospital hooked up to machines."

Strange remained calm and picked up another vial. Hyssop. That sounded right. He set it by the phone. "If it was a perfect world, people wouldn't need our services. This guy may not meet your standards, but he booked the Dignity package for a reason. It's his decision, not yours."

He turned the crank to lower the chandelier and began lighting candles. "Kate, I realize it's kind of sudden, so soon after Heald, but that's just the luck of the draw. Remember that most of your guests need only occasional medical attention. The Dignity package represents maybe one out of every hundred thousand guests. Less. It could be years before you see another one."

Strange set the lighter aside and raised the chandelier. "Aren't you competing in the Iron Fish tomorrow?"

"Yes, sir."

"Then I suggest you put this out of your mind and enjoy yourself."

"But this guy's not right. He shouldn't be a Dignity guest and I don't want any part of it."

"And you don't have any part of it. You just take care of the regular guests. Pearl will take care of everything else that needs doing for this . . . this . . . What was his name?"

"Mr. Oakley."

"Yes. Oakley. He's Pearl's problem, not yours."

Strange hung up the phone, opened the vial of hyssop, and poured it into the hundred-degree water. Then he set the terrycloth robe aside, lowered himself into the tub, and leaned back with his eyes closed, concentrating on his breathing.

When he launched his business, Strange had been shocked that nobody had beat him to it. It seemed obvious. Even sick people liked vacations, but it was difficult to pack a dialysis machine in your carry-on. Or get access to other specialized treatments or supplemental medication, or replacements if your meds were lost or stolen in a foreign country.

In addition, many people traveled to exotic locations to have procedures done more cheaply than back home. They needed a place outside the hospital to convalesce.

Strange pioneered the idea of the medical vacation, a way for people with special needs to still enjoy a quality escape. Personnel, equipment, and supplies were provided according to the requirements of the patient, or as Strange preferred to say, guest. Strange paid existing resort hotels to remodel suites to his requirements and booked them on a priority basis as necessary. So, for a comparatively minimal investment, SV had facilities all over Europe and Southeast Asia. Guests were thrilled to discover that often their insurance covered the medical expenses on the trip.

The SV brand became so popular that they expanded to other specialty vacations, such as weddings, reunions, conferences, sports, or just regular people who liked quality and weren't allergic to sticker shock. Then there was the merchandise. You couldn't swing a bleached blonde on any beach in Europe without hitting half-a-dozen SV shirts.

Then, a year ago, he happened to see a friend in Sri Lanka. His friend had a problem, and as they talked, Strange realized he had the means to help. Accidents weren't frequent, but sometimes they happened, and Strange arranged an accident for his friend during a ski trip in Switzerland. A random, painless accident with no suspicious circumstances to jeopardize the life insurance.

Before the accident, his friend had talked to another friend with the same problem, and six months later she booked the second Dignity package, a mountain bike trip along the route of the Tour de France. Heald's parasailing accident in Monaco was the third. Then Lindsay's base-jumping mishap at the Cave of Swallows.

And now this Oakley. Perhaps Kate was right. Maybe the man had made a poor choice, but that was no one's concern but his own. When it came to the Dignity package, from the beginning Strange had made a point of not second-guessing the guest's decision. They wanted a service, for whatever reason, and he provided it. The sooner Kate let go of the illusion that she had a say in the decisions of others, the better for everyone.

Strange turned on the jets and watched the flame of a single candle dance above him on the chandelier. He was going to have to keep a close eye on Kate for a while.

When Heald listed her as a companion in Monaco, Strange had checked her out. Three years at a Global Health Alliance clinic in the Federated States of Micronesia. Before that, five years at a hospice in the Netherlands with direct contact with terminal patients. She had even initiated the protocols. She was perfect on paper.

Extensive medical experience in the field, and an under-standing of the needs of those in end-of-life care. Just what he needed for the new Cancún location.

But this phone call was troubling. His instincts told him she could be trouble, and Strange didn't like trouble. It was bad for business.

# Chapter Twelve

A noise in the next room woke Jake. Something about that bothered him, but he couldn't quite place exactly why. And there was another thing. It seemed like during the night someone had filled his head with sawdust and scorpions and used one of those dehydrating machines on his mouth.

He opened an eye. It was dark. Really dark. That wasn't right. No matter what hour of the night, light pollution from downtown typically lit up the outlines of things in his bedroom. Did a power failure black out all of downtown? He reached for the lamp and knocked something off the nightstand.

There was that noise again, like someone running into furniture in the living room. Then he remembered why the noise was bothersome. He lived alone.

Jake sat up suddenly and then fell back onto the bed, groaning his repentance. For moving his head. For waking up. For whatever he did the night before.

He should jump up, grab the Louisville Slugger from under the bed, and go in search of whoever was in the condo, but fate had pushed him down the Maslow pyramid into the basement. He would just have to take his chances lying here for a bit and solve the case of the mysterious intruder at his earliest convenience.

The bigger mystery was the cause of his current condition. Jake prided himself on living in balance. With himself. With the world. The universe. Not in a mystical, space-cadet kind of way, just as a functioning human on the planet. It had been years since he'd had a hangover. Not since early college days. Back when he was hanging with Berf.

Of course. Like so many other things, Berf was probably behind whatever happened last night.

As Jake lay there, waiting for the swirling miasma of pain in his head to subside, he realized he was still in his clothes. He pulled his cell phone from his pocket and glanced at it. Four a.m.

He brought up the flashlight app. A cheap clock radio lay on the floor by a cheap nightstand with a legal folder on it next to a headboard that was attached to the wall, not the bed. He flipped on the lamp, but didn't recognize a thing in his room. In fact, it wasn't his room at all.

A crash sounded from the other room and he recognized Berf's voice as he talked himself through the maze of furniture in the living room to the other bedroom in the suite.

Then it came back to him. The wedding. The reception. The money. Cancún. The Iron Fish.

The Iron Fish! The first round would commence at dawn!

Jake staggered to his bathroom, shedding clothes en route, flipped on the faucet, and drank three glasses of water before he remembered he was in Mexico. He set the glass down and backed away like he'd found a rattlesnake in the sink. Surely the hotel filtered the water. If not, then he would develop an intimate familiarity with the coral-themed wallpaper immediately opposite the toilet. And lose the tournament.

With a fatalistic shrug, he stepped into the shower, adjusted it to the equatorial jungle setting, and grasped the pipe behind the shower head, hanging like soap on a rope. The steaming water caressed him like a lobster destined to be the main course. When visibility in the bathroom reached six inches and he began to feel, if not human, then at least somewhere in the same ZIP code as humanity, he emerged, dried off, and delved into his luggage.

He pulled on board shorts and a t-shirt and wiggled his feet into water shoes. Then he donned a safari jacket that held various essential angling implements and a Gilligan hat with a carefully selected array of lures and hooks, picked up his rod case, and emerged from the ocean side of the hotel into the pre-dawn gloom.

A banner tied to the beach volleyball net read IRON FISH TRIATHLON. Above the cabana bar, another banner read REGISTRATION. Under it, a crowd of contestants with numbers pinned to the back of their shirts grazed at the continental breakfast buffet. Behind the bar, Noah, evidently cheerful and industrious at any hour of the day, handed out coffee, fruit juice, Bloody Marys, mimosas, or in some hard-bitten cases, shots.

Jake walked to the registration table at the other end of the bar just as Kate stepped away from the line with her number. Jake was far from one hundred percent, but he had achieved sufficient consciousness to notice that Kate looked even better in the morning than she did by tiki torch light, which, based on Jake's experience, was mathematically impossible. Unless she had made a deal with the devil.

"You signed up to compete?" Jake asked.

"I signed up to win."

From her expression, Jake sensed he wasn't destined for the winner's circle in her Most Eligible Bachelor competition. That was fine with Jake. Sure, she was as cute as a kitten video on YouTube, but he liked them a little less prickly.

Just then the jock from the plane walked up holding a number and a safety pin. "Little known fact. Kate is the reigning champion of the Micronesia Deep Sea Fishing Tournament."

"You're here for the tournament too?" Jake tried to remember his name. Bunyan or Funyun or something like that. After that little incident with the luggage, Jake had figured the guy for free weights, not free casting. Closer inspection persuaded Jake that Runyon could be the type to talk about whether his wine had legs while loading his own ammunition for hunting elk.

And if Kate had made a deal with the devil, Runyon could very well be the devil in question, especially considering the way she smiled at him. Not that Jake cared. Runyon could have her and welcome to it. They probably deserved each other.

Then, to cap off the experience, Frank appeared, a chocolate donut in his hand and a number on his shirt. He stared at Kate and said, "Trophies are hot."

Jake couldn't figure this guy, doubtful that anyone could be as obtuse as he seemed. It was like his emotional development had been cryogenically frozen when he was twelve.

Kate retrieved her gear from a nearby table. It was all new, price tags still on it. She walked to the beach. Runyon followed with his gear, also new.

Frank finished his donut and watched them go as Jake got his number.

"What does she see in that guy?" Frank said, crumbs dropping onto his Hawaiian shirt. "His neck is about is thick as his head. Probably has the IQ of a pet rock with a learning disability."

Jake fought down the smile that crept across his face. "So, Frank, what is it you do?"

Frank brushed the crumbs from his shirt. "Sales." Then he headed back to the buffet.

Figured.

The sun peeked above the waterline, dyeing the clouds pink as Jake walked down the beach past a long line of competitors. He scanned the area, saw breaking waves about fifty yards out, and walked past Runyon and Kate, who were already out in the water and casting.

He stopped about thirty yards past Kate, opened up his case, assembled his fifteen-foot rod, and lodged the case in the sand. Once he'd attached sinker, lure, and hooks, he walked out until the water topped out at his knees and warmed up with a few practice casts.

From his left, Runyon yelled over the noise of the surf. "How's the fishing in Micronesia?"

Jake could barely make out Kate's response. "Incredible."

Runyon yelled back. "I'd like to check it out one day."

Between casts, Jake looked over at the pair. Kate was facing Runyon, who grinned like a high school quarterback chatting up a cheerleader. When Kate returned to her casting, she was smiling.

Jake thought he might be sick but fought the urge. Might attract sharks. He backed up a few yards, set his face toward the sea breeze, cast out about seventy yards, and reeled it in across the break. He breathed in the salt air, the fishy smell of seaweed. It had been a long time, and the water here was a welcome change from fishing the California coast when he was a kid.

After a few attempts, the rhythm kicked in and muscle memory took over, leaving Jake's mind free for contemplation.

From the beginning, he had every intention of repaying it, but he saw now that skimming from the advertising budget had been a mistake, a serious lapse in judgment. He'd never so much as taken a paperclip before now. So how had he leapfrogged to embezzling— that was the word he'd been hiding from. How had he jumped from complete honesty to stealing close to one hundred thousand dollars in a single bound?

Not an easy question to answer. He grabbed the rod with both hands and cast out eighty yards or so. His hand shifted to the crank.

He could blame it on China, on Roger, on the pressure to present the perfect façade of the perfect husband, the quintessential son-in-law. To display the image of perfect executive officer material. The heir apparent.

He could argue that he had been hypnotized by the dream. The corner office. The unlimited expense account.

But they say a hypnotist can't make you do anything you don't really want to do. So is that what he really wanted? Success at any cost?

Out of the blue, the image of Dad at the helm of a sailboat off the eastern coast of Borneo flashed in Jake's mind. The summer Jake turned sixteen. Three months of hiking through jungles, living in hammocks in the trees, fishing, sailing.

That was the life, but who could afford it? A guy who worked his way up from franchise VP to CEO, that was who. Roger was getting on in years, and from all signals, he had his sights on Jake to take the helm. At least, until the wedding.

But Jake could recover. As his head cleared, the events of last evening came into focus. The feeling of hopelessness, the urge to chuck it all in and call it quits. But now in the invigorating ocean breeze, Jake realized it was the stress and fatigue talking. He could do this thing, win the tournament, repay the money, get back on track.

Jake reeled in the line and made to cast again, but suddenly he felt restricted in the safari vest. He shrugged it off and tossed it onto the beach. He cast about seventy yards out and almost dropped his reel when Kate yelled to his left.

She'd caught one. He watched her bring it in when Frank yelled to his right. He had one too. Jake took a deep breath and worked his line, reeling it in with no results. He rushed to cast again, but lost his grip and it dropped into the surf. He bent down, grabbed it, took a strong grip, and cast it out about ninety yards.

As it approached the break seventy yards out, he got a hit. He locked the reel and pulled back. An amberjack leapt out of the water. A big one. He gave it some line and then a sharp tug to turn it around.

That was when the line snapped and Jake fell backward into the surf.

## CHAPTER THIRTEEN

Pearl didn't mind his job. In fact, he liked it. Lots of travel with a full expense account. No heavy lifting. What's not to like? But being out on the worksite before sunrise was where he drew the line. That just wasn't civilized. Shift workers did that kind of thing. And farmers. And morning-drive DJs. And if Pearl had wanted to get up at an obscene hour, he would have taken one of those jobs.

But here he was wiping the sleep from his eyes and walking in the sand. The sun snuck up above the horizon like an overcooked egg. On his left, a snaking line of anglers stood in the surf trying to out-fish each other. On his right, resort hotels with the windows all dark because all the sane people were still sawing logs.

When he was done, he'd have a word with Sully. It wasn't right how they were treating him, a man with his experience and seniority. But don't get him started on that. He had a job to do.

Growing up in Chicago, Pearl had little opportunity and even less inclination for fishing, but he didn't let that throw him. He was a professional, after all. He'd done his research on Sports Fishing TV and had taken pains to dress the part. Waders, flannel shirt, Peterbilt cap, rod case slung over his left shoulder, live bait bucket in his right hand.

Pearl was about to give up when he sighted the Oakley guy in the goofy Gilligan hat just past Kate. Pearl scouted around for cover. By the sea wall, he spotted a clump of greenery at the base of a palm tree behind a bunch of beach chairs. Perfect.

He took a quick glance around, set down the bucket, and tossed his cap over by the chairs. The wind blew it up against the palm, just as he knew it would. He had a second sense about these things.

Pearl grabbed his head like he'd just lost his hat, made a show of searching, spotted it with an exaggerated show of surprise and relief, and threaded through the maze of chairs to the tree. Once there he snagged the cap, made a final reconnaissance of the area, and slipped behind the plants, thankful they were ferns, not agave.

That was his way. Never cut corners. Do your best, even when nobody was looking. It was a matter of family honor. His father had drilled it into him like a Marine sergeant.

Pearl ducked down and pulled the case off his shoulder. He thought about the old man. He had always said that civilization was a life-and-death struggle against the universe. Over generations and centuries, man had made the gradual discovery of what works and what gets you killed.

Survival was a matter of doing the right thing the right way, no matter who was watching. In fact, who was watching had nothing to do with it. It wasn't about right and wrong. It was about alive or dead. And the old man was proof—a cat burglar who supported a family of six sticking with simple B&E jobs that the other guys turned up their noses at. Only one short stretch at Joliet during his entire career. What more evidence could you ask for?

Pearl opened the case and pulled out not a fishing rod, but an air rifle powered with a $CO_2$ cartridge. He loaded it with a tranquilizer dart, a special design for water jobs. The dart, made from cellulose, dissolved in water, leaving no trace that it was ever there. The narcotic delivered a knockout punch within seconds. The victim fell into the water and drowned, making it seem like natural causes. The only pain was the sting of the dart.

Not a bad way to buy the farm, all other things being equal. Which they rarely were, in Pearl's experience.

Pearl pumped up the rifle and snaked the barrel through the vegetation, tracking Oakley as he waded into the surf. He watched Oakley cast a few times, getting the feel of his rhythm. Then he sighted for Oakley's butt. Plenty of meat for the dart to sink into.

Taking a moment to center himself, Pearl regulated his breathing, inhaling through his nose, exhaling through his mouth. Slow down. Enter the moment. Sense your environment while focusing on a single point in time and space. This was no job for some overeager young upstart. That's why you hired someone like Pearl and you paid him right. And treated him right, dang it. But he couldn't think about that right now.

Pearl didn't particularly care for killing folks. Him, he was a live-and-let-live kind of guy, like the old man. But if some bird really wanted to buy the farm—and Pearl considered paying big bucks in advance for the privilege of getting killed a pretty clear statement of desire—then he wouldn't argue the point. The way he saw it, it was your nickel. You want to check out early, we can take care of it for you.

The breathing worked. He could sense that the moment was right. He exhaled and squeezed the trigger like pumping a tennis ball when giving blood. At that precise moment, the Oakley guy must have decided he couldn't fish with his jacket on. He shrugged it off and the dart hit the jacket, not the guy. As he tossed the jacket to the shore, the dart fell to the water.

Pearl swore softly. That was the thing about civilization. It was an attempt to even the odds, hedge your bets on survival. But it wasn't a fair fight. Nobody was immune to Fate. You do the right thing in the right way, you were guaranteed success almost every time. Almost.

But there was always the whatchacallit, the Hindenburg Uncertainty Principle. Randomness. That's what got the old man that one time. Things you can't do a damn thing about. The old man hadn't never heard of the Hindenburg Principle. Pearl had learned about that all on his own.

Pearl reloaded and got settled when Kate hollered, but it was nothing. She just hooked some big fish and was reeling it in. That Kate, she was a good egg. He hoped she stuck around.

Then the Summers guy started hollering. Another catch. Must be biting. Good for them. He hoped Kate won.

He got set and sighted again. Inhale, exhale, squeeze.

Oakley swung back to cast and the rod slipped from his hand. He bent over to get it and the dart zipped over his head into the water.

Pearl swore again, loaded impatiently, and sighted on Oakley as he bobbed around after the rod. There was no shot. He waited. You didn't gain anything by rushing in. The only way to beat Hindenburg was to bet on the side of civilization. Right thing, right time, right way. It was the only chance a guy had against the universe.

Oakley had a fish now, hooked on the line out there on the second break. A big one flipping all over the place. Pearl sighted. Oakley leaned back, working the reel. He presented a stationary target. It was the right time. Pearl sighted.

Inhale, exhale, squeeze.

And Oakley's line snapped. He fell back into the surf. The dart zipped past him and hit the Summers guy in the butt. He hollered something that sounded like "sunny beaches" and dropped his reel. A wave knocked him down.

That ripped it as far as Pearl was concerned. You could only take so much from the universe before you had to take matters into your own hands. Sometimes you just had to give the Hindenburg Principle a swift kick in the nads.

Pearl loaded angrily and shoved the barrel back out through the branches.

Oakley leaned over Summers, trying to pull him out of the surf. His butt was a perfect target. No chance of missing.

Then a large hand dropped on the barrel and snatched the gun. Pearl panicked. Sully loomed in his face, grabbed his flannel shirt, and dragged him up the stairs, past the seawall to a nearby doorway.

## Chapter Fourteen

Sully slammed the door behind them and shoved Pearl across the room. Pearl stumbled into a pile of dirty towels in front of a row of washing machines. The air outside had been cool and humid. Inside the laundry, it was warm and humid, the hum of machinery masking noises and requiring conversations to be made at a shout. Which was fine with Sully, because he was ready to shout.

"What are you doing?"

Pearl got up and adjusted his waders. "Taking the shot."

Sully stood behind a stainless steel laundry table. "How many does it take?"

Pearl walked to the table. "There was—"

Sully slammed the air rifle on the table. With Pearl, you really didn't want to give him free rein to spin excuses. You would be there all day.

"You don't think two guys falling unconscious into the surf for no reason would be suspicious?"

"He was . . ."

Sully raised an eyebrow, the one that shut people down.

Pearl clammed up and turned his head away, which was what he did when he knew he was beat. Which was always.

Working with Pearl was what you call a mixed blessing of a different color. In the plus column, he was small, quiet, efficient, took initiative, an independent worker, didn't smoke or drink or let women jack him up. He was kinda like one of these washing machines. You could shove a quarter into him, push a button, and go do something else while he ran through the cycles.

Sounded like a guy who got top marks on his annual performance reviews, right? Well, it wasn't all beer and beans. He would do something really complicated just fine, then screw up the simplest thing. The problem was, you never knew which thing it would be, so you couldn't head it off. And when he did get to talking, you couldn't shut him up. And don't even get him started about the Hindenburg Principle. He had a thing about that stupid zeppelin.

Sully brought his voice down to a reasonable level. "Look. We got a good thing going here. Salary. Dental. 401(k)."

Pearl glanced up. Sully shoved the gun across the table. Pearl picked it up and walked away without a word, just a blistering glare.

Sully twisted the final thrust in. "Don't screw it up. Like Chicago."

Pearl spun to face Sully, his little eyes hard like black rocks in a fish tank. He spoke quietly, barely audible over the machinery, but you could tell he meant it. "You know that wasn't my fault."

That was another thing. If anything went wrong, it was never Pearl's fault. If he was alone in the desert and peed on his own shoes, he'd blame it on somebody else, even if he had to walk for three days without water to find them.

"What I know is the truck goes down Michigan Avenue with the door open, hot product falling out the back and you behind the wheel."

Pearl raised his voice. It was one of those thin, edgy voices like a stooge from a 1940s gangster movie. It drove Sully crazy.

"He hits the side and gives me the high sign. I drive away. That's how it works. If you aren't ready, don't hit the side. You hit the side, I'm driving. That's how it's done. Hit, go. Hit, go."

Sully silenced him with a fist on the table. "Just remember, this is the one we retire on. Don't screw it up."

"I was just taking the shot."

"Don't screw—"

"Okay, okay. I get it." Pearl shot his cuffs.

"And what is with that getup?" Sully popped the suspender strap on the ridiculous nipple-high rubber pants Pearl had on. And a flannel shirt. In Cancún. The guy really took it too far sometimes.

Sully could just get somebody else, but the next guy would probably be even loonier. And it was hard to find a guy you could trust these days. That was one more thing in the plus column for Pearl. He was as solid as the Sears tower. He wouldn't leak if you aerated him with a pitchfork.

Pearl rubbed the spot where the elastic had snapped. "For your information, they're called waders. It's what fishermen wear."

Sully shook his head and walked out the door. Pearl grabbed the gun and followed. They walked to the sea wall. The guy Pearl shot by mistake was already wading back into the surf. He was one tough cookie.

On the other hand, the sedative was dosed for Oakley, who was maybe half the weight of the other guy, and gauged to last five minutes tops. Just enough time to drown, but not enough to register on a toxicology report unless you knew what you were looking for. And the coroner they used was paid to not look for it.

Oakley was fooling with his line. Kate was standing just behind the water line, watching the big guy, obviously suspicious about his speedy recovery.

Sully nodded at the buzz-cut guy, who was messing with his line. "What do you think about that one?"

Pearl gave him a cool once-over, his little black eyes flashing under his Peterbilt hat. "I'd say watch him like a Mohawk."

Sully frowned at Pearl. "Like a what?"

Pearl's gaze didn't waver. "There's something not right about that guy, that's what. Asks too many questions. Around here, you ask too many questions, people are liable to think you're the kind of guy who wants to find things out. It's bad for your health."

Sully shook his head. "Just watch him, but don't do anything."

Pearl's eyes narrowed. "I'll watch him," he said under his breath. "Like a Mohawk."

# Chapter Fifteen

When it came down to it, and it frequently did, Berf could always say that he had no objections. His general policy was "life without regret," and that was working out along the lines he expected. Of course it helped if you made wise choices.

Like last night, for example. Drink all the weak party drinks you like (as long as you drink twice as much water), get plenty of rest (to bed by four, up by noon), exercise (well, probably the less said about that, the better), and stick to a balanced diet (like these excellent fish tacos).

It was shocking, really, how many people ignored the basic principles of partying. But he was, after all, a Past Master. You couldn't expect the weekend warrior to live up to the high standards of the pro.

Last night he had left Jake in the capable hands of Kate, who seemed like the kind of gal who had been up the creek and over the mountain. If anyone could take Jake's mind off his troubles, Kate was that anyone.

Then there was Rita. Any fool could see she was hotter than Satan's left foot, but Berf had seen immediately that there was something more to this one. And finding that something would be a great way to start this vacation. Let Jake snag the prize-winning fish; Berf had already landed his catch.

It was midday, and Berf strolled with Rita down a *calle*—that's what they called streets here in old-town Cancún—eating tacos she bought from a street vendor and drinking Jalisco from a bottle. She wore tight jeans and a long-sleeved, red-and-white plaid seersucker shirt tied off at the waist.

She reminded him of Drusilla, the daughter of the Basque rancher Don Luis Alvarado. The woman who had caught Tyrel Sackett's eye back in Abilene and got him crosswise with Orrin for a spell. Big dark eyes and long lashes. Old Ty ended up following Drusilla to Santa Fe and marrying her, but Berf wasn't figuring into putting his neck in any loops he couldn't pull out of.

They walked slowly, glancing in shop windows occasionally. Rita shooed away the local kids who tried to sell them gum, bracelets, and cigarettes of dubious vintage.

As they passed, a beefy street vendor in a worn polo shirt with horizontal stripes and hair growing out of his ears stepped in front of Berf and held up a watch. "Rolex. *Para usted, hoy, veinte dólares americanos.*"

Berf stopped. He used to be able to *parlez-vous* along with the best of them, but the space between his cross-border excursions had gotten longer as he got older. "What?" He turned to Rita.

"He has a watch. He will sell it."

Berf regarded the stall, a display of sunglasses, cell phones, and watches. "How much?"

"*Veinte dólares,*" the vendor said.

"Twenty dollars American."

"Twenty dollars? For a Rolex? That can't be real."

The vendor held it out. "*Es real. Mira.*"

Rita took the watch from the vendor and inspected it on all sides. "Looks like real to me." She gave it to Berf. "See the crown under the six?"

There was a crown under the six.

"And the sweep hand. It is smooth. Not jerky." Rita flipped it over and tilted it back and forth. "And the hologram on the back." She gave it back to Berf.

Berf tilted it around, inspecting the hologram. "For twenty dollars?"

Rita shrugged. "Maybe he needs money fast. No time to bargain."

Berf studied the vendor, who smiled like his picture was being taken. It was not a picture anybody was likely to frame and hang on their wall. Except maybe his mama. It occurred to Berf that the only thing worse than buying a fake Rolex from a stall vendor was buying a real Rolex from a stall vendor. "Or maybe he needs to get rid of it fast. Before somebody finds it on him."

Rita shrugged. "Maybe that too."

Berf tinkered with the watch. It had a dial that allowed you to mark when your oxygen would run out. He could use a dive watch, even if it wasn't a real Rolex.

But this wasn't his first rodeo, or even his second. This could be a setup. Berf buys the watch, the *federales* pounce on him, threaten to lock him up in the black hole of Cancún until he gives them a bribe, and the watch ends up costing him five times as much. Minus the watch, which they confiscate. Of course.

He inspected the vendor for signs of incipient larceny. He kinda had the air of that guy who stalked Tell Sackett in New Orleans. Hippo Swan was the name.

Berf kept his eye on the vendor. "Ask him the name of his dog."

The man eyed Berf for a few breaths. "*Lobo.*"

Berf nodded. There were many ways to judge a man, but his dog was the tipoff. A man who had a dog was two steps ahead of the game. Of course, it wasn't a sure thing. Berf's dad had a dog and look at him. Also the vendor could mistreat the dog. But the fact that he named his dog Wolf said something. Berf made a decision.

He scanned the street. Nobody was paying any attention to them. He unzipped his front pants pocket where he kept his wallet when traveling, opened it a crack, peeled out a twenty, and slipped it to Rita while looking the other way.

Then, while she handed it over to the vendor, Berf folded the watch band inside his wallet and slid it into his pocket. A quick reconnaissance showed he had successfully conducted the transaction without attracting the slightest attention.

The vendor thanked him in an explosion of Spanish. Berf nodded. Rita slipped her arm in his and they continued strolling down the *calle* past storefronts selling everything from *talavera* bowls to *lucha libre* masks. Berf tried on some pointy boots. He bought Rita a silver necklace with an opal pendant. Then, as they were searching for a dark, cool bar to spend the siesta hours, Berf came to an abrupt stop.

Rita tugged at his hand, but he let it go and walked across the plaza to an art gallery. There in the window was a 24x30 framed print of *Jackadillo Deals from the Bottom*. A group of mutant animals sat at a poker table. The dealer, an armadillo with the head of a jack rabbit, was caught in the act of pulling an ace from the bottom of the deck. The other mutants displayed various degrees of outrage or amusement.

Rita caught up with him. "*Sí.* Those are very popular."

Berf leaned down to inspect the bottom right corner. It was numbered 23/500 and right next to it was a stylized B.O.W.

"You like?" Rita asked. "I will buy you one." She walked past him into the shop.

Tearing his eyes away from the painting, Berf followed her to a bin where she flipped through a batch of matted prints. She pulled out another copy of *Jackadillo*.

Berf snatched it from her hands and checked the number sequence: 23/500. He dropped it in the bin and found another copy, which displayed the same number.

"Do you want that one?" Rita asked.

"I already have it." Berf dropped it into the bin. "The original. In oil."

Rita's eyes narrowed. "You have the original painting of *Jackadillo Deals from the Bottom*?"

"Yes. And all the others in the series."

Rita laughed. "*Sí, como no?* You are the art collector." She picked it up. "I will get it for you." But when she saw Berf's face, she let it slip from her fingers. "You do not want it?"

"I painted it."

Now she regarded him like she would a man at the cabana bar who bought her a drink with a roll of quarters, nodded to the yacht anchored a thousand yards off-shore, and said, "That's my boat."

Berf jerked the print out of the bin and pointed to the signature. "See that?" He pulled out his wallet and showed her his driver's license. "Berford Oswald Wiggins. B. O. W." He glanced at the sticker. "And you can't get these prints for twenty dollars. They sold for a thousand dollars apiece at the gallery. And look at this. They all say print number twenty-three." He showed her four more, all with the same number. "They're fakes."

He went to shove his wallet back in his pocket when the Rolex fell out onto the floor. He glanced from it to the prints and chuckled. Live by the fake; die by the fake.

Berf picked up the watch and slipped it onto his wrist. It felt pretty solid, even if it was a fake. He pulled the print from the bin and took it to the guy at the counter. "You sell a lot of these?"

The man smiled. He measured five feet both directions and was missing a few front teeth, but it didn't seem to put him off his feed to any considerable degree. You had to admire that kind of determination in the face of adversity.

He nodded. "Very many. It is funny, no?"

Berf gave the man a twenty, winked at Rita, and walked out of the store. He was immediately accosted by a kid who held out a pack of Chiclets.

"Gum! One dollar!"

Berf took the package of gum and handed the print to the kid, whose eyes grew to the size of pesos when he got a glimpse of the sticker. He held out the whole box of gum.

"Keep it." Berf shooed him away and reached for Rita. "It's hot out here. Let's go get some drinks."

She stood in the doorway of the art gallery, studying him. "You made a half million dollars from this picture?"

"It paid for my house. Short sale."

Rita smiled, slipped her arm in his, and snuggled up close. "I know a quiet place. You're buying."

# Chapter Sixteen

Jake nursed a large lemonade at the cabana bar and tried to connect the dots of the strange events on the beach.

First, Frank collapses. He's out for the count and dead weight as Jake and Kate pull him out of the water. Kate checks his vitals. He's breathing and has a steady pulse. Three minutes later he's sitting up and asking about his rod. Kate grills him. No history of blackouts or seizures. No heart problems.

It was a mystery, but not Jake's problem. He was here to get his life back, not play nursemaid to a narcoleptic boor. He checked the scores on the board. Although you'd expect someone with a brand new rig to be a newbie, Kate was in the lead. Maybe she really was the Micronesia fishing prodigy. Frank was a close second. Jake was fifth.

Runyon was down in the thirties, obviously as new to fishing as he was to his equipment. Jake doubted that he'd ever seen a fish that wasn't lying on a plate in a wine and butter reduction. It made a guy wonder why he was here in the first place.

A man in an Iron Fish t-shirt rang a bell to gather the anglers. "Okay, next is deep sea fishing. Your boat assignments are posted." He pointed to a sheet taped to the board.

Jake waded through the crowd, found his name, and hiked down to the marina. He found the boat and hailed the captain, a solid-built man with a complexion like a Maine coastline. The *Sea Beagle* looked to be over fifty feet and was broader in the beam than other saltwater fishing boats Jake had seen. It had four game chairs set up in a V.

He turned to the captain. "Nice craft. Never seen one like it."

"That's 'cause I built her myself, me and the old man." The captain nodded at a wiry old codger icing down beers in a cooler. "Took three years."

"Time well spent." Jake indicated the chairs. "Which one's the lucky spot?"

The captain pointed to the third chair, starboard side closest to the stern, and Jake claimed it.

Frank boarded next. "Hey, partner. You're still hanging in there?" He slapped Jake on the back and took the other chair on the starboard side. "Just watch me. I'll show you how it's done."

This guy just hung on like a three-alarm migraine. Maybe Jake should have let him drown in the surf.

Kate took the chair opposite Jake on the port side. She eyed him. "I'm surprised you entered this competition. People in your situation aren't usually that competitive."

Jake was in no mood to spar. She didn't want him here. That was her problem. "It was on my bucket list."

"Ah," Kate said, like she actually believed him.

From his perch in the chair, Jake stared out into the lagoon. Fifth place wasn't going to cut it. He was going to have to up his game. Fortunately he'd been deep-sea fishing a few times, starting in the South Pacific on his sixteenth birthday. He'd give both Kate and Frank a run for their money.

Jake glanced over in time to catch Runyon taking the chair next to Kate. Great. Runyon and Kate on his left, Frank on his right, just like on the beach. It was enough to make a guy wonder if he was cursed.

All because in a weak moment he had made a single mistake. If he didn't have so much riding on this competition, he'd just catch a cab to the airport right now. But this was his only shot at getting China back. If that included putting up with these bozos, then he'd do it. But he didn't have to like it.

The old man put them through the drill as the captain steered them out of the lagoon and into open water. A few miles out, the boat set a course for a flock of shearwaters and petrels diving for lunch, indicating the presence of smaller fish that were getting it from all sides—from above by the birds and from below by the bigger fish. The old man gave them the signal, and the competition began.

Of course Frank was the first to snag one, a big wahoo that promised a long fight. The old man assisted as the captain steered the boat to best advantage. The rest of them tried to catch up.

As Jake reeled in his line, he heard Runyon yell to Kate.

"I'm a little jealous."

"I'm sure you'll catch one," she yelled back.

"No, not the fish. Micronesia, the clinic, the kids. It's my dream."

Jake tried to control his gag reflex. If he was any judge of character, Runyon probably had half a dozen kids that he had never met spread around the world. Did he really expect her to buy this line? He glanced over.

Kate was watching Frank manhandle his prey. "Really?" she yelled over her shoulder. She glanced at Jake but just as quickly looked away.

"Like you," Runyon continued, "I make sacrifices due to necessity. But one day—"

He was cut off by a whizzing sound. Jake glanced at his line. Nothing.

Kate grabbed her rod and pulled back, checking the fish. "One day?" she said, but it was clear she was focused on bringing the fish under control.

"Yeah. My passion is child trafficking. The sex slave trade."

"What?" Kate jerked her head toward Runyon and lost control of the reel. It whined as the fish, who had a greater stake in the outcome, exploited her inattention. She wrestled it under control.

Jake's line was dismayingly unengaged. He glanced at Runyon. Jake wouldn't be surprised if he was acquainted with the sex trade, but from the wrong side.

Runyon continued, seemingly unaware that Kate had higher priorities. "Yeah, this time next year I'll be back in Thailand leading rescue raids."

Jake whispered a prayer that someone would rescue him from this shouted conversation.

Kate continued to fight with the fish until she was in control. Obviously she knew what she was doing. She was in for a long struggle, but as long as she kept her focus and had the endurance, she would be back in the running against Frank.

She glanced over at Runyon. "Really? You've been to Thailand?"

"Until last year, it was my home."

A barking laugh escaped before Jake could suppress it. He might be trapped on this boat, but there was no rule that said he had to listen to this drivel stone cold sober. He slid out of the game chair, dug around in the cooler for a beer, and watched the crew help Frank hoist his catch in. It was a beauty, almost as big as Frank, which was saying something. Frank stood next to it, smiling for a photo.

Then a whizzing sound caught Jake's attention. The line in his rod was spinning out like an over-caffeinated can of Silly String.

But before Jake could move to his chair, Frank strapped into Jake's chair and grabbed the pole. "I got it."

Jake dropped his beer. "What do you think you're doing? That's my fish!"

Frank pulled back and the fish jumped out of the water. It was gigantic, even bigger than Frank's monster. Frank glanced over his shoulder. "Hang on a second, buddy, and I'll swap with you." He jerked on the rod, pulling the fish closer before it landed, and started reeling in the slack.

Jake grabbed for Frank's arm as the fish hit the water and ran. The line snapped tight. Frank's arm slipped out of Jake's grasp.

Then, inexplicably, confusingly, impossibly, the game chair pulled loose from the deck and Frank, the pole, and the seat all flew over the rail.

Jake stood, his hand suspended in the air like a mime reaching for an invisible box of corn flakes. Then he ran for a life preserver and tossed it in Frank's direction.

Kate raced to the rail and tossed out a second life preserver she had evidently snatched on the way, but Frank was already fifty yards out, clawing his way out of the straps.

As they both watched the chair sink and the figure of Frank recede in the wake, still holding onto the rod, they heard a splash. Runyon was in the water, churning up foam in a line toward Frank.

Jake felt the boat turn. He looked back toward the cabin. There were three ragged holes in the deck where the chair used to be. A scrawny man he hadn't seen before peered out from the hold like a weasel peering from a hollow log. He wore waders, a flannel shirt, and a Peterbilt cap.

The man caught sight of Jake, shook his head, peered closer, and disappeared down into the hold.

Jake turned back to the rail, but Kate stood between him and the water.

She looked from the hold to Jake with an expression he couldn't decipher. "That was your chair. You missed your chance."

Jake shrugged. "I'll have to make it up with the spear fishing."

Kate studied him with a furrowed brow as if she was trying to work out a math problem.

Jake stepped to the rail. Runyon had already latched onto Frank and was pulling him in. Jake let out a deep breath. Despite what he said, he knew there was little chance of him making up the difference now. The fish he would find spear fishing would be slim pickings compared to Frank's wahoo.

Back at the cabana, Jake hung around long enough to see that the top three positions went to Frank, Kate, and Runyon. He didn't bother to wait for his score. As the only competitor that didn't score a qualifying fish in the deep sea portion, he would be dead last by an insurmountable margin.

Jake wandered into the hotel and eventually came to rest in the lobby bar watching, but not seeing, the endless flow of tourists pass by. It was a disaster on the scale of the wedding reception. He was trying to decide whether to order another drink or take a package tour and fling himself off the top of Chichén Itzá when Berf showed up with the girl from last night's party.

"Jake, you remember Rita."

Rita held out her hand. Jake took it limply. "Charmed, I'm sure."

Berf settled into the chair next to Jake and signaled Noah. "The usual."

Noah nodded as if he had known Berf from kindergarten and began gathering an array of bottles and implements.

Berf turned to Jake. "How did it go?"

"It went."

"You're not in first?"

"I'm so far down, I have to look up to see last place. I don't exist."

"There's still spear fishing."

"Is it whale season? Cause that's what I'll need to beat the monster Frank caught."

Noah set drinks in front of Berf and Rita. Berf slid his over to Jake. "You need a drink."

Rita leaned over. "He needs a woman."

Jake pushed his empty glass to Noah, who nodded and refilled it with whiskey. At some point, a guy had to ask himself the big questions without flinching, and the big questions now loomed before him in 200-point type. What was the point? Who was he fooling? Did he ever really have a chance? How high did you have to climb to assure that the sudden stop after the fall would do the trick?

Kate walked up with her clipboard.

"Do you still want the skydiving? There's an opening tomorrow."

Jake glanced up. All eyes were on him. He shrugged "Everything else has been a disaster. Why not jump out of a perfectly good airplane?"

Kate checked a box on her clipboard. "See you in an hour."

When Jake didn't answer, she clarified. "Spear fishing. The final leg of the triathlon."

Jake swirled his drink. "Why bother? Stick a fork in me. I'm toast."

"You're giving up?"

"I'm done pushing Jell-O uphill with a toothpick."

Berf put a hand on Jake's shoulder. "J-Bird, it's your last chance to live large. Go for it." He shook Jake. "Did Tell Sackett give up when he was all alone on the Mogollon Rim, one man against thirty or forty? No, he held his ground and slithered right up in amongst them, and when he stood up to Van Allen, a dozen Sacketts appeared to back him."

Jake shoved Berf's hand away. "Fine. I'll go, if only to shut you up about the Sacketts."

Berf nudged Rita. "You want to go spear fishing?"

Rita shook her head. "I'm going fishing with my brother."

Berf shrugged and pointed at the clipboard. "Can I get in on the spear fishing?"

"Are you certified for scuba?" Kate said.

"Scuba?" Jake asked.

All eyes converged on Jake.

"I didn't know it was scuba."

# Chapter Seventeen

For someone who started out as a Hoboken wharf rat, Gus had to admit he'd had it worse. He checked his chronometer and verified it against the position of the sun. Coming on sixteen hundred. A good four hours until sunset, plenty of time for the excursion.

God bless those contest guys. Gus didn't usually do dive excursions. His thing was more of the sunset champagne cruise for two and such like. But the Iron Fish had run out of dive boats before they ran out of contestants and asked him to pitch in. For a nice little fee, of course. And that suited him right down to the ground.

He lugged the final set of tanks of compressed air from the hold and secured them on the deck. Then he took a seat at the bow of the *Desert Flower*, shook a Camel out of a wrinkled pack, and fired it up. The first hit was always the best, that penetrating scent of freshly lit tobacco and whatever cocktail of chemicals they put in the things these days. He knew they would kill him eventually, but he never figured he'd live this long, so the way he saw it he was ahead of the game.

Gus ran his hand along the railing. He caught a lot of flak for the name of the boat. *How can it be a* Desert Flower *if it's surrounded by water?* Some people couldn't handle irony.

All his boats had been named desert something— *Desert Rat, Desert Maiden, Desert Moon*—all the way back to his first boat, *Desert Derata.* The one he won in a card game in New Jersey after he got sober. Off an investment lawyer with a snootful of high-dollar scotch and more confidence than skill.

He indulged in a little smile at the memory of the blank expression on the lawyer's face. He might have owned a boat a minute before Gus laid down his full house, but he was no sailor, that was plain. Gus had thought of it as poetic justice at the time. A cosmic leveling of the playing field, if just for a moment. That was just after Gus had taken his twelve steps, closed the loop on karma, made his peace with the past. His sponsor had turned him onto Ehrmann's poem, and it had been his daily bread.

*Go placidly amid the noise and haste, and remember what peace there may be in silence.*

But Gus had since discarded such notions as cosmic comeuppance. Every man made his own fate, dictated his own ends. If that was karma . . . well, you could call it what you wanted. Gus called it cause and effect.

On the *Desert Derata* and all boats since, Gus had spent many hours, many days, alone with his thoughts, meditating on balance and purpose, on peace and silence.

There were those who created the noise and haste in this world. There were those who could not abide sixty seconds of silence. Those who filled their lives with the chaotic chatter of civilization like a caveman with a flaming branch, keeping the raging beast of self-awareness at bay.

And then there were sailors.

A sailor knew that true silence is a silence of the soul. You couldn't find real silence in this world. Alone on the sea, hundreds of miles from the voice of another human, there was the crack of a sail, the creak of a mast, the squeak of a pulley, the slap of a wave. Even on a boat becalmed, nothing moving for miles, there was the beating of the blood in your ears, the subsonic groaning of great beasts furrowing the depths.

In true silence, you heard the universe wantonly whisper its secrets. It was the sailor who listened to those secrets, planted them like a seed, watered them with minutes and hours and days and years, and harvested truth. It had always been thus.

*Jesus was a sailor when he walked upon the water.*

That Cohen guy knew a thing or two, Gus would wager.

Gus was roused from his meditations by an argument approaching from the pier. He tossed his cigarette aside and stood. It was the new girl, Kate, and two guys. Gus nodded. Kate was a sailor. He'd put money on it.

As they arrived at the *Desert Flower*, Kate asked, "Why did you sign up for it if you're not certified?"

The guy answered, "I thought it was snorkeling."

Kate caught Gus's eye. "We have a problem, Mr. West. Mr. Wiggins is scuba certified but Mr. Oakley's not."

Gus shrugged. He ran charters for tourists of all flavors after all. "No problem. We have the Scuba-Doo."

The other guy, Wiggins, said, "Ruh-roh!"

Gus looked him over. He'd seen the type before. A congenial smart aleck. Could be a problem, but if it came to that, Gus would deal with it. He was after all a student of Ehrmann.

*Speak your truth quietly and clearly; and listen to others, even the dull and the ignorant; they too have their story.*

Gus motioned them to come aboard and pulled the tarp off the Scuba-Doo. "No license. No face mask. Just jump on and drive. One hour of oxygen."

Developed in Australia, the Doo was really just an underwater moped with a built-in bubble helmet and air tank. As Gus had discovered, the Doo had the power to make even the sexiest person on the planet look like a dork. Too bad it wasn't the Wiggins fellow who would be riding it.

Wiggins responded with a nod and a smile. "Gus, my man, you're a lifesaver."

Gus's expressionless gaze didn't waver.

Wiggins turned to the other guy, Oakley. "There's your Scuba-Dooba, dude."

Oakley wisely ignored Wiggins and stepped next to Gus. "Is this your boat?"

Gus nodded. He liked this guy.

Oakley stroked the lines of the cabin. "She's sweet. I had a Pacific Seacraft once. For a few hours."

Gus felt a kinship with this man, not just because of the boat, but on a deeper level. Here was a guy who understood silence, who had stared into the dark yawning maw of oblivion without blinking or shrinking back.

He rewarded Oakley with as much of a smile as he permitted anyone.

A solid guy with a military air stepped aboard without comment and stood next to Kate.

Behind him a large guy in a loud shirt walked up, scanned the group, and focused on Gus. "You the captain? Let's get this thing going so I can collect the prize money."

# CHAPTER EIGHTEEN

Jake leaned against the rail and closed his eyes as Gus used the auxiliary engine to thread the sailboat out of the lagoon into the open sea. If things had gone differently, if he had not been so stupid as to "borrow" from the advertising budget, this would be his boat and China would be standing in the bow like Rose in the Titanic, he behind her as they sailed into their new life together.

Why was he torturing himself when there was no hope for that now? Jake forced his eyes open but couldn't help but notice Kate at the bow, holding the railing with both hands.

He went forward and joined her without speaking. They continued in silence for a while, absorbing the experience.

"At moments like this," Jake said, "you feel like you could live forever."

Kate studied him. "Change your mind, Mr. Oakley?"

He returned her stare. "About what?"

"About why you came. Is this really what you want?"

The silence grew, and Kate raised an eyebrow like she knew what he was thinking. But how could she? Even his closest friends didn't know about it.

Jake looked away, out to the open water. He didn't know why, but he wanted to tell Kate. "When I was sixteen, I spent a whole summer in Borneo with Dad. We did a lot of sailing. And fishing."

"Borneo? I had you figured more for Singapore. Or Bangkok."

He didn't take the bait. Wasn't in the mood for a fight. "Dad was a sixties Peace Corps worker. Then he got married and had to support a family, so he got a job at Berkeley. Sociology department. But Borneo got under his skin. After the divorce, he taught extra classes for ten years to afford three months back in Borneo. Just me and him."

"Have you been back?"

"Never made it."

"What do you do now?"

"VP of Franchising. In line for CEO. Or was."

"So you decided to climb the corporate ladder instead of find a way back to Borneo?"

Jake tilted his head slightly to catch her eye. "That was the way back. Make enough money to go back and stay. At the right time, with the right woman."

"And now?"

Jake surveyed the water. "Let's just say I don't see that happening. If this is the last thing I see, that's fine by me."

"You're sure?"

"Absolutely." And now that he thought about it, he realized he meant it. The dream with China was lost. He had no plan. From here on out, it was one day, one moment at a time.

"No second thoughts?"

He faced her. "Absolutely not."

Kate studied him for a long time. "I have to suit up."

The others had already donned the wetsuits. He followed.

He would go through the motions, make the futile, last-ditch effort. Then he would bury his past in the cabana bar. If he survived, then tomorrow he would figure out what happened next. And if he didn't, well, at this point, he didn't see a lot of difference either way.

# Chapter Nineteen

Pearl bobbed with the waves in a Zodiac on the far side of the Mesoamerican reef, a quarter mile from the *Desert Flower*, watching it through binoculars. What kind of idiot would name a boat *Desert Flower*? You're in the middle of the ocean, for crying out loud. Call it the *Water Lily* or something.

Hindenburg had been working a number on Pearl. In his whole career, he'd never had a job go pear-shaped like this one. Pearl shivered, thinking back on the day the law had showed up on their doorstep and hauled his dad away for a short stretch. It was all the cost of doing business, sure, but there was a difference between being hauled off for burglary and being put away for murder.

But this time he had hedged his bets to the point that the outcome was a sure thing. Once he knew Oakley and Wiggins were assigned to Gus West, he'd waited until Gus took a lunch break and had rigged everything on the boat. He was ready no matter what the universe tried to throw at him this time.

They had put Jake in the water on that Scuba-Doo. No better sign that the guy wanted to die than to get on that idiotic contraption. If they put Pearl on that, he would die of embarrassment. No need for outside assistance.

Through the binoculars, Pearl watched them hand a spear gun down to Jake, who then disappeared below the surface. The others all flipped off the side like normal scuba guys. They had those little scooter things, like an underwater fan with handles. Nothing sissy about that. James Bond used one. But Pearl was ready, no matter what they used.

Pearl lowered his binoculars and set his watch for forty-five minutes. The Doo had enough air for an hour, and he wouldn't make his move until the air was almost gone.

He opened a briefcase. Inside was a tracking screen and joystick. He raised an antenna and flipped the switch. It showed five blips a mile off the coast.

"Hello, gentlemen. And Kate."

He watched as the blips moved around independently. After a few minutes, the yellow blip moved toward the boat. He watched with the binoculars. Kate surfaced and pulled her catch in. Yellow, Kate. He made a note on the back of his comic book.

She went back out. The orange blip returned to the boat, the Summers guy. Check. The white blip turned out to be Runyon. Pearl gave him a close inspection in the binoculars. He still didn't trust that guy. Blue was Wiggins, who brought in a catch, even though he wasn't in the competition.

So that left red for Oakley. Red didn't come in at all. Shooting a fish from that goof-mobile must have been harder than he thought.

Pearl watched the blips meander around on the black screen like fireflies. After a while, his watch beeped. Forty-five minutes. Oakley would be coming back in soon. At least, he'd try anyway. Pearl had other plans.

When the red blip began moving in a straight line back to the boat, Pearl adjusted a dial to the red light, fiddled with the joystick, and watched the red dot swing around in an arc and head back out.

Pearl smiled. This was the fun part.

Then the blue dot broke away from the others, following the red. Wiggins was keeping track of his buddy. Good man, that one. But Pearl had anticipated this possibility. He'd deal with Wiggins when the time came.

The red dot quit moving. Probably ran into a reef. Pearl backed it up a bit and swung wide to one side, wiggling it a bit to encourage it to fishtail through the obstacles instead of hitting them head on. Poor Oakley was probably getting banged up. But it wouldn't be long now anyway.

Pearl steered the red dot toward Jamaica and open water, where the shelf dropped off. His watch beeped again.

"Mr. Oakley. Your wish is granted." Pearl rolled a wheel, which took the Doo down.

*Take that, Hindenburg Principle.*

# CHAPTER TWENTY

Even before it was possessed by the devil, Jake regretted getting on the Scuba-Doo. It was something Huey, Louie, and Dewey would trick Uncle Donald into riding, resulting in three minutes and seventeen seconds of cartoon violence that would kill a human four times over. So, when it actually was possessed by the devil, it wasn't quite as surprising as one might expect. Alarming, perhaps, even disconcerting, but not surprising.

The Doo was also impossible to spear fish from. He should have known better than to listen to that barnacle Gus. Nice enough guy but obviously a congenital misanthrope. So, while Frank, Runyon, and Kate taxied back and forth between the reef and the boat with multiple catches, Jake puttered around scaring things away and missing shots.

He finally hit an evolutionally challenged flounder just before he got the signal from Berf to head back. That was when the devil hit the Doo. Not that Jake thought such a thing was possible. He just couldn't think of any other explanation for it suddenly heading to Jamaica, except that it was a Voo-Doo.

Okay, maybe that was the lack of oxygen talking. Things got a little fuzzy after that. Jake fought the Doo, but the Doo won. It ran into a reef, bounced off a few more, and even sideswiped a shark the size of a school bus, all the while dragging a bleeding flounder. Which explained why the shark followed. Seeing that monster in the back window of the helmet bubble was like seeing a trooper in the rearview mirror, multiplied by a thousand.

But, as often is the case, Jake's greatest concern wasn't his greatest danger. While worrying about the shark, he had failed to notice that the devil Doo seemed intent on returning to the depths of hell. From the time the Doo revolted, Jake had been too deep to escape and surface without his lungs exploding, but now the light seemed to be fading. When something touched his shoulder, he screamed at a pitch that probably caused dolphins ten miles away to glance over their shoulders with a raised eyebrow.

It turned out to be Berf, the scooter being faster than the Doo on account of not taking detours to bash into things. Berf slipped Jake his mouthpiece and pulled him from the Doo, which continued to sink into the murk, the flounder trailing.

As they slowly ascended, Berf used hand and eyebrow signals to educate Jake on the ways of surfacing without dying, a subject of profound interest to Jake and to which he devoted his complete attention, with the exception of noting when the shark passed below them, following the blood trail of the flounder.

Finally they broke the surface, gasping for air. Jake saw nothing but choppy waves from pole to pole. Now what?

Berf pulled off his mask. "What are you doing?"

Jake noted the sun approaching the horizon. He had no idea how far out they were, but at least they had a direction. But as he raised an arm to stroke to the west, he felt a rumble in the water.

He glanced around, still seeing nothing but water. A second later a geyser erupted, hitting Jake with a wave in the face.

Berf surfaced first. "What was that?"

Jake felt no need to speculate. He struck out toward the setting sun, happy to let someone else investigate. He'd wait until tomorrow to read about it in the paper. Besides, that shark was probably still around.

He had covered about ten feet to the west when a fin appeared, then another, then a third.

Berf pulled up next to Jake. "Looks like your buddy invited dinner guests."

Jake spun around in the water, watching the fins with growing anxiety. One fin broke from the pack and rushed them. Berf revved up his scooter and headed straight toward it, slipping below the surface. Jake saw the fin veer away. Beyond it, a boat appeared above the swell.

Jake lurched up in the water and waved a hand. "Hey!

Berf surfaced. The sharks continued to circle.

Jake waved both hands. "Hey! Over here! Mayday! SOS!"

"I see you," Berf said.

"Not you. Them." Jake pointed to the boat.

"Ah. The cavalry." Berf revved the scooter again. "Hang on."

Jake grabbed Berf's dive belt, but suddenly the motor sparked and died.

Berf slapped the scooter. "Come on!"

The boat pulled up next to them, a woman leaning over the rail. "Berf? Is that you?"

Jake wiped the salt water from his eyes and looked closer. It was Rita, Berf's vacation romance.

"Rita? How did you get here?" Berf said.

"Fishing with my brother, Fernando."

A big guy stepped into view and threw a life preserver attached to a rope. Jake and Berf grabbed it and Fernando pulled them in. As Jake grabbed at the edge of the boat, Fernando grabbed a handful of dive suit and dragged him over the edge. Jake flopped into the bottom of the boat and came face-to-face with a dead body.

"Holy Toledo! What is that?" Jake scrambled away, pushing back against the hull. He glanced at Fernando, who was hauling Berf into the boat. What kind of folks were these guys anyway? Not that he wasn't grateful, but still.

Berf crawled to his feet, noticed the body, turned away, and then turned back. "Is that . . . What is that?" He backed away and almost tumbled back into the water, but Fernando snagged him and deposited him next to Jake.

Rita laughed. Jake found that almost as disconcerting as the devil Doo and the shark.

"No, no, no," she said. "It's a dead man."

That cleared things up considerably. Jake just stared at the body, thinking how close he came to sharing its fate.

But Berf gathered himself into an attitude without moving from his position slumped against the hull and eyeballed her the way a headmaster would a student who has just placed a toad in his middle desk drawer. "Really?"

Rita laughed again. "It is nothing. Fernando finds the bodies in the water for the police."

To Jake's relief, Fernando started the engine. Jake's first priority was to get to shore, and if fate had decreed that it be in the presence of a recovered cadaver, it was a price Jake was willing to pay.

Berf studied the body. "You said you were going fishing."

Rita opened a live well teeming with fish and smiled.

The image of the body was burned in Jake's mind. He had the feeling he would be seeing it frequently in nightmares for years to come. It was not a body of recent vintage. What flesh was left had a bleached, blubbery look. It wore the tattered remains of a scuba suit. A dive watch glistened on the remains of the left arm.

Jake nudged Berf. "Did you see the watch?"

Berf looked at his Rolex, then at Fernando. "Wait a minute. He's your brother? The guy in the market?"

Rita nodded.

Berf eyed Fernando. "Where did you get this watch?"

Fernando silently steered the boat back toward land.

Jake struggled to his feet and staggered to the stern. The sharks had wandered off. A minute later, just off the starboard side they passed a giant dead shark.

He yelled over the sound of the engine. "Hold on. I think that's mine."

# CHAPTER TWENTY-ONE

Kate checked her dive watch and took a few short reconnaissance passes around the reef with the scooter before giving up and getting back on the boat. Mr. Oakley knew he had only one hour of oxygen. Either he had surfaced too far to make it back by now, or he had decided to take advantage of the situation to cash in on the Dignity package.

She surfaced. Runyon held out a hand. She took it and he pulled her aboard.

"How'd you do?" he asked. "Enough to pull into first?"

Mr. Summers leaned against the cabin drinking a beer. "In your dreams." He raised the bottle to her and smiled.

Kate ignored them both as she stripped off her gear, preoccupied with Mr. Oakley. What if he had just decided to ride out the Doo with a fading oxygen tank? It wasn't a bad way to go, as ways go. Disorientation followed by dyspnea, shortness of breath. If he was lucky, he would pass out before the convulsions began.

But despite his obvious intention to see it through, Kate wasn't reconciled to it. Then there was Mr. Wiggins. What was his plan? Suicide by manta ray? Bleeding to death in a final waltz with a moray?

The sadness she felt wasn't like when she worked at the hospice or even when Mr. Heald died. In her experience, these things varied according to the case. Sometimes it was more outrage, joining the patient in defiance in the face of the evil of disease, which, despite being natural, sometimes felt grossly unnatural. Sometimes it was mourning for the loss sustained by those left behind. With Mr. Heald, it was an aching sense of emptiness, the vacuum, abhorred by nature, where Mr. Heald used to be.

But the thought of Mr. Oakley snuffing out his life, as shallow and vapid as it appeared to be, seemed an affront to life, even more so than a wasting disease. When she had first realized what he proposed to do and with so little justification, outrage clouded her manners. But now it was replaced by a draining sadness.

Kate approached Gus. "Mr. Oakley isn't back yet and his oxygen is running out. The Scuba-Doo might have broken down. He might be on the surface somewhere. We need to do a search."

She scanned the horizon. Her eye caught a plume of water a mile or two away. What could cause that? Then a thought came to her. An explosion. Pearl.

She stepped to the highest point on the boat and scanned the water. After a minute, she saw a dark spot. She went back to Gus.

"Do you have any binoculars?"

Gus handed her a set. She focused in on the dark spot. Pearl stared back at her with his own set of binoculars. He lowered them, smiled, and waved.

She lowered her binoculars, but she didn't wave and she wasn't smiling.

# CHAPTER TWENTY-TWO

Through the years, in pursuit of his mastery of the art of the party, Berf had found himself in any number of unusual circumstances. He once awoke in a castle in Denmark in a pile of snoozing Great Danes, a dozen at least. Mostly black and blue. The Danes, not Berf. There was a brindle and a merle too. Then there was the time in Boston when he ended up onstage in his boxers, the black boxers with the red hearts, a big black question mark painted on his chest, singing "Where is the Love?" with the Black Eyed Peas.

But this was a first. In a boat with a dead guy, pulling the shark that almost ate him. As committed as he was to spontaneity, Berf felt this might be a stroke or two beyond the limit of sustainability.

Tell Sackett, the embodiment of The Code by which Berf lived his life, had found himself in some pretty tight spots. Snowed in for the winter in a pocket valley in the Rockies, the Bigelow gang hunting him with a bloodlust. Holed up down in the Sierra Madres with Apaches after his scalp. Stranded up on the Mogollon rim with the whole Swandle and Allen outfit descending on him. But Berf couldn't think of anything in the Sackett canon to compare to this.

He leaned on the rail at the front of the boat next to Jake, as far from the dead body as possible, and stared into the sunset behind Cancún. There were several things here that needed explaining.

"So what was that explosion?"

Jake shook his head. "You tell me."

"And when you went deep-sea fishing, your chair came loose?"

"Yeah. Went right overboard. The whole thing, with Frank in it."

"You think . . . ?"

Berf looked at Jake. Jake looked at Berf.

Berf shook his head. Maybe he had added two and two and come up with Luxembourg. He'd never been one for conspiracy theories. They depended on too many people keeping a secret, and in his experience, a guy with a secret was a guy busting to tell it to someone over a drink. A whole group of people all keeping their mouths shut? "Nah. What am I thinking?"

Jake shrugged. "Either way, you saved my life. I almost died. Really died. Like dead died. Like him." Jake nodded back toward the body.

Berf returned the shrug. "That would have solved all your problems."

"Except for one. I'd be dead."

"From the way you were talking at the hotel bar—"

"I didn't really want to die. I just thought I did."

"So why did you take off like that when your oxygen ran low?"

"I didn't. That Scooby-Doo thing, it just . . . took over."

Berf considered the statement. Jake was a standup guy. One of the best. And as smart as a tack. But he'd been under a lot of stress lately. Lost his job. Lost his wife. Although, considering his wife was China, that was a lucky break. But he could hardly expect Jake to see it that way, for a while anyway. He'd come around eventually. After all, the guy had been voted president of the Young Entrepreneur's Club at UT as a sophomore after generating a record surplus for the treasury through a scheme to offer fifteen-minute time-share options on seats at the Longhorn home games.

But now Jake was talking through his hat. It all came down to one thing. Doos didn't just take over. Usually. But what if this one did? "You could sue them. Pay off your debt. Maybe even get China back."

Jake grunted.

Berf eyed the man who was his frat brother and sometime brother-in-law. "Isn't that what you wanted?"

Jake's face was bathed a warm amber pink in the light of the dying sun. His eyes took on the thousand-yard stare. "I thought I did. But when you stare death in the face and it stares back, it kind of has a way of rearranging your priorities. You were right. China wasn't for me. You have to be careful when picking the right woman. I thought she was a hard-headed woman, but she was really a hard-hearted woman. Big difference." He took a deep breath. "Uh, no offense," he added.

"Offense?"

"I mean, she's your sister."

Offense? This was a moment for rejoicing. "*Mi amigo*, this is what I've been saying."

Jake shook his head slowly. "I got seduced by the whole package. Corporate executive, lakeside home, trophy wife. But that's no way to live."

"Speak on, MacDuff."

"I don't know. Maybe I'll go back to Austin and start a restaurant. Or open a hair salon."

Yes. This was the Jake Berf knew in college, before he fell under China's spell. He held out his hand. "Welcome back, Kemosabe."

Jake stared at it for a long moment, and then took it firmly, and they shook on it.

When they docked in Cancún, Berf left Jake to check in his catch. He headed toward the tiki torches to find a libation suitable to the ordeal he had endured. Not the thin umbrella drinks they handed out for free at the happy hour beach parties, but a true creation. Perhaps he would reveal one of his secret recipes to Noah.

As he emerged from the shadows, he saw Kate sitting at a table talking to Runyon. His hand rested on hers.

The sight of her fraternizing with the enemy when, in Berf's opinion, she should have been alerting the media and sending out a search party got right in amongst him. He stormed up to the table.

Kate stood. "Burt. What are you doing here?"

"It's Berf, and—"

Before Berf could finish the sentence, Jake walked up. "Why? Isn't it included?"

Kate flinched. "But we searched . . . You were . . ."

Jake stepped closer to her. "Right. I almost drowned out there."

Kate frowned. "Why didn't you?"

"Because Berf saved . . . What?"

"Why didn't you drown?"

Berf had expected shock or contrition, maybe even relief. After all, they'd almost died on her watch. But how could you answer a question like that? Why didn't they drown? He could think of five or six good reasons off the top of his head without straining a muscle.

Even Runyon leaned closer, obviously waiting for the answer. Who wouldn't?

Jake rose up to his full height like a senator insulted by a member of the loyal opposition during a debate on obscenity laws. It was good to see him back in fighting form. Evidently getting attacked by a shark suited him. Berf would have suffered a dozen sharks to see Jake returning to form like this.

"You think I came here to die a horrible death, struggling for air at the bottom of the ocean?" Jake demanded.

Kate finally seemed contrite. "Oh. Sorry. I didn't realize—"

"That's not what we signed up for," Jake said, even louder.

That was telling her. Berf stepped up to the plate. "We could sue, you know."

"You changed your mind? You want to cancel?"

That response confused Berf, but Jake didn't back off.

"No, we want what we paid for. A vacation so good you never want to go home. Isn't that what Strange Vacations is all about?"

"So you still want to go skydiving?"

Jake sneered. "What's the plan? Splatter us all over the runway?"

"No, no. Just a nice, pleasant jump. You won't even feel it when you land. Like a walk in the clouds."

"That doesn't sound too bad."

Berf frowned. "It doesn't sound like skydiving." A jump should be all adrenaline. Skydiving, when done right, was the espresso of extreme sports.

"Let me get you some drinks," Kate said. She walked toward the bar.

"Make mine a double," Jake called after her.

"Make mine a sextuple," Berf yelled. He glanced back at the table. Runyon was gone.

Out in the crowd, Frank danced with some lady who must have been blind and maybe deaf. He saw Berf and walked away from the lady, who seemed not to notice. Maybe she was dancing near him, not with him.

"Hey, fellas. Howzit hanging? I thought you were dead." He went for a high five.

Berf just stood there. Jake looked toward the bar.

Frank dropped his hand like nothing had happened. "How did you get back from the dive?"

"We took a cab," Berf said.

"I'll check on the drinks," Jake said and walked away.

Frank watched him leave. "I hear people with the Dignity package are accident prone. A lot of them don't come back."

"Maybe that's why they call it Strange Vacations."

"Is that why you booked it?"

Berf didn't respond. This guy was hard to take at any time, but especially when one was sober.

"How did you hear about Strange Vacations?"

In the last two minutes, Berf had experienced about ten minutes too many of Frank. "Friend of mine."

"When was the last time you saw him?"

"Down here, last week."

"Did he come back?"

Berf frowned. He hadn't seen Spider since then. And when he tried calling, he got that recording. Maybe . . . No, he wasn't going to let this guy seduce him into conspiracy theories.

Frank pulled out a cell phone. "What's his number?"

"It's in the phone book."

"Name?"

"That's in the book too." Berf suddenly felt strange, like thirteen black cats had just broken a mirror under a ladder across his grave. In need of sustenance, he turned to the bar. No Jake, no Kate, no drink.

Two bustomatically enhanced girls in rebel flag bikinis walked by.

Frank called out to them. "Hey, nice buns! How about we get together and make a sandwich?"

Berf walked away. Frank's questions about Spider reawakened the doubts Berf had tried to lay to rest. He found Noah, got a shot of the tequila Spider had given him last week, and dialed Spider's number on his cell. He felt a soft hand on his shoulder.

It was Rita. "Berf! Where have you been?"

Berf shoved the phone into his pocket. "Noah, another for the lady." He motioned Rita to a seat and took the one next to her. "I didn't realize you had a brother in the watch business."

# CHAPTER TWENTY-THREE

Kate waited on a stool while Noah mixed the drinks. Seeing Mr. Oakley and Mr. Wiggins walk up had been a shock. After the explosion and Pearl on the scene, she had suggested the search for show. She assumed it was done. But they had survived somehow and found a way back.

Noah slid the drinks to her and she turned around, almost running into Mr. Oakley. She held out the drinks.

Mr. Oakley took them. "Hey, I . . . I might have been too hard on you back there. Too much adrenaline."

Kate shook her head. "I'm really sorry about how that turned out."

"Well, I guess it wasn't really your fault, was it? I mean, you're not in charge of Scuba-Doos, right? Probably should talk to Gus about it though."

Or Pearl. Or Mr. Strange. "Oh, believe me, someone is going to hear about it."

"Good."

Kate glanced over his shoulder. "I should get back to the party."

Mr. Oakley held out his drink toward the beach as if inviting her for a stroll. Kate stepped forward. He offered her his other arm and she took it. They walked out into the crowd. As they neared the bandstand, he turned to her.

"Want to dance?"

Kate frowned. "What about Burt?"

"Nah. He's a lousy dancer."

"Maybe, but he's back there waiting for that drink."

Mr. Oakley glanced over his shoulder. "Yeah, and so is Jabba the Hutt. Here, you take Berf's margarita."

"I'm on the clock."

"I could punch you out."

"What?"

"Off the clock, I mean. Not you personally."

Mr. Oakley held out the drink.

Kate eyed it. It was top-shelf, and Mr. Strange hadn't really given any rules about drinking. Besides, this was Mr. Oakley's last night. Many times she had sat up with terminal patients through the night, keeping them company, listening to their stories, calming their fears. Was this really that different?

She accepted the drink and took a sip.

"And now that dance." Mr. Oakley took her other hand and pulled her into the mass of swaying bodies.

The band played "Stardust," interpreted through the buoyant tones of a steel drum. Kate and Mr. Oakley danced clumsily, each with a drink in one hand, her other on his shoulder and his other on her waist.

The words bounced through her head like bubbles bursting in time with the music.

*Sometimes I wonder why I spend the lonely night dreaming of a song. The melody haunts my reverie.*

Her thoughts drifted back to the South Pacific, the clinic, the kids. Jim. They had met when she was in medical school. She had been struck by his confidence and his vision for taking medicine to the dark corners of the world.

Enough to follow him to Micronesia, where it soon became apparent that what she had taken as confidence was in fact arrogance, a common enough trait in the medical profession. But, although she and Jim no longer shared a mutual admiration of his genius, they still shared a passion for reaching the underserved populations of the world.

And as she fell out of love with Jim, she fell in love with the children.

As the song ended, she realized that during the few weeks she had been in Cancún she had thought of returning to Micronesia more often than she had the entire year in the Netherlands. Maybe she should quit thinking about it and do something instead.

Then she realized she was standing there in the silence, holding onto Mr. Oakley. She released her hold and took a sip of the drink. "So how did you get back?"

The band started a salsa number.

"A passing fisherman." Mr. Oakley seemed to shudder. He slammed his drink, took hers and slammed it, and tossed the cups aside. "Let's go out with a bang."

He grabbed her and led into a salsa dance. Kate barely kept up, but he was good enough to keep her from making too much a fool of herself.

"Did you learn this in Borneo?" Kate asked as he pulled her closer for a spin.

"My mother taught me."

She struggled for a while, then broke free. She wasn't wired for salsa. She kicked off her shoes. "Here's what my Dad taught me."

Kate began an Irish jig, her feet softly thudding in the sand. It fit surprisingly well with the music. Mr. Oakley tried a few steps, got his legs tangled, and went down, sprawling in the sand. Kate laughed and pulled him to his feet.

"Here, try this." She demonstrated a simple move. Mr. Oakley copied it. "Now add this." She did another move.

Before long they had sixteen bars of a simple sequence they could repeat. Berf appeared with Rita, and Kate waved them in. Soon there were four of them doing a jig conga line to salsa music.

The steel drum player pointed at them with a mallet, laughing. Kate saluted him and several more dancers joined the line.

When the song ended, the band transitioned to "A Kiss to Build a Dream On."

Kate stepped back to catch her breath and watched Burt and Rita move off into the shadows, dancing like a couple out on the town for their first anniversary.

Mr. Oakley grabbed Kate's hand and pulled her into a lazy, swaying dance. "I think we got off on the wrong foot."

Kate smiled. "Oh, you dance okay. For a gringo."

"I meant last night."

Kate still wasn't reconciled to Mr. Oakley's decision but felt a little guilty for how she had handled it. "I'm sorry. I wasn't professional."

"No, I was being petty. All that stuff about China and the boat. Ridiculous when you think about it."

Kate stopped dancing. "What do you mean?"

"You were right. A lot of people have it much worse." Mr. Oakley tried to resume dancing, but Kate didn't move.

"So you've changed your mind? You don't want to do it tomorrow?"

"No, no. We're on. Tomorrow I'm jumping out of a perfectly good airplane."

Kate stepped back and took a deep breath. This guy sent more mixed signals than a mis-wired traffic light. It was time to settle this once and for all. "Then what are you saying?"

"Berf is right. Live each day like it's your last. If you think about it too much, you won't have the courage to do what must be done." Mr. Oakley grabbed drinks from a passing tray. He gave Kate one and held his up in a toast.

Kate half-heartedly raised her glass but didn't drink. It was a sorry excuse for an answer. "Are you sure about this? Maybe you should think it over."

"I've never been more sure about anything in my life."

"Why not give it a few days?"

"It's time to embrace the next thing. Whatever it turns out to be."

They stood close. Kate studied him. She'd seen al-most two dozen people make this decision, but usually with resignation and relief, never with such enthusiasm and vigor. Except for Mr. Heald.

Maybe that was it. A different kind of patient, a different environment, a different way of dealing with it. It would take some getting used to. She wasn't sure she liked it. It seemed to lack the gravitas that she felt the situation warranted.

Mr. Oakley leaned toward her. "Thanks, Kate, for everything."

He bent over for a kiss, but Kate pulled back. He kissed her on the forehead and smiled.

"By the way, I won the Iron Fish. Five-hundred-pound shark."

He winked and walked away.

Kate watched him go, then headed to the resort. She didn't feel like dancing anymore.

# Chapter Twenty-Four

When Runyon saw that Kate would be kept occupied for a while dancing with the pencil-necked geek, he moved through the shadows, quietly but quickly, to the SV office. It was a small detached building near the hotel, facing one of the side roads used by service vehicles.

After a quick bit of reconnaissance, Runyon easily jimmied the door, slipped in, and closed it behind him. He was in a front office with a desk, a water cooler, and filing cabinets. He made quick work of skimming through files but didn't expect to find anything there. She wouldn't be that careless.

With two decades of field experience, he had a sixth sense about these things. When he was first offered this job, he almost turned it down. After all, the cover photo of the Global Health Newsletter showed a woman with an honest face and plenty of natural assets. She obviously ate right and worked out. He could tell, despite the loose scrubs.

Then there was her bio. She had lived all over Europe—Ireland, France, Germany, the Netherlands—before disappearing from civilization, down into Micronesia, taking care of kids. She'd packed a lot into thirty years. Runyon liked that.

But he'd been in enough tight spots to know that beauty could hide a multitude of sins, and of course the female was the deadlier of the species. The dossier had filled in the missing links. She was one canny customer. He'd have to be on his guard.

But finally he took the job. After that hostage thing in Chechnya, he thought a few weeks in the Caribbean would be just the ticket. And he was right. So far things were going according to plan.

He closed the filing cabinet and walked through a door to a larger inner office. Several desks, a printer, fax machine, copier, and a computer. Bingo. He moved the mouse and the screen came up to an SV logo and a password prompt. He tried a few simple passwords without success. Sometimes people wrote their passwords down. He opened a desk drawer and the overhead lights came on.

Runyon looked up. The weasel-faced goon he'd seen lurking around stood in the door, one hand on the light switch, the other holding a gun. A Glock with a silencer. Runyon waited. In cases like this, the less said, the better. Never volunteer anything, not even a lie.

Weasel sneered at him. "To what do we owe the pleasure of you digging through our drawers?"

Runyon stood slowly and backed away, his hands up. Out the back window, he saw Kate coming from the beach. "Filing a complaint. I heard it was the vacation to end all vacations."

"I can arrange that. Personally."

Runyon paused, timing his next line. "Actually, I was looking for Kate." Kate walked in. "Kate, there you are."

She seemed shocked to see the gun. "Pearl, what are you doing? Put that away."

Weasel didn't put it away. He spoke without taking his eyes off Runyon. "He was messing with stuff."

Runyon smiled at Kate, keeping his hands up to make the situation as ridiculous as possible. "I couldn't find you at the party. I thought you might be here."

Weasel sneered again. "How did you get in?"

"It was open."

"That was probably my fault," Kate said.

Weasel seemed doubtful. His eyes darted to Kate and back to Runyon.

Runyon lowered his hands slowly. Weasel wouldn't do anything with a witness. "How about I buy you that drink now?"

Kate spoke sharply. "Pearl, put that thing away. Now!" She turned back to Runyon. "The drinks are free."

"Then I'll buy you two drinks."

Runyon stared pointedly at Weasel and waited until the gun was reluctantly lowered. Then he walked out with Kate, leaving Weasel behind to lock up.

# CHAPTER TWENTY-FIVE

Jake left the beach feeling better than he had since the wedding. Or, more specifically, since the reception. The disaster with the Doo, the shark, and the corpse had been the triple whammy he needed to put him right. And winning the $100,000 prize hadn't hurt either. It would square him with The Lawn Arranger.

Roger had made it clear that he considered losing a hundred grand a bargain if it meant that Jake would leave immediately and never return. But from the moment Jake got on the plane, he had intended to return to Austin, repay the amount he stole, and regain China's trust and affection.

He still intended to return and repay, but he was done with the rest of the plan. The idea of life with China seemed more and more absurd. What had he been thinking? It had happened like these things do, a little at a time, like boiling a frog, only he was the frog. Now he could see how the frog could sit there and blissfully be parboiled into a fancy appetizer. Even an independently-minded frog like himself.

He would start a new life, in Austin or somewhere else. He wasn't that picky at the moment. But whatever he decided to do after this vacation, the last thing he needed was the threat of prison hanging over his head.

Jake hummed "Someone Saved My Life Tonight" as he let himself into the suite and checked Berf's room. Empty, of course.

When he walked into his room, he saw the annulment papers on the night stand where he had dropped them the night before. He grabbed them and sat at the table, staring out the window across the Caribbean. Was he sure? Yes. Any lingering doubts? Perhaps.

No, not really. It was time for brutal honesty. He had been wrong. He'd picked the wrong woman, or she had picked him. Trying to salvage it now would simply be a matter of pride, trying to prove to China and everybody else that he had not blundered. There was no room in his life for that kind of self-deception, not now.

He picked up the hotel pen, signed the annulment papers boldly, slid them into the envelope, and sealed it.

# Chapter Twenty-Six

Kate opened the door of her suite absently, thinking about Runyon. A bit of an ox in a teashop, to be sure, but well-meaning. In her mind, the work he did for the unfortunate and disadvantaged in the neglected parts of the world covered a multitude of sins of the social graces kind. He had a good heart.

An envelope lay on the floor. A fax. She picked it up, flipped on the light, and read it.

TO: KATE COLLINS
   WE REGRET TO INFORM YOU THAT MR. DYKE HEALD PASSED AWAY RECENTLY. HIS WILL SHOWS YOU AS THE PRIMARY BENEFICIARY OF HIS ESTATE IN EXCESS OF €200 MILLION. PLEASE CONTACT OUR OFFICE AT YOUR EARLIEST CONVENIENCE.

Kate sank to the couch, staring at the fax through tears. He had been crazy, of course.

Dyke Heald was ninety-four and regretted not having had the sense or decency to die before now.

If he had realized he would end up in the middle of the Netherlands in Het Gooi, trapped inside this absurdly gigantic bedroom and chained to the bed via various medical contraptions, he'd have charged a bull elephant barehanded in Botswana a decade ago.

The old granite pile of a mansion was a sprawling gawdhelpus postmodern structure set in a dazzling patchwork of lawns, gardens, and canals. Designed by his third wife half a century ago, may she rest in peace.

Heald signed the last of the papers his lawyer set in front of him and then shooed him away. The new nurse, Kate, dropped a dozen pills into an array of paper dispenser cups, placed them on a breakfast tray, and crossed the room.

He regarded it with undisguised contempt. "What is this crap?"

"Yogurt and skim milk."

"That's not breakfast, that's torture."

Kate set the tray in front of him. "Here's your medication."

"What? And ruin my breakfast?"

Kate shook her head. "First the pills."

Heald dumped the pills into the yogurt, stirred it, and ate. He choked a little but forced it down.

She smiled as if he had done exactly what he asked. "Good. Now your blood pressure."

"Is your passport up-to-date?"

Kate pulled open the Velcro of the cuff. "Of course. Why?"

"Pack for warm weather." He handed a Monaco brochure to Kate. "Do you have a bikini?"

Kate handed the brochure back. "Why? You want to borrow one for your trip?"

"Our trip." Heald held up two tickets. First class. One had her name on it.

Kate held out the cuff. Heald lifted his arm. She wrapped it and pumped it up. "Even if I wanted to go to Monaco with you, I can't. Every penny goes to—"

"This is no life for you, girl. You're working yourself to death. You deserve better."

Kate shushed him and put on a stethoscope, watching the clock and releasing the air pressure.

She reminded Heald of his fourth wife. Now there was a feisty one, and make no mistake. He should have quit with number four.

Kate wrote a number on a chart, pulled off the stethoscope, and ripped the Velcro open. "I deserve to win the lotto and pay off Dad's bills, but I'm here."

Heald put his hand over Kate's, stopping her when she tried to pull away. "Kate, I mapped the Amazon, explored the Marianas Trench, climbed Everest. Five years ago, I became the oldest man to climb Kilimanjaro. I even killed a hyena with a bicycle chain and a tire pump in Syria." He wasn't halfway through his résumé, but sometimes less was more. Not often, but occasionally. He'd learned that much in nine decades.

Kate smiled and put away the sphygmomanometer. "What's more, you braved the wrath of Mrs. Brill and said the veal was overdone."

"This isn't a fitting way to spend the twilight of life. Not for someone like me. Like us."

Kate stiffened. "Like us?"

Yes. She was a kindred soul, whether she knew it or not. "You're not at home in this sterile museum any more than I am, and you know it. We were made for the wild places. To go out in a blaze of adrenaline, not fade away into a dusty oblivion."

Kate softened. She reached out to smooth the counterpane. "Yes, but we don't get to choose how we die."

"Some don't. Others do. You know that."

Kate pulled her hand back and looked hard at him. "What are you saying, Mr. Heald?"

Heald turned his gaze to the window, out past the gardens and fountains. "I'm saying I want to take one last trip. And I'd like you to go with me." He pointed at the medical equipment. "Somebody has to inflict all this stuff on me while I travel."

Kate picked up the tickets he had dropped on the counterpane. "Are these non-refundable?"

"Life is non-refundable."

"Why Monaco?"

"Why not Monaco?"

"But an overpriced tourist trap? You?"

Heald waved the brochure. "All expenses paid. Plus a bonus. A large one."

"What about your son?"

"Jack?" Heald threw the brochure down in disgust. "He's useless. This place suits him all right. And he can't wait to get his hands on it."

"I bet Jack would like Monaco. Sounds like his kind of place."

"Then let him book his own vacation. I won't spend my waning days on the Mediterranean listening to the drivel of a mama's boy who knows the price of everything and the value of nothing."

Kate weakened. "But the tickets are for tomorrow."

"I'm not getting any younger."

"Separate bedrooms?"

"However you want it."

"What should I pack?"

Heald appraised her, again. He might be ninety-four, but he wasn't dead. Or blind. "Start with a bikini."

The two-hour flight had been a minor ordeal, but he survived it and the drive to the hotel. At lunch, hunched over the soup course, Dyke Heald knew that he looked more like a pterodactyl with an oxygen tank than a man. But despite the journey he felt younger than he had in decades.

Kate Collins sat across from him at the best table in the best restaurant in the best hotel in Monaco. They had a window seat overlooking the Mediterranean. Azure waves rolled up to pristine sand. A cruise ship announced its departure with a deafening blast of horns. Sailboats skittered across the sea. Farther out, container ships dotted the horizon. On the beach, lithe, tanned beauties stretched out in the sun or splashed in the surf.

But none of the sights compared to this woman. Instead of her scrubs, she wore the formal black dress he had bought her for this trip. Despite all that, she somehow retained the air of a kindly nurse, not the one who checks your pulse while staring at her watch and thinking of what to fix for dinner, but the one who looks you in the eye and asks when was the last time you took a dump because she really wants to know.

The expectation of her company every day could almost tempt him to change his mind. But that was nonsense. She was here because she was paid, very handsomely, to be here. Heald knew that, but Kate always left him with the feeling that she had come just to see him, to talk to him, to be with him again. He didn't know how she did it, and he didn't want to know.

He wanted to enjoy the illusion. He wanted to believe, even though a long lifetime of lessons had created in him a cynic, not a true believer. He knew the feeling was self-delusion. People like Kate, or like what she seemed to be, didn't really exist. Did they?

"I wish I had met you when I was younger. Oh, to be seventy again."

Kate smiled. "When you were seventy, I was seven."

There it was again. A line like that from any other woman would have been mocking. But from Kate, it sounded like she also felt a nostalgia for what might have been. Like, if Heald had told her he had a time machine that would right-size the age difference in her direction, she would be game.

"Thanks for coming. I didn't want to do this alone."

Kate pushed her soup bowl aside and leaned forward. "I still think you should have brought Jack."

The last thing Heald wanted to talk about was Jack. "I wanted to enjoy it. Jack always plays it safe, like his mother. We should have named him Nancy, Junior. No, you are the perfect companion. One in a million. And a lot better looking."

"I'm sure Jack would be fun if you gave him the chance."

"Oh, he's had the chance. Many of them, I assure you."

The waiter cleared the soup and brought an antipasto salad. Kate selected the appropriate fork.

Heald picked through the salad and stabbed a slice of prosciutto. "I have the feeling that this trip is going to open new doors for you."

"How exactly?"

"When you get home, I think you will find that things are very different. I wish I could be there to see what you do."

Kate put her fork down. "Why wouldn't you be?"

"Not many grains of sand in the top of the hourglass for me."

"You're doing great."

"I haven't been great since aught three. Not counting these last months with you, of course."

"Are you hitting on me, Mr. Heald?"

"Perhaps. While there's life, there's hope."

They smiled and ate in silence through the rest of the salad course. The urge was overwhelming to tell Kate everything, but that would be a mistake. There was the small chance she would try to stop him, but that wasn't the main reason. For her own protection, she needed to remain ignorant.

The waiter brought a mango sorbet.

"Fresh mango was one of my favorite things about Micronesia."

That sparked the one thing that puzzled Heald. If he ever wanted to know, he would have to ask now. "I've always wondered. Why a children's clinic in Micronesia? You could have chosen to do anything you wanted."

"I could and I did."

Heald stared at her blankly.

"Choose the thing I wanted," she said.

"Why not something bigger? You have so much potential. You're selling yourself short."

"Nothing is bigger than changing the life of a child."

Such was the force of Kate's conviction that he found himself agreeing with her, believing she was right, despite the fact that he knew there were much bigger things and that she had the power to do them. That was when he realized he had fallen in love with her.

It had been a long time since he'd made that mistake, not in fifty or sixty years.

He stared down at his sorbet, knowing he had lost. "When will you go back?"

"It will be a few years, probably."

"What if I'm not ready to let you go?" It wasn't what he had meant to say. He meant to ask what if she could change thousands or millions of lives instead of a few dozen. Would she still go back? But maybe it was really the same question.

"I'm not the only home-care nurse in the Netherlands."

"Perhaps not. But that doesn't mean you aren't unique. I should know. It took me two years and over sixty interviews to find you."

"What was wrong with the last one? Pinching the silverware?"

"She was fine, but she wasn't suitable for this trip."

"She didn't have a bikini?"

Heald smiled as the waiter brought out the lobster. Perhaps Kate was irresistible because she was unattainable. And perhaps he was an old fool who should keep his mouth shut. But it was too late to be coy now.

Kate eyed him suspiciously. "You've been searching for two years for somebody to take to Monaco?"

"Not Monaco, specifically. I was looking for the suitable companion for a final vacation."

"And I won the competition."

"Kate, one of your uncountable charms is that you are completely unaware of your own power. It is fortunate for mankind that you have chosen to use it for good. Those children in Micronesia have no idea how blessed they are."

Kate was silent.

At least that part of it was out. Perhaps he could finish his meal without further humiliating himself.

After the seventh course and an espresso, Kate and Heald walked slowly down the beach to the pier. Their conversation had returned to his more usual banter and Heald felt more relaxed. They headed down a row of slips, past all manner of boats, to a speedboat set up for parasailing.

Pearl, a weasel-faced goon dressed in black and sporting a captain's cap, met them at the gangway. Heald knew him for what he was the second their eyes met. He'd encountered dozens like him the world over—three parts Uriah Heep, two parts wharf rat, one part Al Pacino. Ironic that after dominating such vermin the world over, he should at last be delivered into their hands.

Heald parked his oxygen tank and stepped gingerly in the boat, nodded to what appeared to be a linebacker at the helm, and allowed Pearl to strap him into the harness.

Kate watched from the pier. "Mr. Heald, are you sure about this?"

Heald yelled over Pearl's shoulder. "I've never been more sure about anything in my life. Go out with a bang, I say!"

"It's just that it seems so dangerous."

"If I can't do something dangerous when I'm ninety-four, when can I?"

The captain throttled the boat up.

Heald waved. "Thank you for coming, Kate."

"You be careful out there, Mr. Heald."

"I didn't come here to be careful. I came to have the time of my life. And this is it."

"Then have the time of your life."

Heald blew her a kiss. Kate blew a kiss back.

They pulled away from the pier and headed to open water. Heald looked back to the pier. Kate watched, her hand shading her eyes.

When they were far enough out, the captain hit the throttle and Heald rose into the sky like an ancient bird of prey. He clung to the bar and scanned the horizon. He could see Nice to the west, the cruise ship steaming past. To the north, Mont Agel rose above the Monte Carlo skyline. Staring straight down, he could see through the blue-green water to ribs of white sand terracing out to the deeps.

Even in the midst of a commercialized tourist trap, Heald sensed he was surrounded by beauty, true beauty. This moment could have come in his bed in his mansion in the Netherlands and his final vista would have been the stippling on the ceiling, with a tangle of tubes and beeping machines as his companions. No. Absolutely not.

Heald breathed deeply, the rush of wind in his face forcing air into his lungs. He looked down, saw Kate, still there, still watching, still with him. Her time to make choices was coming. If there was something beyond, some way of seeing back, perhaps he would get the chance to see it.

Jack was in for a big surprise.

Heald waved to Kate. She waved back. Then he felt a stab in his upper arm. A tranquilizer dart protruded from it. He got in one last sighting of Kate.

*And now we find out*, he thought.

Kate wiped the tears from her cheeks and set the fax on the desk. Mr. Heald had been a good man, maybe like Runyon in his youth, traveling the world, having adventures, but clearly crazy. This would have to be sorted out.

And all that talk about doing big things, bigger than the clinic. It all made sense now. She pulled out her mobile and chose a number in Amsterdam from her contacts.

Her mother answered and Kate told her the news.

"Then it's all settled," Mum said. "Your problem is solved and you can go back to the clinic tomorrow."

"I'm coming home tomorrow to sort this out. He has family. It should go to them."

"Kate, you know I'd love to see you, but you should reconsider. It sounds completely legal. The man can give his money to whomever he wants, and who is more deserving than you?"

"I didn't call for advice, Mum. Just to let you know that as soon as I hand things off to Mr. Strange, I'll be booking a flight."

"Well, at least use some of the money and upgrade to first class. They can't begrudge you that."

# Chapter Twenty-Seven

The phone rang. Michael Strange looked up from the massive spreadsheet projected on the wall of his Cayman suite. The numbers said Sri Lanka would be the best location to expand the Dignity package. He had excellent terms with a resort there and access to local talent for the more specialized aspects of the project.

He picked up the phone. "Strange."

"Mr. Strange, something has come up and I need to go home immediately."

The Collins woman was becoming an unexpected fly in his otherwise very acceptable ointment. He should have been more cautious about bringing on someone with such an obvious humanitarian bent. "That's not possible at this point."

"It's an urgent financial matter I have to take care of personally."

Whatever her financial concerns were, they could hardly compare with the spreadsheet on the wall. "Every person is critical. Leaving is not an option."

"I'm sorry, Mr. Strange, but I have to go. I'll brief Sully."

Strange checked his calendar. He would have to deal with this himself. "I'll fly out in the morning. We can discuss it over dinner." Given the concerns she raised yesterday, he couldn't afford to let her go without impressing the need for discretion.

There was a pause, then finally, "I guess I can wait one day."

"Good. I'll see you tomorrow. Don't say anything to Sully."

Strange hung up and dialed the phone while pulling a suitcase from a closet. Sully answered immediately.

"Yeah."

The man was lacking in the social graces but ruthlessly efficient and the only one who could control Pearl without strangling him.

"I'm coming in tomorrow. Keep an eye on Kate."

"Something happen?"

"Just don't let her leave. Got that?"

"I got it. Oh, boss."

"What?"

"Pearl caught a guy sneaking around the office."

"What did he do?"

"Nothing. Kate showed up."

This changed things considerably. "What did she do?"

"Took him out for drinks."

An urgent financial matter, she said. Or was it an insidious financial scheme? "Find her and don't let her out of your sight until I get there."

Strange hung up and tossed the phone aside. He finished packing and zipped up the suitcase. He turned to go but thought again. Who was this guy snooping around? The more he thought about it, the less he liked it. Whatever he and Kate were scheming, he would have to shut it down.

He stepped to the closet, opened the safe, pulled out a gun, and put it in his briefcase. He hoped he didn't need it, but there was no room for mistakes in this business.

# CHAPTER TWENTY-EIGHT

Despite the events of the day before, Jake woke up at dawn feeling like somebody had invented a day just for him. And who knew, maybe they did. It was like the first day of school, all excitement and anxiety and the smell of pencil shavings and paste.

Time to move on from "Hard Headed Woman" to "Morning Has Broken." He sang it in the shower, dressed in board shorts and a guayabera shirt, and went downstairs to deal with the prize money.

Half an hour later, he headed to the breakfast buffet in the cabana with a hefty check in his pocket and a hefty appetite in his soul. To his delight, Kate was there, sitting at a table alone, a neglected breakfast at her side, a stack of paperwork in front of her. He threw some food on a plate and walked to her table.

"May I?"

She looked up, startled. "Sure." She moved a folder to a chair and continued with her paperwork.

Jake moved everything from the tray and arranged it on the table. "I can't wait to get suited up and go up in that plane." He cut his cantaloupe slices into bite-sized chunks. "Funny, when I was a kid, I was so scared of heights I wouldn't get on the top bunk. Even in high school." He cut off a big slice of omelet and stuffed it into his mouth.

In the silence, Kate paused in her work. "Yeah?"

Jake swallowed. "So Dad took my girlfriend and me skydiving. With her there, I was too proud to back out. Dad suited up, but when it came time, he froze. He almost crawled out of the plane when it landed."

Kate raised an eyebrow. "He didn't jump?"

"Nope. Turned out he was scared of heights too. But went up in that plane anyway."

Kate returned her paperwork. "Did he ever conquer his fear of heights?" she asked as she made notes.

Jake's breath caught for a second. It had been years, but still it sneaked up on him sometimes. "No. He just went back to his classroom at Berkeley and never got in a plane again." He took a sip of coffee. "Five years ago, he went to a conference in the city. Had lunch in the rooftop restaurant. The elevator broke. He fell thirty stories, but his feet never left the floor."

Kate looked up, stunned, and touched his hand. "Jake, I'm sorry."

Jake nodded. He was grateful that he kept short accounts with his dad. After the divorce, they had drifted apart, but the Borneo trip changed all that.

"I learned one thing. There's no point in fearing death. Even if you don't go looking for it, one day it will come looking for you. So you might as well face it on your own terms, not hide in a corner somewhere."

Kate's face softened and she let the pen slip from her right hand. "Sometimes you remind me of a very wise man I once knew."

"And the other times?" He liked the way she looked at him at this moment. Not like the looks he got the last two days, mostly anger or confusion. "Every time we're together, we're always talking about me. Here, answer this. If you won the lottery, could do whatever you wanted, what would you do?"

"Go back to Micronesia," Kate answered without hesitation.

Jake glanced at the paperwork she had pushed aside. A photo peeked from the edge of the pile. He pulled it out and inspected it. It was group shot, Kate in the middle of a bunch of kids in a clearing of a tropical jungle. It was creased. He unfolded it to reveal a guy, probably a doctor, on the other side of the group.

"Is that your boyfriend?"

Kate snatched the photo from his hand. "That's the doctor at the clinic."

"Your significant other?"

Kate stuffed the photo into the folder on the chair, picked up her pen, and resumed her work. "Jim is his own significant other. Nobody else could love him as much as he does."

Jake, anxious to keep the connection he seemed to have established with her, tried to recover from this conversational misstep. "So you were glad to leave?"

The pen slowed to a stop, but she kept her eyes on the papers. "I wish I'd never left."

"Why did you?"

"Dad got sick."

"How's he doing?"

"He died. Slowly. Expensively."

Now it was his turn to be embarrassed. "Oh. I'm sorry. I didn't—"

"Of course you didn't." She stood and gathered the papers. "I really do have a lot of things to do."

Jake touched her arm. "Kate, I'm sorry about your dad."

Kate tried to pull away.

Jake stood. "He must have been a good man. I'm sure he deserved better, and a person like you, well, you deserve better too."

She frowned at him. "What do you mean, a person like me?"

"A giving person. One in a million."

Kate pulled away more slowly. Jake let her go, his breakfast forgotten. As he watched her rush into the hotel, he thought maybe he would hang around a few more days.

A noise caused him to turn back to the table. Frank was there, plate overflowing, watching Kate walk away.

"Gotta love the women's movement. Especially from behind."

Jake was in no mood for Frank. "Isn't there someplace you need to be?"

Frank sat down and started eating. "Nah. I'm on vacation. What are you doing today? Scuba diving again?"

"Skydiving."

"Never done that. Sounds like fun."

"You wouldn't like it." Jake abandoned his breakfast and followed Kate into the hotel.

# Chapter Twenty-Nine

Runyon sat in the lobby bar having a post-lunch whiskey. Some people might call that irresponsible, but Runyon never drank more than one in any six-hour period, and experience had shown that he could function better on a shot of whiskey than ninety-nine point nine nine nine percent of the population when stone-cold sober.

He'd stake his life on it. In fact, he had. More than once. Sometimes that one shot of whiskey was all it took to make the other guy relax, and before the sucker knew it, he had a Bowie knife at his throat and his *cojones* in a vice.

So, no, this dram of whiskey wasn't a problem.

If Runyon's information was correct, and it always was, Kate would be out by the airport escorting a group of skydivers. The perfect time to find what he needed.

Getting in with Kate had been a cinch, of course. She was crazy about him. He'd always been good with women like that. Look tough but act sensitive. It threw them off their guard. Things were going good, but he wanted to know more before he made his move.

Because Runyon knew enough to know that you never knew. The only sure thing about women was that you couldn't be sure about women. He would wait until the time was right to surprise her. He smiled and sipped his whiskey.

At that moment, Kate walked across the lobby, followed by Jake and Berf. And Pillsbury, the Frank guy, the walking epidemic of stupidity, attitude, and trouble. Runyon knew his kind. So clueless that you just shook your head and then you were blindsided by the chaos that inevitably erupted around this type.

Like collapsing in the surf while fishing or flying overboard in a fight chair, hanging onto the pole like it was a ticket to paradise. If you weren't careful around guys like Frank, you could find yourself bleeding to death, collateral damage of his karma. Best to keep a wide perimeter.

Runyon killed the shot and walked to the entrance. They all got into a Strange Vacations SUV and pulled out. He watched them head south on Kukulkan Boulevard toward the airport. As he turned away, an unexpected movement caught his eye. An old yellow VW minibus pulled out from a service road and followed. He shrugged. Not his problem.

Runyon strolled down the sidewalk, down the service road, past the SV office, and peered in the window. Weasel was inside. Runyon kept walking. He'd try again later. Kate wasn't going anywhere, not while she had this sweet deal.

# CHAPTER THIRTY

Berf kept his eyes glued to the roadside scenery to avoid having to respond to Frank's incessant inanities. He regretted that he hadn't had the presence of mind to call shotgun. It was his practice to never ride anywhere except the front seat, and this experience validated that principle.

The thirty-minute drive felt like a decade in an oubliette. After a few miles, Frank lapsed into a petulant silence. Berf thought back to the questions Frank had asked last night and then to the strange things Spider had said last week.

The ultimate adventure. The final frontier. Transcending the threshold past the point of no return.

What kind of talk was that? Being preoccupied with the wedding, Berf hadn't paid it much mind at the time. He pondered on it for a spell, but after a good 90 to 120 seconds, he was no closer to making any sense of it. Whatever it was, it didn't sound like anything that had happened to him or Jake so far.

Berf cast a surreptitious glance at Frank, fished his phone out of his pocket, and tried Spider's number again.

He got the same "service disconnected" message as the last time. He thought about calling around Austin to track him down, but he needed privacy for that little exercise.

He put away his phone and gave his mind free rein to graze. The next time he noticed a thought passing by, it was of Rita. He shook out a loop, lassoed the thought, and checked its brand. She seemed a likely lass, cute as a cloth button and clever as a Nelson riddle, but definitely a candidate for the irregulars bin.

Berf had dated his share of chicks who roamed out where the buses don't run, but none like Rita. There was something about her he couldn't quite tie down. Great dancer but knew all the checkpoints for spotting a fake Rolex. Even better kisser but also rode the Mesoamerican reef retrieving corpses. And that brother of hers, well, Berf had met some sketchy drifters on the trail in his time, but on his list of cowhands he'd like to hook a boot heel over the bar rail with, Berf would put Fernando dead last on the list. Maybe even further down.

If he kept popping up, Berf would have to weigh Rita's many charms against enduring the unnerving glare of her brother. And right now it was a close thing.

As they pulled into the parking lot of the skydive place, Berf tried to remember which he had more of, painted canvases or jumps. It was an odd statistic, unlikely to make Harper's Index, although he might suggest it. After doing the research, of course.

Kate parked the SUV on the side of the hangar and escorted them inside to get suited up. Frank immediately grabbed a parachute and tried to put it on. A guy in a jumpsuit ran over to turn it right-side up.

Kate ushered Berf and Jake into a side room. It looked like a supply closet for airplane parts. "Okay. You boys sure about this?"

"Heck, yeah! Are you kidding?" Berf said.

Kate stepped to Jake. "Last chance to back out."

Jake shook his head. "No. I need to do this. It's time."

Kate nodded and opened a small box. She took out a paisley pill, glanced up at Jake, dropped the pill back in the box, and left the room.

Berf and Jake looked at each other.

"What was that?"

"No clue."

They turned to leave, but the door opened and a guy came in with two packs and dropped them at their feet.

Berf had seen this guy around the resort a few times in the last two days. He had thought that the Runyon guy had reminded him of Hippo Swan, the guy that tried to take Tell Sackett down in New Orleans, but this guy was the real deal. He seemed to be armor plated. If Berf were consulted on the matter, he would recommend that this guy be called Rhino Swan.

Berf made a mental note to apologize to Runyon at his earliest convenience.

The hulk held out the box formerly presented by Kate, pulled out a paisley pill, and dropped it in Berf's palm.

"What's this for?" Berf asked.

"Anxiety. Makes the landing easier." He sounded like a rhinoceros looked.

Berf handed it back. "No need. I'm an old pro."

"Keep it, pal. Even old pros get nervous on a jump like this one."

The guy unzipped a pocket in Berf's suit, slid it in, and did the same for Jake.

Then they joined the rest of the gang, and after a safety briefing, they boarded the plane.

Jake, Berf, and Frank sat on a bench by the jump door. On the other side, Kate sat next to the two bustomatically enhanced girls that Berf had seen around and whom he had come to think of as Thelma and Louise for the sake of convenience. Such were their assets augmented that the zipper wouldn't go all the way up on their jumpsuits. They looked like something from a sixties James Bond movie but with new hairstyles.

As the plane lifted off, Frank nudged Berf. "Hey, check it out."

Berf ignored him, but nothing short of a nuclear holocaust would dampen Frank's enthusiasm, and maybe not even that. After the big one came down, all that was left might indeed be cockroaches, chickens, and Frank. And who could tell the difference?

"How'd you like to get those cantalones in your *pantalones?*" Frank asked.

Berf slid down the bench.

Frank yelled over the prop noise. "Hey, chicas. How 'bout we buddy jump?"

He started singing "Jump For My Love," making dancing movements on the bench. His voice was like the love child of Tiny Tim and William Hung auditioning for *America's Got Talent.*

Then, to the shock of everyone, Frank jumped up and did some surprising dance moves given the tight space and the unsteady footing.

From the right seat, Dustin, the jumpmaster, yelled at him. "Sit down!"

Frank danced in front of the girls.

The plane began circling. They were at the drop zone. Dustin stepped into the back and pulled the door open, just as Frank did a knee slide. He came within inches of sliding right out of the plane.

"Jump for my love. *Whoa!*"

Berf lunged off the seat to grab him, but Dustin stepped between Frank and the open door. Frank hugged Dustin's legs.

Berf got a good look at his face. Whatever game he might or might not have been playing was over. He was as transparent as black ice, giving Berf an unwelcome view into the face of abject terror, of soul-crushing, testicle-wilting fear.

"Jiminy Christmas, that's a long way down!"

Dustin shoved Frank back to his seat. "Get ready to hook up. You're going first."

Frank clenched the seat like his life depended on it. And maybe it did. "I'm not going anywhere."

It happened all the time on the trail. Some greenhorn drunk on his own ego, talking big, cutting a wide swath, his guns tied down, pearl handles facing out, calling out anyone who glances at him crossways. Never figuring he might be the one to bleed, to die in the middle of the street at high noon.

Like that Reed Carney back in Abilene, who got crossways with Tyrel Sackett and had more grudge than sense. So he calls out the wrong guy, and before he can even clear leather, the barrel of a pistol looms in front of him like an express tunnel to hell.

But when you've made it to that point, it's a little late to rethink your strategy. And that's where Frank was right now.

Thelma yelled, "Jump, dirtbag!"

Frank's bravado was obliterated. "Can't you take a joke?" He seemed to be trying to form a molecular bond with the skin of the plane. "Nobody said it was this high up."

Thelma yelled, "It has to be this high up or you'll die, Einstein."

Contrary to all his instincts, Berf felt some measure of pity for the loser. Nobody deserved to be that humiliated in front of two allegedly hot chicks. Even Tyrel had pity on Reed and gave him a chance to fork his saddle and ride out.

Berf leaned over to Frank. "Don't feel bad. It could happen to anyone. I know just what you need." Berf pulled out the paisley pill.

Frank stared at it like it was cyanide. "What's that?"

"Something to get your nerve back."

"I don't want my nerve back."

"You only live once."

Dustin tired of the delay. "Okay. Who's first?"

Berf yelled, "He is," and pulled Frank to his feet.

Frank shrugged weakly. "Are you sure this will work?"

Berf nodded.

"I'll try anything once." Frank grabbed the pill.

Berf heard Kate yell, "No!"

Kate slammed into Frank, pulling at his arm, but he had already swallowed the pill.

He shuddered and focused on Kate. He seemed to regain his confidence immediately. "Hey, baby. Yeah. Yeah, man. I feel great! Let's do it!"

Frank stepped to the door. Dustin held out the clip to latch his chute to the static line.

Kate reached for him. "No! Stop!"

Berf stood to help her, but Frank's eyes rolled up in his head and he tumbled out before Dustin could clip him in.

"Uh-oh," Dustin said, watching Frank cartwheel out the door.

Berf looked out the window. "What happened to him?"

"You gave him the pill!" Kate yelled at him.

Berf shrugged. "I didn't need it, and he sure seemed to."

Dustin pointed at Jake. "You! Go!"

Jake pointed at Berf. "First one to pull his chute is buying dinner tonight."

Kate spun around to Jake. "Dinner? You're planning dinner?"

Jake jumped. The jumpmaster turned to the girls. "Let's go! Now!"

The girls jumped together.

Kate whirled around. "He's planning dinner?"

Berf nodded. "That's Jake. He takes the long view, like Orrin Sackett. Me, I'm just a drifter hunting for my next cattle drive." He stepped to the door.

Kate reached for him. "No! Wait!"

"Go," Dustin yelled.

Berf jumped. It was a thrill and a terror. You went from sitting around haunted by a vague dread to plummeting to the earth at an increasing velocity, the only thing between you and certain death a scrap of nylon.

Berf didn't know if it was possible to feel more alive than when staring at possible death.

His philosophizing was interrupted by something grabbing his arm. He squealed like a stuck pig. Kate had latched onto him.

"Your chute!" she yelled.

Berf sneered, "I can outlast Jake."

"Yeah. All the way to the ground."

Kate jerked his cord. Nothing happened. That wasn't good.

Berf fumbled for the backup line and pulled. More nothing. "*Sacré bleu!*"

Kate yelled, "Hook up with the girls!" She pulled in her arms and legs and dived.

The girls were a good way down, doing a ring of two. Berf streamlined, gaining on them. The thrill of possible death had turned to the sickening certainty of actual death. That was a different thing entirely.

He tried to focus on tracking the girls, but this was more adrenaline than he had on his schedule for the day, and it was hard to concentrate. As he approached the girls, he went spread-eagle, slowing as he crashed into them.

The girls screamed. Berf grabbed Thelma and swung around under her, hugging tight.

She struggled and screamed, "What are you doing?"

Berf wrapped his legs around hers. In a voice muffled by her jumpsuit he yelled, "Pull the cord!"

"Great. Just great." She pulled the cord.

It was a mighty jerk and Berf almost lost his grip. Then they were gliding, and Berf realized he might not die after all. The relief was so great he almost relaxed his grip.

Instead he hugged her tighter and said, "I want to have your babies."

Thelma shivered from pole to pole. "In your dreams, pervert."

# Chapter Thirty-One

Jake trailed Frank, admiring how he had gone from quivering wimp to fearless daredevil, and yelled, "Way to push the envelope, Frank!"

He was also determined to wait Berf out. He looked up. There were no open chutes. Tough crowd. Jake checked the altimeter and became concerned. He planed closer to Frank. No matter how brave the guy was, you had to pull the cord eventually. "You should pull your chute. Hey!"

There was devil-may-care and then there was devil-take-your-hide. Frank had definitely passed the line, which didn't surprise Jake when he thought about it. It seemed to be his defining characteristic.

Then Frank rolled over and Jake saw he was unconscious.

Jake reached out and pulled Frank's rip cord. Frank suddenly disappeared from view, jerked up into the sky, floating away. Jake was alone and falling and much too low for his comfort. He pulled his cord, but no chute appeared. He kept falling at a gazillion miles per hour.

The rush of adrenaline was nauseating. Resisting the urge to throw up, Jake frantically groped for the backup. "Ah, ah. Don't panic. Don't panic. Inhale. Exhale. Find the backup. Find it. *Find it!* Ahhhhh!"

Jake found the backup rip cord. It came loose in his hand. "Ahhhhh! No! No! No!"

He went spread-eagle to slow his fall. He wasn't sure why. What would he do with the extra three seconds of life it might buy him?

Suddenly Kate appeared next to him.

"Hold on, Jake!"

"To what?"

She reached out and hugged him to her. "Hold on. This is going to be one big yank."

Jake clung to Kate like a spider monkey on crack. Kate pulled the cord. Jake felt his grip slip. He clawed his way back to a tighter hug and was suddenly sailing serenely instead of plummeting to his death.

Jake held on and let Kate guide them to the drop zone. He could tell she tried to set up the landing, but they were coming in hot and the impact blinded him. They rolled for an eternity, the chute trussing them up like a turkey. Jake clawed his way out and kissed the ground.

As Kate staggered out of the wreckage, Jake stood in time to see Berf and one of the bimbos hit the ground in a heap and tumble to a stop. The wind filled the chute and pulled the girl back. Berf rolled free.

Berf jumped up and did an end-zone dance. "Oh man!" He ran to the girl and kissed her. She released the chute and pushed him away, punching at him.

Frank thudded to the ground between Berf and Jake, his chute settling over him like a shroud.

Jake stood there, trying to figure out what just happened. His chute didn't open. But they checked and double-checked and triple-checked these things. He shrugged his way out of the pack and stared at it.

Kate stormed up to Jake and shoved him, knocking the pack to the ground. "What do you think you're doing?"

He glared back. He was the one who had almost died, not her. "First? Changing pants."

She charged over to Berf, dragged him away from the girl, and spun him around to face her. "You gave the pill to Summers!"

Berf stood there, his breath coming in and out like a bull facing a particularly troublesome matador. "Yeah, I did. He needed it. I didn't."

Kate shoved him aside and moved on to Frank, who lay on his back, the chute billowing out behind him. She unzipped Frank's jumpsuit. His wallet fell open.

An FBI badge flashed in the afternoon light. "What?" Jake said.

Berf stepped up. "What happened to him?"

Kate turned on him. "He took the pill."

"So?"

Kate grabbed Berf with one hand, Jake with the other, and dragged them toward the SUV.

"And we thought the scuba dive was bad!" Berf said.

Jake shook his head, but he couldn't seem to clear it. Too much was happening too fast.

As they approached the SUV, Berf held up a finger. "Wait. What happened to Frank?"

Kate whirled around and faced Berf. "The FBI agent? He's dead."

"FBI?" Berf said.

"Dead?" Jake said.

"When you made the reservation, what deal did you ask for?"

Jake looked at Berf. Kate followed his gaze.

"Uh . . . It was Dustin or something . . . Destiny. That's it. Destination of Destiny. Or something."

"How about Dignity?"

"Vacation with Dignity. Like I said."

"You asked for the package. Why didn't you take the pill?"

Jake held onto the SUV with one hand and rubbed his eyes with the other. None of this made sense. It was like Alice down the rabbit hole. One pill makes you taller. One pill makes you smaller. And one pill makes you dead.

He pulled the pill out of his zippered pocket. "This pill? Was supposed to kill us?"

Kate looked her most exasperated yet. "Of course."

Jake stared at her, unable to form a coherent thought. Things fell into place, like hidden tumblers lining up inside a vast machine. It was as if he were viewing a mosaic of random tiles, seemingly meaningless, but then took a step to the left and suddenly it all coalesced into an unutterable insight into the meaning of life.

As all of this lurched fitfully together in Jake's adrenaline-ravaged brain, the expression on Kate's face went through a terrible transformation. The outrage turned to confusion, then incredulity, enlightenment, denial, realization, and horror in quick succession. Just to watch her almost broke his heart. No, it did break his heart. He didn't know why, but it did.

Her voice dropped to a barely audible whisper. "You mean . . . you don't want to die?"

Berf started. "Is that a rhetorical question?"

Her hand flew to her lips. "But you said . . . No! It can't be!"

Kate grabbed the pill from Jake's fingers, fumbled with the keys, scrambled into the SUV, and tore out of the gravel parking lot in a cloud of dust.

Jake watched the dust roil behind the car. Something was going on here. Something was definitely going on here. But whatever it was, Kate was not the instigator. There was a hidden hand. Dark things were afoot.

Berf glared at the departing SUV. "Can you believe that? I have a good mind to write to my congressman. Or at least the Better Business Bureau. Words will be exchanged. Measures will be taken." He spun around as if headed to a car, then stopped. "Think there's a taxi around here?"

Jake looked back to the drop zone. In the wind, the chute tugged at Frank's body. The owner of the skydiving shop hollered at Dustin, who was still trying to disconnect his chute. The girls watched from a short distance.

There was one thought left in Jake's head. Time to get the heck out of Dodge.

# CHAPTER THIRTY-TWO

Kate paced the inner room of the SV office as far as the cord would allow. Pearl kept an eye on things in the front office.

She had no idea how this unfathomable mistake had been made, but it had to be dealt with immediately. Surely a corporation the size of Strange Vacations had the resources to put it right, insofar as a thing like this could be put right.

Kate whispered fiercely into the receiver. "I don't know how they got the pass phrase, but they know it."

"Then they get the package," Mr. Strange said, matter-of-factly.

She shook her head involuntarily. "No. You don't get it. They don't want to die."

"It's no longer optional."

Kate stopped cold, eyes wide open. "What?" This was as incomprehensible as the insane jump.

"In twenty-four hours, Cancún will be crawling with FBI agents. If you want to stay out of prison, we can't have Wiggins and Oakley telling stories."

Kate quieted down. So this was how he was going to play it. She modulated her voice into a meek tone. "I suppose you're right."

"Work with Pearl. Get it done before midnight."

The line went dead before she had a chance to answer. Kate hung up the phone and rushed out the door. She planned on getting it done much sooner than midnight.

# CHAPTER THIRTY-THREE

Berf grabbed his clothes from the drawer by the fistfuls and crammed them into his suitcase. It was the same suitcase and the same clothes, but somehow it didn't all fit anymore. He grabbed a random handful and tossed it aside. Better.

From the other bedroom, Jake yelled. "Next time you want to do me a favor—"

"How was I to know?" It wasn't like it was in the fine print or anything.

"Really do me a favor and stick your tongue in a light socket."

A woman's voice. "Hello? Jake? Burt?"

Berf stormed out of the room, a wad of shirts in each fist. It was Kate, peeking in the front door.

"It's Berf! Berf, Berf, Berf, *Berf!*" He tossed the shirts like confetti. "Let me write it down so you get it right on the headstone."

Jake walked out of his bedroom with a suitcase. "Kate?"

Kate closed the door behind her. "I have a plan."

Berf jerked the shirts up off the floor. "No, thanks, we already have a plan. It's called *getting the heck out of here!*" He stormed back to his bedroom, shoved the shirts in the suitcase, and zipped it shut.

"Mr. Strange still wants to kill you."

Berf grabbed his bag and came back out. "Tell Mr. Strange to take a number." He pushed past Kate and out the door.

He made it downstairs and to the lobby before he looked over his shoulder. Jake had almost caught up. Kate was close behind him. He turned to the door and ran into Runyon. It was like hitting a loaded beer truck. Berf didn't have much use for the guy, but he didn't wish anyone ill regardless of race, color, national origin, religion, sexual orientation, or hat size.

He fixed a gimlet eye on Runyon. "If you got Dignity and you know what's good for you, you'll leave now."

The guy looked like a calf staring at a new gate. "What?"

Let him figure it out. They'd get around to him eventually. Berf blew out the door to the waiting taxi. The trunk was open. The bellhop stepped forward to take the bags, but Berf ignored him and tossed the bag in from five feet away.

Kate caught up. "Mr. Strange thinks you'll talk to the FBI."

Berf slid into the back seat. "Fat chance. When the FBI shows up, all that will be left of us is a butt print in the drop zone."

Jake threw his bag in the trunk and tossed a handful of bills and coins at the bellhop.

Kate tried to stop Jake. "But I have a plan."

Jake pushed past her, jumped in the taxi and shoved a handful of bills over the seat at the driver. "Airport. As fast as you can get us there."

Berf looked at Kate. "We did your plan. It sucked." He slammed the door as the driver gunned the engine.

Kate's voice faded as they launched. "But they'll be—"

One thing about Mexican taxis—they knew how to expedite delivery. The driver employed a combination of techniques to navigate the competing interests on the road, including hand gestures, horn, well-chosen phrases, and an oversized dose of macho.

Berf bounced off of Jake while searching in vain for a seat belt.

Jake shoved Berf back to his side of the taxi. "How did you get this vacation deal?"

Berf grabbed the armrest and glanced at Jake. "Spider. He told me it would get us a killer deal."

Jake wedged himself in place with one arm on the back of the seat and the other against the window. "Spider? The guy who drank lighter fluid to light his belches?"

"Hey, that was in junior high." There was a statute of limitations on some things. Could you really hold something against him he did fifteen years ago, before he was even old enough to get a driver's license? It wasn't like he was running for president or anything.

"The guy who snowboarded off the cathedral roof? He's a walking death wish."

One did encounter certain difficulties when attempting to establish the credibility of a source, particularly when that source was Spider. Berf let it go. "When I tried to call him, his number was disconnected."

"His number was disconnected at birth, Buckwheat."

At that moment, Berf's head bounced off the driver's headrest as the taxi went from sixty to zero in a millisecond. He looked up to see what they had hit. Nothing, evidently. The limo in front of them was still a few inches from their bumper. A guy in a tailored suit with a skunk stripe down one side of his hair narrowed his eyes at the taxi, and then got into the limo.

Jake shoved the door open. "Here we are."

It seemed like an hour before the driver made it from the front seat to the trunk. When he popped it open, Berf elbowed him aside, tossed Jake a bag, and took the other. They were at the ticket counter before the man had closed the trunk.

Jake shoved a credit card at the agent. "Two tickets on the first plane to the U.S."

Berf dug in his bag for his passport. A hand fell on his shoulder.

"Excuse me, sir. Come with us." A hulking guy who could be FBI flashed a badge so fast it left a vapor trail.

Berf melted into three kinds of regret. "What?"

"It's just routine." The man seemed familiar. He grabbed Berf's arm.

A guy who was a double for one of the zoot-suited weasels from *Who Framed Roger Rabbit* grabbed Jake. He seemed familiar too.

Jake pulled away. "Hey! You were on the boat when the chair came loose." He peered at the guy holding Berf. "And you were at the skydive!"

Berf inspected the guy with a hand on his shoulder. He was the one with the pills. *The pills of death.* Berf struggled.

The Weasel had a little more trouble with Jake, but seemed to know a secret technique that encouraged compliance. They were halfway to the door when Berf heard the clacking of heels on the floor and a feminine voice.

"Berf, honey. Where have you been?"

Rita rushed up and latched onto him. He was happy to see her. He was happy to see anybody, but especially her. The Hulk tried to push her away, but she clung to his other arm.

"Berf, darling! Where are you going? What about the wedding?"

As glad as he was to see her, he disapproved of someone who would dry gulch a guy in a tight spot. "Wedding?" He wasn't opposed to weddings as a rule, except in cases where he was the victim. Plus he wasn't dressed for the occasion and hadn't even received an invitation.

The commotion attracted the attention of the other travelers. In the departures area, it seemed that commerce had halted, everyone frozen in place as they awaited his reply.

Jake pulled free from the Weasel and faced the crowd. "They're getting married."

Smiles and cheers all around. The glare Jake shot at Berf would have motivated a water buffalo to tap dance.

"Yeah. The family is waiting." Berf smiled at the crowd.

Someone pushed a few onlookers aside and Fernando strode toward them.

The Hulk spun Berf around to face him. Berf regarded his reflection in the dark-midnight-of-the-soul shades the guy had on.

"Why were you at the ticket counter?" he demanded.

"Ah, yes. Uh . . . the honeymoon!" Berf reached for Rita. "Hawaii, darling. It was a surprise—"

A collective "Awww" arose from the crowd. A smattering of applause turned into an ovation. Fernando arrived and grabbed Jake's arm. The Weasel tried to hang on, but the Hulk shook his head and they both let go.

He adjusted his shades. "We'll take care of this later."

As cheers erupted, the wedding party dashed out the door. Berf took a backward glance as they exited the building. The Hulk and the Weasel watched them leave. The Hulk was as impassive as a hangman. The Weasel looked like a hillbilly plotting a campaign of revenge unto the tenth generation. It was a chilling vision that stuck with him as they followed Rita and her brother to a beat-up yellow VW minibus. Fernando got behind the wheel, Rita took shotgun, and Berf leapt into the back seat.

Before Jake even got the door closed, Fernando rocketed away from the curb and Berf was once again struggling to maintain balance as the driver negotiated traffic with his best impression of an X-wing fighter pilot hurtling through an asteroid belt. He was trying to process the implications of everything, but it was difficult to maintain his concentration while adrenaline coursed through his veins, his pulse raced, and he bounced around in the back seat like an ice cube in a cocktail shaker.

Somehow Kate got the impression they wanted to die and did her best to make it so. Must be something to do with the Dignity package. Thankfully she now knew they didn't want to die, but Mr. Strange still wanted to kill them, doubtless for good reasons, misguided though they might be. And evidently the Weasel and the Hulk were Strange's tag-team angels of death.

So the airport was out. Driving would take a few days, but Berf had that route mapped in his DNA. He knew, and was known in, all kinds of off-the-beaten-track places. They could disappear for a week or so if required. But they would need cash to stay under the radar. Maybe Rita or her brother wouldn't mind making a road trip and a few extra pesos.

Jake leaned forward to say something, but Berf beat him to it.

"Rita, I don't know how you found us, but I'm glad you did."

Rita swiveled in her seat, flowing with the motion of the van like a natural-born equestrian. "Yes. Now we go get married."

Berf's smile of gratitude froze. "That was funny the first time. Not so much the second."

Jake caught Fernando's eye in the rearview. "I'm going to tell you a story. Okay?"

Rita nodded. Fernando grunted.

Jake took a breath. "It goes like this. Berf booked a vacation . . ." His eyes glazed over.

Berf shook his head. What was wanted at a time like this was less backstory and more incentive.

"Here's the thing—" Berf started, but Jake started up again.

"Okay. This morning, right after breakfast, we . . ." He stopped, took a breath, and tried again. "Right. Here it is. We have to leave the country."

Rita and Fernando looked at him blankly.

Jake's voice rose. "Now. Like right now. Like, are we going north? How far is it to the border?"

Berf pulled Jake back against the seat and scooted forward. "Right. Now, Fernando, is it? Right, then, Fernando, how would you like to make a few hundred bucks tax free?"

Fernando stared into the mirror, his face a mask. "This is how it works. We help you get away, you marry my sister."

Berf opened his mouth, but the only sound that came out was the noise of a fish with a bone caught in its throat. Jake sighed and shook his head.

Then Berf caught the expression on Rita's face, and hastened to explain. "Honey, I'd love to get married, but I won't be much fun if I'm dead."

It was Rita's turn to goggle like a goldfish in a party dress three sizes too small. "What?"

Jake stepped in. "They want to kill us. They arrange accidents for people."

Then Rita stared at him for a few seconds. She exchanged a few phrases with Fernando in Spanish, then turned back to Jake.

"You stay, you have the accident?"

"Yes."

"But if you go back home, can they not arrange the accident there too?"

Berf's mind melted into a medium grey as the implications of her suggestion seeped through him, sucking up all his energy and his will to fight. Strange Vacations had his home address, and even if they didn't, how hard would it be to find him? A mentally negligible intern with internet access could do it. Even the Weasel or the Hulk could do it. "She's got a point there."

"You need files, recordings," Rita said. "Proof. You put them away. Then you escape danger."

Berf raised an eyebrow. Evidently this wasn't her first shakedown. Now that he thought about it, she kinda reminded him of the dark-eyed woman that latched onto Tell Sackett when he was crossing the Mojave with a bait of gold. Dorinda Robiseau was the name. And everyone knew how that turned out.

But as he thought on it, he realized she was right, no matter how she came by the knowledge. They had got lucky with the pill mix-up, but how many times could you depend on luck to pull your grits out of the fire? Then he remembered the conversation on the boat the night before.

"Jake, the screwy Doo. Do you think . . ."

"I didn't, but now I do."

"And the chair on the boat."

Jake's eyes took on a distant aspect. "I'd forgotten it, but right after Frank went overboard, I saw that scrawny little guy peering out of the hold."

"And that was your chair." Berf shook his head. "The Weasel and the Hulk have been trying to kill us since we got here."

He saw it now. There was no running from this crowd. He'd have to stand and fight. Get enough evidence to put them behind bars, every man jack of them. But what could he do? Bug their offices? Video them killing somebody else? Steal their files? "We need someone on the inside."

"Hey," Jake blurted out. "What about Kate? She could get us proof."

Berf loved Jake like a brother, but sometimes he needed a good whack with a switch from the peach tree. "The one who tried to kill us?"

"But she changed her mind."

# CHAPTER THIRTY-FOUR

Jake peered through the windshield at the SV office. It was just dark enough for a light to show through the blinds. Had to be Kate. They'd searched the resort, discretely of course, and come up dry.

He crawled over Berf and cracked the door open. "If I'm not out in five, call 911."

Fernando shook his head. "No police. We come in."

"Sure." Jake stepped out and walked to the office door. It was unlocked. He waved back at the van and slipped inside.

There was a front office, but it was dark and deserted. The light came from an open door on the back wall. Jake walked through the door into a back office and in on an interrogation.

The Weasel held Kate in a chair. The Hulk unrolled a strip of duct tape. Blood trickled from his cheekbone and a stapler lay on the floor. He leaned over to tape Kate's arm to the chair.

"We don't have to do it this way. Just tell us where they are."

Jake hollered, "Hey!" And then realized there might have been a better way to intervene.

Before the syllable ended, the Hulk whirled around and Frisbee-ed the duct tape at Jake. It hit him in the forehead. He fell against the door, stunned. The Hulk rushed around a desk. Jake fled to the front office, slamming the door behind him. Halfway across the room to the door, he stopped.

What was he doing? Running away from a woman in distress? He didn't believe in Berf's ridiculous Code, but sometimes you had to resist instincts and do the right thing. Despite the fact that he was clueless as to how to stop the avalanche that had just kicked open the door and crashed into the room, Jake turned to face it.

When he saw the fury in the man's face, Jake flinched and backpedalled into a water cooler. As the Hulk bore down on him, Jake sidestepped and shoved the entire cooler into the man's gut. The Hulk went down and the water bottle toppled off, soaking him.

Jake heard noises from the back office, but the Hulk was scrambling to his feet. Kate would have to deal with the Weasel until further notice. The Hulk slipped in the water and Jake stepped to a filing cabinet and tipped it over. The Hulk was trapped.

For good measure, Jake dragged a desk over and added it to the pile. The Hulk groaned. Never content to leave a job half done, Jake grabbed a full water bottle and swung it against his head. The Hulk settled down immediately and quit making disconcerting noises.

Jake staggered to the back office. Kate had the Weasel in a swivel chair, cocooning him in duct tape as she spun him around. His nose was bleeding and a broken keyboard hung over his shoulder, the cord wrapped around his neck. On the floor lay a dented tower computer, a smashed monitor, and a few dozen copies of the Weasel's face smashed against the copier glass. She had clearly been equal to the task.

Jake held out a hand. "Come on."

Kate ripped off a final bit of tape and slapped it over the Weasel's mouth. She joined Jake and they walked through the front office past the pyramid of office furniture piled on the Hulk as they passed. "Nice work. How did you knock him out?"

"Hydrotherapy." Jake toed the water bottle.

"I don't envy Sully the headache he's going to have if he ever wakes up."

"Who is Sully?"

"Mr. Strange's right-hand thug."

"Is the other guy Strange?"

"Mr. Strange is the CEO of Strange Vacations. That's Pearl back there. He does the dirty work."

Jake stopped. "Pearl?"

Kate shrugged and pushed the door open. Jake led the way to the van. They jumped in. As was his custom, Fernando zoomed off before the door was closed.

Berf shoved over behind Fernando. "'Bout time, J-Bird. For a while there, we were thinking you might have stepped in a prairie-dog hole and broke your leg."

Kate slid next to Berf, and Jake squeezed onto the end of the seat. Rita inspected Kate over the seat back. Kate returned her gaze without comment. Fernando watched in the rearview.

After an uncomfortable silence, Kate asked Jake, "Who are they?"

"Well, you know Berf."

Berf tipped an imaginary hat. "Pleasure to see you again, ma'am."

Kate nodded.

"And this is the cavalry." Jake gestured. "That's Fernando."

Fernando caught her eye in the rearview. "He's going to marry my sister."

Kate's face was full of confusion and consternation.

Jake shrugged. "And that's the sister. Rita."

"You're going to marry Rita?" Kate said.

"Oh, no," Jake blurted. "Not me. Berf is going to marry Rita."

Berf stirred from his corner against the window. "Berf is not . . . Oh, never mind."

Kate shifted her disapproving stare upon Berf. "Are you really going to marry Rita?"

Rita's gaze shifted to Berf. Fernando moved the rearview to get Berf in his sights. Jake joined the crowd in waiting for Berf's answer.

For a person who was often the center of attention, Berf seemed uncharacteristically uncomfortable. "Well . . . we haven't really . . ."

Rita blew out a puff of air. "But Berf, you said . . ."

Fernando impaled Berf with a deadly glare through the mirror. Jake had never seen anyone play a rearview with such power. Not even his mom, the queen of the withering stare.

"Maybe we should talk this over a little more," Berf said. "I mean, think about it. Marriage is a sacred institution, the inviolate bond between a man and a woman. What you're shooting for in a case like this is something along the lines of Tyrel and Drusilla, not Orrin and Laura. It's not like picking out a puppy at the pound or choosing a color for the dining room."

Fernando spoke over his shoulder without taking his eyes off the road. "We have a deal. You break the deal, I take you back to the *matones*."

Jake sensed the fabric of their tenuous coalition unraveling. "Berf, maybe you should—"

"Looky here, I'm as agreeable and accommodating as the next feller, but that doesn't mean I'll just stand by and be dry-gulched. It takes two to tangle."

Fernando slammed on the brake and wrenched around in the seat, reaching back at Berf. "Are you calling my sister a whore?"

Rita threw herself between Fernando and Berf. "Fernando! No! He does not mean it."

Fernando bristled but pulled back and waited.

Jake leaned across Kate and whispered hoarsely. "Berf, it looks like it's time to take one for the team."

Berf's reaction was not unlike that of a lamb that has just been asked to lie down with a lion in a unilateral gesture of goodwill and is considering asking for something in writing beforehand. "Are you actually listening to what you're saying?"

Jake shushed him. "You could do a lot worse."

Berf switched to a stage whisper. "You're not the one who has to—"

"Look at her," Jake whispered.

Berf looked at her. He appeared to soften. "True. I have done worse. But it wasn't permanent."

Jake tried another approach. "If you get married, your mother will quit harassing you night and day about settling down."

Berf considered this. "Or I could just move to the Himalayas and hire out as a Sherpa."

Rita leaned across the gap and whispered, "The women in my family, we know how to make our men happy."

Fernando nodded, adjusting the rearview. "Papa died with a smile on his face. May he rest in peace." He crossed himself.

Berf seemed lost in another solar system.

Jake whispered, "He said his father died with a smile on his face."

"I'm doubtful, not deaf."

"What exactly are we negotiating?" Kate whispered.

"It's complicated," Jake whispered.

"We will help them to not be killed by the accident," Rita whispered.

"If Berf will marry Rita," Jake whispered.

"Why are we whispering?" Kate whispered.

They all watched Berf, waiting for the smoke to go up. He closed his eyes and seemed to retreat within himself, as if searching for some escape clause.

In the faint light of the dash, Berf's jaw muscles flexed a few times. He clinched his fists, drew in a deep breath through his nostrils, and blew it out slowly through his lips while opening his hands, palms up like he was letting go of something.

Then he opened his eyes. "Oh, all right," Berf boomed. "If you get us out of this alive, we'll get married."

Rita leaned across the seat and hugged Berf. Fernando stepped on the gas, and they resumed their journey through the night.

Berf extracted himself from the hug and leaned against the window. "But if you don't," he added. "Then it's off. And I mean it!"

"So how do I fit into this plan?" Kate asked. "They're coming after me just as much as you." She glanced at Fernando, who studied her in the rearview. "Do I have to marry someone to get rescued?"

Right then Jake wished he had a cosmic *Get Out of Jail Free* card he could play and teleport them all to Austin. Yes, he was up against it, and so was Berf, but so was Kate, even though Berf couldn't see it. She was a nice person who had obviously been lured into this Strange Vacations scheme through false pretenses, and now she was in just as much danger as the rest of them.

They didn't have much hope, but what little hope they had rested on Kate. He placed what he hoped was a comforting hand on her shoulder. "Our only chance is to get evidence that Strange Vacations is trying to kill us. You are the best person to do that."

Kate recoiled. "Me?"

"Yes. Then we go to the cops and let them take care of it."

"No cops," Fernando yelled.

"No." Kate shook her head. "No offense, but I'm not interested in dying in a Mexican jail."

Fernando glanced back. "No cops. FBI."

Berf stirred briefly from his funk in the corner. "That's out. We killed the FBI agent."

Rita whipped around to face the back seat. "The FBI agent is dead?" She glanced at Fernando.

"It was an accident," Berf said. "He was freaking out over the jump and—"

"There will be more," Kate said. "Lots more. Mr. Strange is expecting them."

"Who is Mr. Strange?" Rita asked.

"Her boss," Jake said. "Good. We just have to stall until the FBI gets here."

Kate shook her head. "I'd rather not die in an American jail either."

"Why would you go to jail?" Jake asked.

"For starters, I work for the guys who are trying to kill you."

"Yeah," Berf said. "And up until this afternoon, she was trying to kill us too."

"We can explain all that," Jake said. They were making this unnecessarily complicated.

"In case you haven't noticed," Kate said, "FBI agents aren't particularly adept at nuance."

"Perhaps, but we can—"

Kate overrode him in a voice much louder than required for the inside of the minibus, as old and noisy as it was. "Let me spell it out for you. Yes, it's illegal to kill people who don't want to die. But in most countries it's also illegal to kill people who do want to die. Especially if you haven't consulted everyone who might be affected by the decision, documented everything in triplicate, and followed legally approved protocols." In a softer voice she added, "And there's probably a good reason for that."

"You'll be saving yourself as much as us," Jake said. "If Mr. Strange isn't in jail, he'll hunt all of us down, you included."

Kate took a deep breath and seemed to grow to twice her size. "I don't know how you got into this, or what you thought you were doing, and I'd like to help you if I can, but you got yourselves into it without me."

She took another deep breath and let it out slowly. "Look, you don't deserve to die because of a misunderstanding, but I don't deserve to spend my life in prison either."

Jake shook his head. She wasn't seeing the bigger picture. If Frank really was FBI, and if more agents were coming, then they had been building a case against Strange Vacations for a while. They would be gunning for the top guys. "If you get the evidence against Mr. Strange, you can use it to bargain for immunity. And I'd say Micronesia is as good a place as any to disappear under the witness protection program."

Kate considered this for a moment. "That's not a chance I'm willing to take. But I will help you get the evidence. Then you get me out of the country. I'll take it from there and you go to the FBI on your own."

Berf said, "I don't know if that will work. Will that work?"

Jake scanned the small band of conspirators, but nobody answered. Would the FBI take the files as proof, or would they demand insider testimony to confirm it? He didn't know how these things worked. "Maybe you could cut a deal with them in exchange for—"

As he was speaking, Jake could see that Kate was no longer listening. Her eyes clouded over into a thousand-yard stare focused deep within. It was like after the jump, when she grabbed the pill and ran away to the SUV.

Kate shuddered. "How did this happen?"

Berf cleared his throat. "Well, first you tried to kill us—"

Jake interrupted. "Technically, she didn't try to—"

Kate spoke in a distant voice, like she was at a séance, channeling her great-great-great aunt from Romania. "'You're just an activity director,' he said. 'Pearl will take care of the sensitive details,' he said."

Berf leaned forward to talk around her. "I mean, technically, she did try to kill us."

Jake tried to wave him into silence. This wasn't helping. "That's not the point."

"But—" Berf said.

"Okay, okay," Jake said. "Technically she did, but she didn't mean to."

Kate's voice switched into a higher octave. "Just help people like Mr. Heald . . ."

Berf shook his head. "No, you'll have to stipulate that she meant to at the time."

". . . who have the right to choose their own end," Kate said.

"But only because she thought we meant to," Jake said and held up a finger to silence Berf.

"They said the code. They get the package." Kate was approaching hysteria. "But you didn't want the package."

"No, we didn't," Jake said softly.

"And Sully found me and—"

Jake enfolded Kate in his arms, shushing her. "Kate. It's okay. We'll go to the FBI without you."

She pulled back as if puzzled to see him there. "I'm so sorry, Jake. I didn't know."

"I know."

"I never would have—"

"Of course not."

She seemed to return from whatever nether-land of horror she had fallen into and glanced around the group self-consciously.

Berf cleared his throat. "Ma'am, I appreciate this is a delicate time for you, and we all wish you the best in your future endeavors, but one question remains outstanding. How do we get the files?"

From what Jake could see of Kate's expression, Berf wasn't going to displace anyone on her friends and family list. "They locked me out of the system, but if we get Mr. Strange's laptop and his ring, we can get the records."

Berf frowned. "His ring?"

"The ring has a receiver that gets the encryption key from a satellite and sends it to the laptop. Without the ring, the laptop is useless."

"So how do we get them?"

After a long silence, Fernando said, "Frederick, *quizás?*"

Rita nodded. "Frederick has the in-room spa appointment with Mr. Strange tomorrow."

In a heartbeat, Kate lost her penitent tone. "How do you know that?"

Jake wondered the same thing. Who exactly were these people?

Rita shrugged. "We know things. Sometimes."

Regardless of who they were, Jake failed to see the relevance of Frederick and the in-room spa. "So?"

"You do the spa, not Frederick," Rita said, as if pointing out the obvious.

There was nothing obvious about that suggestion.

"But what about Frederick?" Kate asked.

Rita dismissed this question. "Fernando can take care of Frederick."

"You know him?"

"Oh, yes. He is always glad to see us."

The conversation stopped as Fernando pulled up to a shabby apartment building deep in a local Cancún neighborhood. Rita got out. Jake followed, helping Kate out of the door.

As Berf slid across the seat, Fernando grabbed him by the arm. "Come with me, brother."

"Me?" Berf cast a wordless plea toward Jake.

Fernando smiled. "We must know each other better."

"Really?"

Jake shrugged.

"Shotgun," Berf said, then hesitantly climbed into the front seat.

# CHAPTER THIRTY-FIVE

Kate followed Rita and Jake into the flat. The phone was ringing. Rita answered it and immediately began arguing in Spanish. She started a pot of coffee and then disappeared into a bedroom, still yelling at the phone.

Kate leaned against the counter and scanned the room, avoiding Jake's eyes. The apartment was better than her accommodations in Micronesia, a rusting Quonset hut, but she would have never considered living in a flat like this in the Netherlands. Anyone with a choice would abandon this dump. There was too much collateral drama built into the neighborhood surrounding such flats.

Whoever Rita was, she was clearly not on the take. Maybe Berf really was her ticket out. Well, good for her if she could make it work. It might be the only worthwhile thing Berf did with his life.

The coffee machine belched and sputtered, and a few tendrils of steam curled up from the basket. Jake poured a cup and offered it to Kate. She shook her head and walked to a set of French doors off the main room. There was a balcony, an iron railing with peeling black paint. She leaned on it and took in the moonlight-silvered city.

In the rare moments when despair had her surrounded, when she faced her dread and stared into the heart of it, Kate always found some glimmer of hope peering back. It wasn't a lemonade-from-lemons thing. It wasn't a silver-lining thing. It wasn't a denial-of-the-facts thing. It was a real thing. Hope was always there, buried in the muck right along with you, an unlikely silent companion, at home amidst the chaos, even through the gates of hell.

It didn't say, *Buck up, everything will be okay.* It didn't smile and ask, *How are we feeling today, love?* It just sat nearby and held your hand and said, *I'll be here for the worst, and I'll be here after that too.*

From the deepest pit you could still see stars. You just had to know where to look.

Kate searched from the front to the back of this situation, searching for the stars, but as far as she could tell, it was all clouds.

If she had any sense, she would walk out the door to a major street and get a taxi to the airport and a flight to Micronesia. But as much as she wanted to, she couldn't just leave these two bozos to the mercy of Mr. Strange, a man who evidently had no mercy in him.

But what could they do, the three of them, five if you counted Rita and Fernando, against a powerful multibillionaire and his hired goons? She gave up thinking and just let the moonlight settle into her bones.

Then Jake stood next to her. She spoke without taking her eyes off the view. "It's like something from a fairy tale."

"Even a slum sparkles in the moonlight."

Not everyone had the vision to see beyond the surface to the true reality. "It's as real as the view at noon."

Jake leaned against the door frame, sipping his coffee. "So which is true? Is it a slum or a fairy tale?"

"Why can't it be both?" Didn't the best fairy tales start in the slums? And sometimes they stayed there and still lived happily ever after. Or as much as was possible in this world.

"Even if it is a fairy tale, the evil wizard is out there plotting to kill us and make it look like an accident."

She abandoned the point. He wasn't her project. He was just an unfortunate victim of a colossal misunderstanding. That stirred other thoughts she would rather leave undisturbed. "I should be worried, but I can't quit thinking about Mr. Summers."

"Frank? That wasn't your fault."

"It's all my fault." It all started with getting greedy, wanting to take the fast lane back to Micronesia.

"He was FBI. He knew the risks."

"And I almost killed you and Burt."

"You were just doing what you thought we wanted."

The moment Mr. Strange ignored her objections about Jake, she should have left. "I knew you didn't belong." She shook her head. "I'm just glad it's over. I can't imagine what I might have become if I listened to Mr. Strange for a year."

They fell into silence. Jake seemed restless. He sipped his coffee, scanning the street in both directions.

Rita's voice floated out from the bedroom, still in the throes of an argument. Jake turned and leaned back against the rail. Kate could feel his eyes on her. He seemed to want to say something. Then he finally did.

"If we . . . When this is over, what will you do?"

Her answer was immediate. "Go back to the clinic."

"Disappear to Micronesia forever?"

"Who wouldn't want to disappear to paradise?"

"You need some help down there?"

She pulled her gaze from the city and transferred it to him. "You? We don't have reserved parking for your BMW. No executive washroom. No 401(k). No exit strategy."

"I don't have a BMW anymore. Or 401(k). And I'm good with whatever plumbing is available."

Was he serious? Was he delusional? He'd spent one idyllic summer on a sailboat and evidently had spun some kind of fantasy from it. Even in paradise you had to get the food, cook it, and deal with the waste, all kinds of waste. And in a third-world paradise, those things were not easy to do. "So what are you? A CEO or a Peace Corps volunteer?"

"Why can't I be both?"

Jake reached for Kate's hand. She was so shocked, she didn't react at first. She just looked at his hand on hers, then at his face, wondering what was behind this sudden change.

"Kate, I've been thinking—"

The front door slammed open. They turned from the window. Fernando came in and dropped some boxes on the kitchen table. Berf followed with more boxes.

Fernando said, "We have the stuff." He sniffed the air, spotted the coffee pot, and began searching for a cup.

Kate pulled her hand from Jake's grasp.

Berf leaned through the doorway. "Frederico is un-available tomorrow. Maybe longer." Then he stepped to the balcony and whispered. "Between you and me, if you're thinking of going up against Fernando for any reason, just remember this one thing: bad idea."

# CHAPTER THIRTY-SIX

When Jake awoke the next day, he thought he'd been asleep for ten minutes, but according to the clock, it was noon. They had planned late into the night. Then the women slept in the bedroom. The men slept in the main room on whatever they could find.

As the others prepared lunch, Fernando waved Jake into the bedroom and closed the door. "Take off your clothes."

Jake squared off against him. "This has been weird enough, Fernando."

Fernando shook his head disgustedly and pulled a digital recorder from a duffel bag.

Jake nodded with relief, stripped down to his boxers, and thought back to his conversation with Kate while Fernando wired him with a mike. If Berf and Fernando had not interrupted them, everything would have been settled.

This whole trip had been a wakeup call, but it all happened too fast for thinking. It was just all reaction and survival. First the Doo and the shark, and then the jump and Frank, and then the airport and Sully, and then the SV office and Sully, and then everything else. It was like bam, bam, bam. One thing after another with no break to collect your wits and see what it all meant.

But he could see it now. It was Fate. He saw it last night when Kate melted down in the van. He was focused on getting out of this thing alive when he suddenly saw beyond himself and his dilemma.

Kate was stuck in this thing too, just like them. He didn't know how she got into it, probably for a good reason, not that he had to know, because he could see she wouldn't do it unless it was for a good reason. A very good reason.

It was that moment in the van when she suddenly seemed so fragile and lost, and he just wanted to hold her in his arms and make it better, and he had. That was the moment. That was when he realized he wasn't going back to Austin. What was left for him there?

He'd already sent the prize money to the bank. He would hire a lawyer to sell the condo, settle his debts as best he could, declare bankruptcy if he had to, and go do the world some good for a change. So what if his credit was ruined for ten years? What would he need credit for? He'd have Kate, a good woman, a hard-headed woman, the best kind, and he'd be making a difference in the world. Not that lawn care wasn't useful. Sure, people needed that. But this was different.

Once they got the laptop and the ring, he would get her alone and put his cards on the table, and that would be it.

He watched as Fernando taped the lightweight recorder to his back and ran the wire under his arm. "Why do you have stuff like this? What do you do?"

He still wasn't sure about these guys. Did they really think Berf would marry Rita? Not that it was a bad idea. Actually, Rita was better than most girls Berf got mixed up with. But was that really the story? On the other hand, why else would they do it? Anybody who lived in this dump would be desperate for their ticket out of here.

Fernando taped down the wire. "I have the electronics store."

Jake picked up the empty box. It was stenciled *La Propiedad de AFI*.

"Property of the AFI?"

"Auction. Old stuff."

Right. There was another angle here. This wasn't his first rodeo. "Tell me, Fernando. How many times have you married Rita off?"

Fernando stopped and turned a face chiseled from granite on him. "In Mexico, questions are bad for your health, my friend."

# Chapter Thirty-Eight

Michael Strange sat at the desk in his Cancún resort suite. He was on the phone with Sully and he was not happy.

"No, no. Lutz rides the turtle. King wants the pyramid. Yes. Yesterday, but then this thing happened."

These petty details were precisely the things he should not be doing. That was why he hired Kate. His instinct had been way off with her. Given how things had worked out, it should have screamed like a rocking chair had rolled over its tail the moment he set eyes on her.

Strange clicked the computer, bringing up photos of Oakley and Wiggins. They were the real problem. If they hadn't gotten cold feet at the last minute and then feigned ignorance, Kate wouldn't have had second thoughts and gone rogue.

There was a knock at the door. He checked the time. Must be Frederick. Strange walked to the door, still on the phone. "Has Pearl found those clowns?"

The knock repeated, louder, more insistent. That wasn't Frederick.

"I want them in my room today." Strange hung up the phone and opened the door.

It was two guys. A slim bald guy dressed in pastels and a skinny hippy in paisley and straight hair down to his elbows. The bald guy stared at him like an ostrich recently tickled on the back of its head with a blackjack.

"Well?" Strange asked.

The guy shivered to life, flipped up a card, and read from it. "Mr. Strange?" He sounded like he was gargling marbles.

# CHAPTER THIRTY-SEVEN

The door jerked open and Jake was toe-to-toe with Michael Strange. If James Bond were twice as fashionable, three times as cool, and had a skunk stripe in his hair, he still would be no match for Strange. Now that they had met, it was unnerving just being in the same ZIP code with him. The slight possibility that perhaps he was in over his head flitted through Jake's mind like a bullet on its way somewhere else.

Back in college, at Berf's insistence, Jake had done a little theater. As they got dressed this afternoon, he had felt the familiar pre-show jitters. It was coming back. He could do this, he thought at the time. Then the door opened and Strange stared at him like he was a caveman in a NASA moonwalk diorama, and his confidence wilted and blew away.

"Well?"

Then Jake remembered the first night he walked onstage as Ali Hakim in *Oklahoma!* and looked past the lights just like he'd been told not to. Hundreds of faces all focused on him. It was like bungee jumping into a black hole. He'd very nearly tumbled into the orchestra pit, but Berf, playing Curly McLain, had sprung onstage, grabbed his belt, and hauled him back.

"Remember the fourth wall," Berf had whispered fiercely into his ear, then loudly adlibbed some plot-appropriate excuse for being in the scene and shoved Jake at Ginger, who was playing Ado Annie.

Jake realized that the door opening was nothing more than the curtain going up. As long as you didn't think about what was beyond the fourth wall, you were fine. Otherwise, you were toast. Maybe literally in this case. But he couldn't think about that. He had to stick to the script.

Jake reached into the breast pocket of his pastel pink blazer and snapped a card out. "Mr. Strange?" He was glad to hear his voice was holding up, and the accent he had worked out with Berf's help sounded right on the money.

Strange stepped forward and peered down the hall. "Where's Frederick?"

Jake slipped the card back in his pocket. "Frederick has the indisposition. Oysters and the month without the R. Very inconvenient for him. But good for you. I am Feldspar. You have heard of me? This way, Ahnri."

Jake picked up a bag and flowed past Strange with a flourish. He scanned the room, saw a laptop on the desk by the windows, and pointed. "Over there is good. Better for the view." Jake noticed with a considerable amount of alarm that his and Berf's photos were prominently displayed on the laptop, but he suppressed the instinct to run out the door screaming.

Berf walked in, dragging a portable massage table and a large case. Jake turned to Strange but a noise distracted him. Berf had dropped the case and the table. He was staring at the laptop.

Jake reached into his bag and whipped out a thick, white terrycloth bathrobe, holding it out to Strange, blocking his view of Berf. "Down to the boxers, Mr. Strange."

Amazingly, Strange took the bathrobe and disappeared into a bedroom.

Berf was frozen in place, mesmerized by the laptop like a bird before a cobra. "He's got our pictures right there."

Jake didn't break character for a second. "I can see that, Ahnri." He extracted towels and lotions and oils from his bag.

Berf shivered out of his trance and set up the massage table. Jake opened scented oils and lighted candles. They worked in silence until Strange returned in robe and midnight blue silk briefs.

Jake slapped the donut pillow. "On the table, Mr. Strange. He will scream for joy and beg for mercy, eh Ahnri?"

Berf smiled nervously and slapped the table. Jake shook his head. Berf's hippie outfit was a bit much, but you worked with what you could find. There weren't a lot of options in the vintage clothing shop and even fewer in the costume shop. But it would work if Berf would work it. He'd been completely convincing in the dress rehearsal, where Fernando had played the part of Strange.

Strange draped the robe over a recliner and mounted the table, face in the hole. Berf closed his eyes and bowed his head, his fists balled at his side, and breathed in and out deeply a few times.

This was better.

The tension in the room dropped several degrees and then Berf suddenly exploded out of his meditation and attacked Strange's muscles like a pianist playing Rachmaninoff's Prelude Op. 2 No. 5—dramatic movements, hair flying.

Strange groaned. Jake draped a hot towel over his head. Strange moaned.

Yes, this might actually work.

If Strange had been entertaining doubts about their authenticity, Jake was certain they had been erased by the end of the massage. Nobody could go through an experience like that and have the ghost of a thought left in his mind or a micron of tension left in his body. Jake almost envied him.

They transferred his limp form to the recliner. Jake shampooed his hair while Berf arranged smooth heated stones on his body and face.

There was a knock at the door. "Housekeeping."

The door opened and Kate pushed in a cart. She wore the same uniform as the regular staff. Her red hair was hidden under a black wig. Jake ignored her, staying in character. She caught his attention with a strange gesture, her hand twisting around above her head, and nodded at Berf.

Jake checked, but Berf was doing fine. He was bent over Strange, removing his rings in preparation for the manicure. He set them on the end table, but slipped the big one into his pocket. So far, so good.

Kate was at the desk. She emptied the trash can, straightened items on the desk, and slipped the laptop on the cart under a stack of linens. She coughed and made the strange gesture again. Berf looked up.

Now Jake could see what Kate was getting at. Berf's wig was askew. Jake pulled a hand up from his shampooing and rotated it above his head, nodding at Berf as he did so. Berf frowned for a second, then responded with an *aha* expression and broke into a frenetic hand massage.

There was nothing for it but to try to distract Strange and hope he didn't notice. "Frederick tells me you have the unusual business, Mr. Strange."

Strange frowned. The stones quivered. "What?"

Kate had gone back to her cleaning, but now she whipped around, drew a finger across her throat, and shook her head frantically. He ignored her and adjusted the flower in his lapel holding the mike.

"Very special vacation packages, he says."

Strange elbowed his way up to a semi-sitting posture. The stones fell from his face and body. Kate put down the ashtray she was cleaning and pushed the cart slowly toward the door.

"What does Frederick know about it?"

Berf continued to massage Strange's hand like he was milking a particularly troublesome cow. Strange looked at Berf, his fingers squeezing, his head rotating, hair flying around like a dervish in a trance.

"Stop that."

Berf didn't stop. Strange clamped his free hand down on Berf's head. The hair stopped but his head kept going.

Strange frowned at the wig in his hand. "What is this?"

Berf froze, startled that he had been parted from his hair. He caught Strange's stare and dropped his hand.

Strange held up the wig. "Hey."

Berf grabbed the footrest of the recliner with one hand and jumped up, flipping Strange back. Strange somersaulted with the chair. His feet hit Jake on the chest.

Jake staggered back, arms flailing, and careened into the bedroom, falling onto the bed. He got up and rushed back out the door. Strange was on his feet. He turned in a martial arts stance, looked at Jake, and squinted at the top of his head.

Jake realized his skullcap had become dislodged and was pushed down over his eyebrows. He raised a hand to adjust it as Strange unleashed a scissor kick that sent him flying back into the bedroom. The last thing he felt was the thud of his head bouncing off the foot of the bed.

# CHAPTER THIRTY-NINE

A mounting sense of dread stalked Berf from the moment he saw their pictures on the laptop. It was all the more unnerving because it was a completely new sensation for him. Up to this point, life had been relatively kind.

Not that he had never known disappointment. Sure he had. What grade-school kid who has been forced to dress in a raccoon suit and conjure up lawn furniture against a green screen for the purpose of broadcasting his humiliation on television for the amusement of his peers has not tasted the bitterness of injustice, has not felt that life is a cruel trick played upon the unwary innocent, has not sensed a brooding malevolence at work in the universe, or at the very least a hollow meaninglessness pervading the tedium of his every waking hour?

But despite his environment as a child—the marsh-mallow ubiquity of his mother's spirituality to the dismissal of reasonable objections, the tunnel vision of his father's ambition to the disdain of other pursuits, the mimetic obsession of his sister's pretensions to the displacement of authentic relationships—Berf had remained at the core the type of fellow who sees not a glass that is half empty, but rather a glass that could use a little topping off and steps up to do the needful.

On the whole, life was better taken with a grain of salt, with lime and tequila, if possible, but at any rate not taken so seriously as to prevent the enjoyment of the moment as it wafted by on the breeze of eternity.

But when he saw his own face staring back at him from Strange's computer, it whisked the sand right out of him. Sure, he snapped out of it and soldiered on, but he couldn't shake the sense that it would end badly. And it had. Maybe he was trying too hard, compensating, but the bare facts were that the wheels came off, the thing went off the rails, and they were in the soup up to the gills.

Flipping the recliner over would disable a normal human, but Strange was some kind of Jackie Chan stand-in. He slung Jake in and out of the bedroom like a yo-yo.

He and Kate had to get out with the goods while Strange was occupied with Jake. It was their only chance. With the laptop and the ring they would have bargaining power to get Jake back and stop the madness.

Kate was frozen in the middle of the room, in shock. Berf made a dash for the front door and called out to her. "Kate, come on!"

The last thing he felt was an express train making an unscheduled stop against the back of his head.

# CHAPTER FORTY

Kate had her doubts about the plan from the beginning, but she didn't have a better one, and on top of all that, she was a de facto prisoner. That much was obvious, though unstated. Her best chance of getting through this was playing along, preventing any suspicion of less than total commitment until an alternative presented itself.

In her experience, the Gordian knot of a dilemma was addressed not through cunning or devious plots but by cutting through the tangle of ego and self-interest with sincerity and compromise. But the dramatic failure of that approach became apparent when Mr. Strange ordered the execution—there was no other word for it— and was driven home with the attempt to torture information out of her.

She had been looking for ways to get Jake and Burt out of the country and coming up empty when Sully and Pearl had found her. Being taped to a chair was merely a dramatization of the inner reality that she was out of options. Or rather down to one option, to take as many of them with her as she could before they took her out.

When Jake stepped through that door as Sully ripped off a length of tape, he represented more than escape from torture. He was the possibility of a plan. Then she heard the plan. They were all crazy, of course, the whole lot of them. And not just the lot she had fallen in with— Jake, Burt, Rita, and Fernando. The others were crazy too—Sully, Pearl and most of all, Mr. Strange. What else could you call it?

What they came up with in the wee hours of the morning wasn't much of a plan, but it was all they had. Mr. Strange was a powerful man. There was no point trying to run from him. He already had a file on her an inch thick. Even Micronesia would be no sanctuary. In fact, going to a remote island with a rudimentary police force and justice system would make his job easier.

But from the moment she said "housekeeping" in her best Mexican accent and pushed the door open, she saw it was hopeless. Burt with his hair pushed back on his head like a hippie Benjamin Franklin, Jake adjusting his flower microphone. It was like going up against the KGB with a spy ring composed of the Marx Brothers, the Keystone Cops, and Elmer Fudd.

When it began to unravel, she just focused on her part, getting out of there with the laptop. Then Mr. Strange transformed into a kung fu master, and despite herself, she stopped, astounded at the disproportionate firepower.

Then Burt made a dash for the door, yelling, "Kate, come on!"

Mr. Strange picked up one of the stones from the massage and threw it. It hit Burt at the base of his skull and he dropped in the doorway like someone had pulled the plug on a Hoover, blocking Kate's escape path.

She looked at Mr. Strange.

He looked at her. "Kate?"

Mr. Strange stepped to the desk, grabbed a pistol from his briefcase, and motioned her to the room where Jake lay sprawled on the floor at the foot of the bed.

"Mr. Strange, this isn't euthanasia. It's murder."

Mr. Strange shoved Kate into the room without comment, dragged Burt over, threw him on the bed, and slammed the door. She heard some noise from outside the door and tried to open it. The knob spun, but the door wouldn't open.

"Michael!" she said, hoping the use of his Christian name would stir some Christian sympathies. "Think about what you're doing."

She could hear him moving around, doing something, but he didn't respond. Kate ripped the wig off her head and threw it across the room. She went in the bathroom, soaked a washcloth with cold water, pulled Jake out of his heap on the floor, and wiped his face. His eyes fluttered. When he came around, she stood up. His head thumped against the footboard.

"Ow!" Jake leaned against the bed, peeled the skullcap from his head, and tossed it on the mattress.

It hit Burt in the face. Burt pushed it away, groaned, and wrestled up to an elbow. "What did he hit me with, the refrigerator?"

Kate walked to the other bed and glared at Jake. "What was with that routine? 'Mr. Strange, speak into the flower, please!'"

She turned to Burt. "And you with the circus act."

Burt crawled to the edge of the bed and sat up. "Is he coming back?" He dragged the desk chair to the door and wedged it under the doorknob. Then he dug in his pocket and held up the ring. "It worked. Now what?"

Jake got to his knees, struggled to his feet with the help of the bed, and used it for support as he inched to the phone. He dialed.

Jake said, "We're locked in Strange's bedroom."

Kate heard a noise. The door opened, swinging out into the main room. Burt's chair defense fell at Michael's feet. He was wearing pants now, a shirt in one hand, the gun in the other. He pointed it at Burt.

"You. Wiggins. Over by the window." Burt moved next to Kate. Michael pointed the gun at Jake. "The phone, Mr. Oakley."

Jake turned back to the phone and yelled, "And no anchovies this time!" He slammed the receiver down.

Michael stepped across the room and ripped the phone cord from the wall. "I would say don't do anything stupid, but it's too late for that."

"You can't keep us here," Jake said.

"I don't plan to. Not for long."

Kate stood up. "Michael, you can't do this."

He regarded her coolly. Maybe with a trace of contempt, but whatever it was, it passed quickly. "No, you couldn't do it. But I can."

Michael backed out, kicked the chair into the room and slammed the door. Jake grabbed the chair and smashed it against the window. It bounced off, hitting him in the face.

The door opened. Michael kept the gun on Jake, took the chair, and left without a word.

Kate shook her head. "Next idea?"

Burt snorted, then winced and touched the back of his head gingerly. "Do you have any suggestions, your majesty?"

They were really out of options now. "No, just a few regrets. Like going along with this plan."

Burt sat down on the bed. "Life is too short for regrets."

"It's apt to be very short if we don't get out of here."

Jake ignored them. He was at the door, leaning his shoulder against it and wedging coins into the gap between the door and the jamb near the knob. He tried turning the knob. It didn't budge.

"Let's see him get in here now," he said and began scanning the room. He went in the bathroom, came back out. He looked up. His eyes came to rest on the vent in the ceiling above the door. "Boost me up."

Every time she thought they had exhausted all available idiotic ideas, they came up with another. "You're kidding."

Burt shook his head. "You can't climb through an air duct. It's a whatchacallit . . . urban legend."

Jake stripped off his jacket. "Yippie kai yay."

Burt shrugged, groaned up from the bed, and made a step with his fingers interlocked. Jake climbed up, sat on Burt's shoulders, ripped the vent cover off, and wriggled in, slowly and quietly. It took about a minute for the whole process.

Burt watched as Jake's feet disappeared into the gloom of the duct and said, "Well, what do you know?" He smiled at Kate. "Okay, you next."

Kate backed away. "I'm not climbing up there."

"It's your funeral." Burt manhandled the dresser under the vent. A few drawers fell out in the process. He climbed up and scrambled into the duct.

Michael's voice came through the door, "Hey, what are you doing?" The knob rattled, but the door stayed shut. Kate smiled, surprised, but she didn't go for the duct.

Unlike Jake, Burt didn't take pains to be quiet. They could probably hear him out on the beach. Kate climbed on the dresser and looked in the duct. Burt's shoes were a few feet in, thumping against the walls as he crawled. She heard voices echo in whispers.

Jake: "What are you doing?"

Burt: "Go on. I'm right behind you."

Jake: "Go back. It won't hold both of us."

Burt: "Hurry up before he figures it out."

Kate climbed down, found a pen, sat on the dresser, and started digging the coins out of the door. She heard Michael's voice from the main room. "You're kidding, right?" There was an ominous creaking sound from the ceiling. She dug faster. "I'll be doing the gene pool a favor," Michael yelled.

Kate pulled the last coin out, turned the knob, and pushed the door open. Michael stood ten feet away, the gun still in his hand, staring at the ceiling. He glanced over, surprised to see her crouched on the dresser in the doorway.

"What?"

That was all he had time to say. With a wrenching screech, the support rods gave way and the duct crashed through the ceiling, flattening Michael in a mound of ceiling tiles and ductwork.

Jake and Burt crawled out of opposite ends of the duct.

Burt dusted himself off. "Problem solved." He grabbed the laptop from the cart and opened the front door.

Sully stood outside, hand raised to knock. Pearl stood behind him. Burt swung the door shut, but Sully shoved his foot in and pushed it open, knocking Burt into Jake. They were quickly apprehended at gunpoint.

Sully checked the room. "Where's Strange?"

The duct moved. Sully kicked it aside.

Michael climbed from under it. He dug around and found his gun. "Pearl, get them in the bedroom. And strip them."

Pearl pulled a gun from a shoulder holster and smiled. Kate had always tried to take people as they were, to make allowances for cultural influences and life experience, to walk a mile in their shoes before making judgments, but Pearl had made her uncomfortable from the moment she saw him hooking Mr. Heald up to the parasail in Monaco. He seemed to be the worst parts of a hyena, a coral snake, and a man.

"Right this way, ladies. And let's see those skivvies."

# Chapter Forty-One

Berf had to admit that things looked bad for the home team. In fact, he couldn't remember when things had ever been worse. Not even the time he drove the family car into the lake right after Dad had spent half a month's salary to have the engine overhauled.

As Pearl escorted them into the other bedroom, urging them to disrobe, Berf thought back on the plan. The truth was, it was Rita's plan. That was some consolation, but he had gone along with it. In fact, during the dress rehearsal, he had expressed the unguarded opinion that it was sheer genius. Perhaps that had been overstating it.

Okay, yes, it was a long shot, but he was the king of the long shot. You didn't invent a new art form by playing it safe. What seemed like nailing the long shot was really reading sign, feeling the coming change in the prevailing wind, sensing the unseen currents beneath the seeming calm.

When you found yourself in a tight spot, knowing when to talk and when to keep quiet was the key. In general, when you held the money cards and everybody knew it, you kept quiet and let the weaker party talk themselves into a corner. An impassive stare during a long period of silence could erode even the most cocksure opponent.

But when the cocksure opponent held a gun and told you to strip down to your underwear, a penetrating stare was a less compelling tactic.

The problem was that talking from the weaker position was chancy. The weaker your position, the more careful you had to be with your words and how you said them. It was like walking a half dozen Labradors through a minefield. The farther you went, the more likely the whole thing would blow up, and once you were out there, going back was just as chancy. Even standing still could get you killed.

The next ten seconds would be critical. Every word had to count.

Berf followed Kate and Jake into the other bedroom. It looked lived in—a used coffee cup and newspaper on the nightstand, a towel draped over the chair.

The Weasel stood in the doorway, the gun pointed in their general direction. Berf cleared his throat. "Look, Pearl, is it? Okay, Pearl, I think there's been a mistake here."

Pearl smirked. "Sure there has, and you're the one that's made it." He motioned with the gun. "Now let's see some skin."

There it was. Once some people got an idea in their head, there was no talking to them. Jake unbuttoned his shirt. Berf followed suit.

Pearl swung the gun to include Kate. "You too."

Jake stepped forward. "Now look—"

Strange walked in. "Mr. Oakley, I don't think you're in a position to make any demands." He unplugged the phone, grabbed the chair, and left the room.

Berf glanced at Kate and shrugged apologetically. Some things just couldn't be negotiated. As Berf pulled off his shirt, he noticed that Jake had stopped, his hands suspended above the buttons, his eyes glazed over.

Pearl gave him a menacing growl and wiggled the gun in his direction. Jake pulled off his shirt, exposing the wire taped to his skin. Berf had forgotten about that.

Pearl frowned. "Turn around. Careful like, with your hands up."

Jake complied.

"So that's how it is." Pearl ripped the digital recorder from where it was taped in the small of Jake's back and jerked the wire.

Jake winced as the tape ripped free. Pearl dropped the recorder to the floor, stomped it several times, and kicked it out the door.

Sully walked up to the door and picked up the remains. "This doesn't look good."

Strange stepped into view and examined it. "It's just a recorder. No transmitter. We're fine. But it means they have friends. They're not smart enough to come up with this on their own."

That was a cheap shot, but what could you expect from hired killers?

Pearl eased into a greasy smile. "Snap to it, ladies and gentlemen."

Berf stepped out of his pants and stood in his red silk boxers, trying to avert his eyes. The thing was that even in her underwear, Kate was more clothed than half the women down by the pool, but somehow it just didn't seem like the same thing. After all, those women had chosen to dress that way, but Kate hadn't. He forced his gaze to the other side of the room, where Jake stood in black cotton boxers.

Pearl kicked their clothes out the door, followed them out, and closed it. There was the sound of a chair being wedged under the knob.

As soon as the door closed, Berf ran into the bathroom and returned with a bar of soap. He handed it to Jake. "You fake a seizure. When they come in, I'll bean them with the mirror." He pointed to a gigantic mirror on the wall in a thick wooden frame that probably weighed 150 pounds.

Jake shoved the soap back to Berf. "How about I just flush you down the toilet and you swim for help?"

Berf blinked and a better plan popped into his head. Sometimes it worked like that. He raised a finger in the air, said, "Got it," and dashed back into the bathroom.

"It was a joke," Jake yelled after him.

Berf dug through Strange's toiletry bag and extracted a bottle of aftershave. Next to the sink, he found a tray of candles. He snatched up the book of matches and sprang back into the bedroom.

Kate stood by the door, looking like she wanted to say something but couldn't think of anything.

Berf would give her something to cheer about. "You're going to love this." He soaked the bed with aftershave and lit a match.

Kate yelled from her corner. "What are you doing?"

Jake lunged across the room as the match landed on the bed. It went up like a BBQ grill. He wheeled on Berf. "Are you trying to kill us?"

Berf smiled. Sometimes you just had to take a little initiative. "Problem solved."

Kate glanced around the room like she was searching for intelligent life. "Brilliant!"

"What she said," Jake said.

Evidently Berf would have to connect the dots for them, although it couldn't be more obvious. "It'll set off the smoke alarm."

"It just beeps in here. It's not connected to anything."

"You sure about that?" Berf glanced at the sprinkler head. "What about that?"

"That won't go off until it's like 400 degrees in here."

Berf frowned. "Fahrenheit or Celsius?"

Kate stepped between them. "If you're going to do their job for them, don't forget to make it look like an accident. Smoking in bed perhaps?"

The fire raged. Berf grabbed the bathroom mat and tried to beat down the flames, but it just encouraged them. Kate grabbed the trashcan and ran into the bathroom.

Jake dashed to the window, cranked the side louvers open, and peered between the slats. He started waiving his hands, presumably to get someone's attention.

Berf sprinted into the bathroom, where Kate sat on the edge of the tub, running water into the trashcan. Berf jerked the shower curtain rod off the wall and ran back into the bedroom.

The smoke level had lowered the visibility ceiling to six feet.

Berf shoved the rod under the bedspread and held it up to the sprinkler. Jake ran past him into the bathroom. Berf knelt down below the level of the smoke and pushed the flaming bedspread closer to the sprinkler. He hoped it got to 400 soon because his arms were starting to quiver from the strain.

Jake rushed out of the bathroom, caught a face full of smoke, and dropped to his knees, coughing. He crawled around the bed to the window, dragging a round vanity mirror. He climbed to his feet, keeping his face in the louvers for outside air, and caught the sun in the mirror, flashing it down into the courtyard.

Kate stumbled in with the trashcan full of water, but the smoke had got her. She dropped the trashcan and staggered to the window for air.

Then the sprinkler clicked and water gushed out.

"Ha!" Berf exclaimed. The plan was basically good. It just needed tweaking.

From beyond the bedroom door came a cry of alarm and indecipherable directions yelled angrily.

Kate began beating on the window. "Derek! Up here!"

The door crashed open. Sully stepped in, gun drawn. "Let's go!" The upper half of his body was suddenly enveloped in smoke. He doubled over, coughing.

Berf lurched to his feet and flung the smoking blanket over him.

Sully fired wildly. A lamp fell over. The giant mirror shattered.

Berf beat at the bulge that was Sully's hand with the shower rod. The gun thudded to the carpet as Sully stumbled back against the wall.

Jake ran crouching across the room and slammed the closet door into the lump that was Sully's head. Sully folded into a misshapen pile under the bedspread. Berf kicked the gun away. It slid under the bed.

Smoke poured out the open door. As it cleared, Berf swung the curtain rod forward and peered out the door. The room was empty. He turned back. They were half-naked and soaking wet.

In other words, they didn't look that different from the people around the pool. "It's clear. Let's go."

# Chapter Forty-Two

Runyon stared at the hardbodies around the pool without seeing them. Twenty-four hours ago, Kate took that busload of losers skydiving, which was the perfect time for another go at the files, but the Weasel was infesting the office. The last time he'd seen her was when the losers had lit out in a taxi for the airport and she had followed. Then she just disappeared.

Kate seemed like the real deal, twenty-four carat, completely legit. He'd never met a girl like her. He couldn't count the number of girls in his life that seemed to be Mother Theresa but turned out to be Mata Hari.

Women were slippery. Just when you thought you had them, they slithered through your fingers and retreated to the middle distance, laughing as you grasped empty air. Kate seemed different, but of course she would. All women were different, incomprehensible in maddeningly unique ways.

Men were easy. They all wanted power. They might call it something else—money, success, respect, love, world peace, whatever, but when you stripped it down to the bare metal, it was power, and power worked in predictable ways. You could plan for it, compensate, adapt, conquer.

But you could never figure out what women wanted, and if you did, they changed it. With them, it wasn't about power, even when it was. For women, power was not the end goal; it was simply one of the infinite facets of the diamond that seduced them. Just when you had their motivation figured out, the jewel swiveled and something else caught their eye.

It always seemed to come down to daddy issues, but Runyon had even less of a clue about how that worked. It sounded like a psychobabble black hole you would never get out of, and he faded like a wisp of smoke if it ever got to that.

But he was sure the clue was in the SV files. If she was legit, he would see it there. If she was just another of the infinite variations on crazy that was woman, it would tell him the degree of crazy he was dealing with. And unlike the emotional minefield of relationships, clandestine investigation was his element. Thirty minutes in the SV files would tell him more than thirty years of conversational jousting.

But his go at the files was aborted by the Weasel. The little rodent actually did the I'm-watching-you thing, two fingers moving out from his eyes and pointing at Runyon. Runyon knew his type, all swagger and bravado when he thought he had the odds, but folded up like a cheap umbrella in a simoom when the tsunami hit.

Runyon's ruminations were interrupted by a light flashing in his eyes. He scanned the pool area for the source. Nothing. The bar? Nothing. Then he heard a banging. He looked up. Smoke poured from the side louvers in one of the rooms. A third floor room.

A face behind the glass. Kate. Seventh window from the end, third floor, seaward side. He sprang from the chair in a dead run, pulled every fire alarm he saw along the way, and slammed through the stairwell door, knocking chips of concrete out of the wall. He took the stairs three at a time, using the rail to spin around the corners, and blasted through the third floor door, barely breathing hard.

Through years of training, Runyon could consciously trigger the power of the limbic system to summon adrenaline on demand. He doubted there were three other humans on the planet that could do that. Maybe none. It was impossible to run a survey to know for sure. But it meant he could instantaneously draw on resources that served others only when their reptilian brain kicked in. It had saved his life more than once. Now it was going to save Kate.

Seven doors down, smoke curled into the hall. He veered, pushing off the doorjamb into falling water. A mess of ceiling tiles and ductwork was piled in the middle of the room. He raced past it to a bedroom. A dresser blocked the door. He kicked the mess aside. The room was empty. He sprinted to the other doorway.

Jake stood by the door in black cotton boxers, soaking wet. Berf, in red silk boxers, was just beyond. At his feet was a lump of smoking bedspread with feet protruding. By the window, Kate stood in bra and panties, white, her red hair plastered to her head. Her luminescent skin was dappled with water drops and freckles. She looked the alabaster goddess he had imagined her to be, although he had expected to discover the truth under quite different circumstances. In that moment, he violently wished that she was everything she seemed to be.

"You okay?" he asked between breaths.

Jake said, "Yeah. We'll take it from here."

He would say that, the pencil-necked geek. Where was his honor? A closet door was open behind him with a rack of high-dollar tailored suits. Runyon pulled out a jacket and covered Kate.

She pushed a tendril of wet hair from her face and smiled. "Thank you, Derek."

Runyon ushered her toward the door. "This way."

Jake stepped in front of them. "We can handle it."

Kate pushed him aside irritably. "Come on."

Runyon smiled at the back of her head as she walked out the door. He shouldered Jake aside, touched Kate's arm as he passed her, and led them to the end of the hall and into the stairwell. They followed down the stairs.

On the way down, Runyon tried to imagine a scenario to explain what he had found in the bedroom—Kate and those two clowns half-naked with a body wrapped in a scorched bedspread, the ceiling of the main room destroyed, and a dresser blocking the doorway of the other bedroom. Nothing from his vast mental library of bizarre circumstances provided a clue. Was it something kinky or were they in some kind of trouble?

On the ground floor, Runyon stopped on the landing, just inside the fire door. Beyond, through the wire-reinforced glass, the fire alarm blared and the lobby was a roiling panic of bodies rushing in all directions. He turned to the group.

"I need a 10-43 on this situation. What's going on?"

Jake pushed past him, grabbed the bent handle, and pulled the door open.

"We're getting out of here now, that's what's going on."

# CHAPTER FORTY-THREE

Fernando sat in the van in front of the hotel, inspecting the flow of people pouring out the front doors. Something was up, and he wondered if it had anything to do with the phone call from Jake. They were being held in Strange's room, but there were many questions. How many hostiles? What was their current status?

He recognized a face in the crowd—Strange, disheveled and wet, holding a briefcase and scanning the vehicles. A black SUV pulled out of the parking garage and screeched up to the entrance. Strange pulled the door open, climbed in, and waited a second, watching the entrance. Then he slammed the door. The SUV sped away.

Fernando glanced across the road to Rita, who lounged on a motorcycle as if taking a siesta. Their eyes locked. She glanced to the entrance. He nodded. She lowered her visor and followed the SUV. Fernando returned his attention to the entrance.

In a long history of stupid decisions, helping these imbeciles might be the stupidest thing he had done, ever. They would get themselves killed, and him and Rita too, if he wasn't careful.

It was Rita's fault. She ran the thing and had from the beginning, the whole while pretending he made all the decisions. She came by that first night, actually early that first morning, and said, "What do you think?"

What could he think? It was obvious what he was supposed to think, and when Rita was in the picture, people tended to think what she intended for them to think, even if, like that Bantam rooster she dragged around on a string, they didn't realize it. Especially if they didn't realize it.

Of course he went along. Fate brought Rita to him, and Fate decreed he do her bidding. One day Fate would take her away. If she didn't get him killed first.

They never discussed tactics. Rita relied on him to intimidate when the circumstance called for it, and he obliged. It was what he did best. He could drive anything on ground, water, or air, had a taxi driver's knowledge of every alley and back road in the province, could work any machinery or gadget he picked up, and was an excellent shot, although he hoped it wouldn't be necessary to demonstrate that particular skill.

He wasn't so good at planning. He left that to Rita.

Something odd caught his attention. A guy in black boxers and nothing else ran out of the front door, followed by a guy in red boxers, and a girl who seemed to be wearing nothing but a man's suit coat. With a shock, he realized the nearly naked people were the idiots he was waiting for. Behind them a fourth guy came out and stood with them. This one was trouble, a delivery truck with military hair and a tan.

The guy in black boxers, Jake it was, spotted the van, dashed over, and climbed in. The others followed, including the guy who acted like hired muscle for the cartels. The guy Rita had been playing, Berf, rode shotgun, the other three crammed in the second seat.

Fernando didn't like it. The odds of Fate dealing from the bottom of the deck just doubled. Tripled. He shook his head, shoved the van into gear, and lurched away from the curb.

Fernando caught Jake's eye in the rearview. "Why is he here?"

The woman answered first. "He rescued us."

Jake shook his head. "No, he didn't."

The muscle said, "What's going on?" He turned to the woman. "Are you in some kind of trouble?"

She pulled the coat tighter around her. "Yes."

"Don't tell him anything."

That was Jake. Or maybe Berf. Fernando wasn't sure which. He should have let Rita drive the van. "What happened?"

Jake eyed him in the rearview. "Total disaster."

Berf twisted around in the seat. "Not total. I got the ring."

"Let's see it," Jake said.

Fernando frowned at Berf. *Only the ring?*

Berf shook his head. "It's not handy at the moment. Maybe in a few hours. Give or take."

"You swallowed it?" Kate asked.

Fernando whispered, "*Madre de Dios*." He should stop the van right here, tie them to the tool box, throw them into Nichupte Lagoon, and drive away. And he would have if he didn't have to face Rita after. Then again, maybe he didn't. It all depended on how much gas money he had.

He checked the gas gauge. A quarter tank. His cell phone rang. Rita.

Jake said, "So all we need is the laptop."

Fernando answered the call. "Where are you?"

"The Strange Vacations office. They have the laptop."

# CHAPTER FORTY-FOUR

Berf was right behind Fernando on the stairs and through the door of the apartment.

As they filed in, Fernando pushed Rita's bedroom door open. "Find some clothes."

Kate dug through the closet first, found a sundress, and disappeared into the bathroom. Jake actually found some guys' jeans and a shirt that fit surprisingly well, but that was it for the men's clothes.

Berf pulled out a sweatshirt and held it up. "Do you think I'd look good in purple?"

Jake dug a pair of flip-flops from the closet floor. "Absolutely. It brings out your eyes."

Berf put it back, grabbed the baggiest pair of jeans in the closet, sucked in his stomach, and inched the zipper up. He stepped to a mirror. "Does this make my butt look big?"

Jake walked out. Berf found a loose white blouse with ruffles and big cuffs, pulled it on, and checked himself in the mirror. The effect was like a matador who shopped at Goodwill. Well, it was that or Moby Grape. Not much of a choice.

Berf had adopted a nonchalant manner to help buck up the team, but the truth was that inside he was a hopeless mess of quivering jelly. Not that anybody would know by looking at him, but now that he was alone, he dropped the façade and collapsed into the chair by the window.

He was at a loss to explain the labyrinthine twists of the past two days. And try as he may, he could find no analog in the chronicles of the Sackett clan. Sure, the Sacketts had sometimes come upon reversals and betrayals. That episode with Tell and Dorinda Robiseau was a perfect example. Talk about wheels within wheels. And that whole thing with Nolan and the Karneses was practically an object lesson in double- and triple-crossing. But a Sackett never came up against anything that broad shoulders, a steady gun hand, and a Code couldn't overcome.

Until now. Here he was wearing women's clothes, hiding out in a Mexican slum from a band of ruthless killers who would hunt him down to the ends of the earth, and no Sackett clan to ride to the aid of the brand. In fact, all he had to work with was a woman of dubious virtue who happened to be his fiancée, a watch-pirating, body-snatching, van-driving henchman who was his future brother-in-law, and a testosterone-laden mercenary.

And Jake. But he was the reason they were all here in the first place.

It was a lesson was what it was. A lesson on the paving propensity of good intentions. He made a note of it for future reference. Wish no man ill and do what one could, but don't overdo it.

Berf pulled himself erect and walked into the main room.

Kate was just walking out of the bathroom, quite appetizing in Rita's dress. The afternoon sun slipped below the horizon, momentarily painting her in a golden glow before it vanished, and the room sank into twilight.

She caught sight of Berf and stopped dead. He resisted the urge to model his outfit for her. Instead he flipped on some lights and dropped onto a couch next to Jake.

Fernando stood with his back to the room before an open armoire. Inside, a full arsenal lined the doors and back wall. He reached past the shotguns, rifles, and automatic weapons and pulled out a handgun that looked like it could stop a tank.

Things were escalating at an alarming rate. Two days ago, they were partying on the beach to the mellifluous tones of a steel drum. Now he was wearing women's clothes and gearing up for Armageddon. Not to mention everything that had happened in between, like getting engaged.

Fernando closed the armoire, set the gun on top of it, and turned to the group seated around the room.

"This is what is going to happen." He pointed to Berf. "Stay here and squeeze out the ring." He pointed to Jake. "Stay here with him." He pointed to Kate. "We go get the laptop." He pointed to Runyon. "And you go away."

Kate frowned at Fernando. "Who are you?"

"What the hell is going on?" Jake demanded.

Runyon took a broad stance. "That's what I want to know."

"Shut up," Jake said to Runyon.

Berf nodded. After the stress of the last few hours, me-too banter from a Charles Atlas wannabe was not what you wanted to see on the menu.

Runyon ignored Jake and spoke directly to Fernando. "You got some kind of operation in progress."

Fernando scowled. "Go away."

"And you're taking a civilian into harm's way. I'm not cool with that."

Berf hadn't considered that angle. Up to now, he had seen her as part of the Strange Vacations team. He glanced at Jake.

Jake returned the glance with a raised eyebrow. "Yeah, me either. She can stay here and I'll go."

Berf put a restraining hand on Jake's shoulder. There was such a thing as being too enthusiastic. "Think before you talk, J-Bird." He agreed that Kate shouldn't be drafted on a commando mission. He was equally sure Jake shouldn't go on the mission either.

"Right," Runyon said. "Because we really need a salesman on our side when it all goes down."

"There is no *we*, Rambo," Fernando said. "*Dejame en paz.*"

"Sure thing, hombre. But first, tell me how many of them are there?"

Kate said, "Three."

Berf held up two fingers. Somebody wasn't keeping score at home. "I took Sully out."

Runyon said, "Sure you did."

Berf straightened up and perched on the edge of the couch. Who did this guy think he was anyway, and why did he care? Did he set off the alarm that ran the bad guys off? Did he subdue Sully with a burning bedspread? Did he pummel Sully into submission with a shower rod? Taken in order from left to right, no, no, and no. All he did was show up and say, "Let's go." Any idiot could do that, which is obviously why he was given the job. And any fool could see he was doing this just to impress Kate.

Berf stood to protest, but Runyon had already turned to Fernando. "You're going in alone against three guys?"

"Two guys," Berf interjected.

"I'd say you could use some backup. With experience."

Kate nodded. "It's true. Derek's led rescue missions against slave-trade gangs in Thailand."

Berf shook his head. Runyon was more like the hired muscle for a gang than a righteous warrior. "I'd check Snopes before I hit forward on that email."

Runyon cracked a smarmy smile. "Let's just say it's not my first rodeo."

"You've got to be kidding me," Jake said.

Fernando studied Runyon like he was working out a particularly challenging Sudoku puzzle. "What's it to you?"

"I'm here for Kate," Runyon said.

Jake waved an arm and looked around the room. "For crying out loud. Is anyone but me hearing this?"

Let him go is what Berf advocated but didn't say. It might reduce the population by one surplus poser. Nobody else responded either. The room fell silent for a few minutes.

Fernando looked them all over. He pulled out his cell phone, thought a bit, and put it back in his pocket. He opened the armoire again and pulled out an Uzi. "Okay. Here's how it will be."

Jake jumped to his feet. "What? You're actually listening to this joker?"

Fernando handed the gun to Runyon. "Rita covers the front. I cover the back. You go in with Kate. She IDs the laptop. You get out. Zero body count. Understand?"

Jake said, "Wait a minute. Who do you work for?"

Fernando's glare would have silenced most people. "Don't worry your pretty little head about it, *jefe*."

Jake wasn't most people.

Neither was Berf. "Rita covers the front?" After all, she was his fiancée. He ought to have a say in the matter.

Jake took a step toward Fernando. "We have a right to know. It's our lives on the line."

Kate stood next to Jake. "I'm not going in there until I hear the whole story."

Runyon checked the Uzi, set it against the wall behind the chair, and leaned back with his hands behind his head. "Sounds reasonable to me."

Fernando closed and locked the armoire. "We're with the FBI."

"What?" Berf dropped onto the couch. Rita was an FBI agent? How could he have spent three days with her and not had a clue?

"You're FBI?" Jake said.

Fernando shrugged. "Freelance. The FBI doesn't have the jurisdiction here. We get the information for them, they use it."

"Frank?" Kate said.

Fernando nodded. "He was our contact. You can't always choose your clients in this business. If they can pay, you don't ask questions."

Frank really was FBI? Berf didn't actually believe it at the airfield. Impressive. "He wasn't the sharpest Oreo in the box, but what a genius at keeping a cover."

Jake said, "So what happens to Kate?"

"We just want the evidence. We give it to the FBI, they pay us. What they do with it is their problem. What happens to Strange or the rest doesn't matter to us."

Kate took a deep breath and let it out slowly. Then she nodded. "Let's do it."

Jake turned to her, his voice cracking. "Are you crazy? A job Mr. Happy Pants outsourced to Pancho Villa, with ad hoc backup from Ramboner?"

Runyon stood up. "Look, Gumby, we'll get the job done while you help dig that ring out of your friend's—"

Jake shoved Runyon. "I'll show you a ring or two."

Runyon shoved back.

Fernando stepped between them. "Shut up, girls. It's time to roll."

Berf stood up. There was enough in the past twenty-four hours to make a busy twenty-four days, but one thing remained uppermost in his mind. "Wait a minute. What about Rita?"

Fernando said, "What about her?"

"Does this mean she doesn't want to marry me?"

Then the door slammed open and the room filled with guys pointing guns.

# Chapter Forty-Five

Michael Strange peered through the tinted glass at the shabby buildings that rolled past. Sully drove, despite the broken nose and black eye. Pearl monitored the tracking device and issued directions from the back seat.

Strange had been surprised to find the trail leading them deeper into the city and rather unsavory neighborhoods. He had expected to find a hiding place on Hotel Row, or perhaps find them at the airport again, or the bus station if they were keeping a low profile. What contacts would they have in the heart of Cancún? Kate had only been here a few weeks, and the other two only three days.

This should not have happened. You hired the best people, and they got things done. If your top man allowed himself to be severely beaten by a trio of half-naked, unarmed civilians, then what did that say? It came down to a failure of management at the highest levels, which meant Strange himself. It was an unpleasant fact, but Strange had not become the czar of an internationally successful specialty-vacation empire by avoiding unpleasant facts.

And Pearl, who started out so well, failed at four successive attempts with Oakley and Wiggins and killed an FBI agent in the process, a mistake that went beyond lost revenue to possible loss of freedom for all of them.

And finally Kate. Words failed when it came to explaining that mistake. Her background made her the obvious choice. Her financial need indicated she would likely accommodate the moral flexibility required for the position. But there were clues, had he been paying attention. That whole Micronesia thing reeked of moral crusader. The thought made him shudder.

It was clear he would have to shut down the Dignity package for a year or two. He would let Sully and Pearl go. They were professionals. They would move on to their next engagement.

Kate was another matter. He couldn't count on her to meekly return to her clinic, even if he paid off her debt and set her mother up for life, a minor personal expense he would never miss. But a woman with scruples was a dangerous thing. Wouldn't listen to reason.

Wiggins and Oakley would have to disappear too. Unfortunate for them, but it couldn't be helped. Lucky for Strange, the tracking device that came with the encryption ring led him to the source of his problems. They would join him in his private plane for a trip to the Caymans, conscious or otherwise, as the occasion required, and make an unscheduled exit at ten thousand feet and a hundred miles from land in every direction.

"This is it," Pearl said.

Strange looked out the window at an ugly, squat apartment building across from a variety of questionable eateries and retail hovels. Curiouser and curiouser. What were they up to?

Sully parked the SUV on a corner and they followed Pearl as he led them first one way and the other until they found an entrance to the courtyard, located the wing of interest, and filed up the narrow staircase.

The apartments opened onto a covered walkway overlooking the courtyard. Sully and Strange drew guns as they slipped noiselessly along. Pearl stopped in front of a door, pocketed the tracker, and pulled out his gun. On a visual count of three, Sully kicked in the door, charged through, and peeled off to the right. Pearl followed, diving to the left. Michael gave it a few beats, then stepped in.

He stood in a tiny kitchen with a cracked and dingy linoleum floor. On the other side of a bar, five people stood in a circle in the living room. Kate, Wiggins, Oakley and two other guys. One appeared to be local, the other Austrian or maybe Australian, both hired muscle. Fast work. Perhaps he had underestimated Kate. It was a pity about her. This could have been such a sweet deal.

Strange walked into the main room. Sully and Pearl backed him up.

"Feldspar, isn't it? And Henri? I almost didn't recognize you." Strange was momentarily stunned by Wiggins's clothes, ridiculously tight jeans that throttled his calves and a billowing blouse that barely reached his waist. He looked like a beatnik flamenco dancer. All he needed were the boots.

"I'm afraid you have something that belongs to me." Strange said. "Let's produce it without any unpleasantness, shall we?"

Wiggins was the only one who spoke. "What? I don't have anything. Do you, J-Bird?"

Strange waited, then spoke over his shoulder. "Which one is it, Pearl?"

"This is only accurate to three meters."

"That's easily remedied. Everyone against the wall."

There was initial resistance and some strong glares, but they moved against the wall. Strange scanned the group. They wouldn't give it to the hired help. It was most likely Wiggins. The clucking chicken always hid the egg.

"Okay, Mr. Wiggins, walk to the kitchen. Slowly."

Wiggins flinched, looked around at his comrades, and walked slowly to the kitchen.

"Bingo," Pearl said.

"Let's have it," Strange said.

"I . . . I . . . I can't actually get to it at the moment."

No, surely not. Even he couldn't be that stupid. "You swallowed it?"

"We could cut him open," Sully said.

"Oh, I think that can be avoided. Check the medicine cabinet."

Sully disappeared into the bathroom, came out with a package, and handed it to Strange.

Strange held out the box. "Here you go, Mr. Wiggins. This should speed things along."

Wiggins stared at it fearfully but didn't reach for it.

"Don't force me to seriously entertain Sully's suggestion." He stepped toward Wiggins. "I hear it's got a nice chocolate flavor."

Wiggins reluctantly took the box, opened a packet, and chewed the laxative.

Then the lights went out. All of them.

There were shouts and scuffling. Strange shoved his way to where he had last seen Kate, found a handful of hair, and shoved his pistol against her head.

"I've got Kate, so don't try anything," Strange screamed into the cacophony. He felt a hand slip around his throat and a muzzle against his head.

The lights came back on. The yelling died down as everyone got a bead on the situation.

Strange had Kate's head pulled back with a fistful of hair. His gun was against her temple. He craned his head for a glance behind. The hand on his throat belonged to the Austrian, who had an Uzi in his other hand. Sully had his gun against the Austrian's head, the Mexican thug had his gun to the back of Sully's head, and Pearl brought up the end of the conga line with his gun against the Mexican's head.

Oakley was still against the wall. Wiggins still stood by the bar, holding the laxative box.

"How about you let go of Kate and put down that gun, Percy?" the Austrian said.

"You first, Percy," Sully hissed.

"I'm right here, gringo," the Mexican growled.

"Just try it," Pearl wheezed.

"Let's keep our wits about us, if we will, gentlemen," Strange said.

Then the lights went out again.

Strange spun around, moving his grip on Kate from her hair to an arm around her neck and raising the elbow on his gun arm to shove the thug's gun away from his head. Kate kicked at him with her heels, but she wasn't wearing shoes, so it didn't slow him down. He slammed his back against the wall and jammed the gun against the base of Kate's jaw. There was shouting and thrashing in the dark.

The lights came back on.

Pearl and the Mexican had their guns against each other's heads. Sully and the Austrian had their guns against each other's heads. Strange leaned against the wall by himself, holding Kate. Everyone was breathing hard and staring harder.

Strange said, "We're leaving now." He edged away from the wall, slowly moving toward the door, keeping Kate between him and the others.

"I don't think so, Percy," the Austrian said.

"You cancel each other out. I have Kate. We win."

"It's not a soccer match," the Austrian said.

"And I'd rather it not end like Hamlet," Kate said.

"Let's go." Strange backed toward the door, pulling Kate with him. Pearl and Sully inched away from the other two. "Sully, you cover them. Pearl, you get Wiggins and Oakley."

Pearl lowered his gun and scanned the room. "Where'd they go?"

# Chapter Forty-Six

The second time the lights went out, Jake edged along the wall past the testosterone-and-adrenaline-fueled scrum of gunmen, grabbed Berf, and dragged him out the door, banging both of them into the jamb along the way.

Berf screamed and clawed but nobody heard him in the riot of yelling, grunting, and thumping. Jake hissed, "It's me!" in his ear and pulled him down the walkway to the stairs and out to the street.

On the sidewalk Berf pulled away. "What are you doing?"

Jake grabbed his arm and pulled him along. "I'll tell you after we get out of sight."

They ran through the neighborhood, dodging down alleys and side streets until they were several blocks away. Jake slowed to a walk.

It was a desperate gamble, dragging Berf out of the room and leaving Kate behind, but when you're up against three guys with guns, you took the long odds or you went along for the ride. A long ride off a short pier.

For a brief moment, a thought flitted through his head. Grab a cab. Get to the embassy. Contact the press.

Bust the whole thing wide open. But if he did that, Kate would go down along with the rest of them. And he wasn't having any of that.

He scanned the street. Most everything was closed. A carpet store. A dentist. A cell phone store. A liquor store. A bar that was open. Pretty sketchy from the outside. A flickering neon *Cerveza* sign, dingy stucco walls, a battered metal door.

"There," Jake said.

"No."

"You have a better option?"

Berf spread his hands and spun a slow circle in the mercury-vapor light. "Look at me. I go into that bar wearing this and I'll either be pummeled or propositioned. Or both."

There was no time for negotiation. Jake pulled the door open and walked in. It slammed behind him. The inside was dark and smoky. A handful of locals leaned on the bar. A few more sat at tables. They all stared at him without expression. There was no noise other than the TV over the bar. He nodded, walked to the back of the room, and took the table in the corner, his back against the back wall. All eyes followed him. He noted a couple of other doors. Maybe one led to a back exit. He leaned back and watched the front door. The locals went back to their conversations.

The front door opened, and Berf walked in boldly, like this was his main hangout. The locals glanced back at the door. This time Jake saw a few puzzled expressions. Berf scanned the room, nodded at the bartender like he was a family friend, spotted Jake, walked casually to the table, and sat down with his back against the side wall. He watched the locals, who continued to stare.

"Why are we here? They have Kate back there."

"I know that. It works like this. They have to kill all of us, or none of us. If even one of us gets away and reports them, they're sunk."

"They're already sunk. They probably killed lots of other people. What difference does it make if they kill one of us without the others?"

"It's an assisted suicide thing. The other people wanted to die. We don't. With us, it's murder."

"And you think that makes a difference?"

Jake's confidence flagged for a moment. He certainly hoped it did, but in this crazy game, who knew what the rules were? Or if there were any rules?

"Plus, you have the ring. As long as we have that, they'll keep Kate alive for leverage."

Berf nodded. A woman walked up and stood next to their table.

Berf smiled at her, a smile that would have owned the room if he hadn't been wearing Rita's clothes. He leaned toward Jake, keeping his eyes on the woman. "You got any cash?"

"My money is in my pants back in Strange's room, just like yours."

"Check your pockets."

"You check your pockets."

"Look, J-Bird. See how tight these pants are? If there was any money in the pockets, we'd be able to read the date on the coins without having to take them out."

Jake smiled at the woman and checked the pants, pulling out a few bills, to his surprise. He dropped them on the table. "*Dos cervezas, por favor.*"

The woman took the money and went to the bar.

The front door opened. Jake tensed to spring out a back door.

# Chapter Forty-Seven

Rita throttled the bike down and put some distance between her and the black SUV. Kukulkan Drive was not the best place to inconspicuously tail a car with a motorcycle. More than twenty kilometers of road with few intersections or motorcycles. She hung back until they got to the mainland and Bonampak.

After the phone call last week from Agent Summers, she had entertained visions of a nice commission, something that could last her a year if she continued to keep her expenses down, leaving her free to develop other contracts without resorting to less desirable work, like recovering bodies.

Four days ago, she met Summers, got the full briefing and the advance payment. Her unease increased the longer Summers talked, but the money softened it. He might have seemed like a flake, but he had a budget and he was FBI. She called the branch office, asked for his extension, and that checked out. His mailbox greeting was unmistakably the same annoying voice.

Summers put her onto Berf, telling her he was a Dignity client and would lead them to the main players. Berf was a lot of fun, but not much help. He led her to Jake, who was just another client, and Kate, the activities director. From the start, Rita saw that Kate knew something but wasn't in the inner circle.

It wasn't until Fernando tailed them to the skydive that she connected Pearl and Sully to the scheme. That was the big break, but it came with an unfortunate downside—Summers got himself killed. Now how would she get the rest of the payment? It was always like that. So close to making it but denied by the incompetence or prejudice of others.

But this time she wouldn't let it slip away. She would pull it off, bring the evidence to Summers's boss, and maybe even get more contracts.

It turned to touch-and-go when she realized Strange and his gorillas were headed to her apartment. What had tipped them off? She became paranoid for a few minutes until she saw the scrawny one holding a GPS system as they exited the SUV. Evidently the ring could be tracked, a detail that would have been nice to know earlier.

She chose to remain unseen in case she needed to work them undercover later. Instead, she counted on the chaos of cutting the lights to shake things up, maybe in their favor. But Fernando had armed only the cowboy, so they were outgunned. It was understandable that he didn't give a gun to Berf or Jake, but why not Kate? Rita would bet that Kate knew her way around the block if it came to that.

The second roll of the dice produced results. It got Berf and Jake out of the apartment. They still had the ring and a shot at getting the laptop. But the ring could be tracked, so they needed to act quickly. She left the standoff to Fernando and tailed Berf. When he went into the bar, she waited to see if he was being followed. It seemed clear, so she went in.

Rita saw them immediately. She waved at the gang and the bartender, Luis. She knew they would be amused when she joined the gringos, especially when she saw what Berf had on. She pulled up a chair and sat next to Berf with her back to the side wall, facing the bar.

"Berf. I never would have suspected you for a cross-dresser."

Lilia brought three beers and some change to the table. Rita took one. "Gracias!" Lilia gave her a questioning look and returned to the bar.

Berf had an expression she hadn't seen before. What was it? Anger? Hurt? Sorrow?

"You're working for the FBI?"

"Yes. We will help stop Michael Strange in his death business."

"So was I just part of your cover? Is that all it was?"

This was too sweet. Really it was. She had never expected a player like Berf to get invested in their fling. He was obviously a man of many short-term partners, and he had been so terrified of the whole marry-my-sister ploy, she was shocked at the sense of betrayal in his voice and on his face.

In fact, she was surprised the marriage scheme had worked, but she had counted on their desperation. An offer of help of this magnitude from outsiders without an ulterior motive would have been too suspicious. Better he think it a scam targeted at his money than to guess the truth.

But now he knew the truth. It would have come out eventually, but she was counting on him being relieved, not crushed. In her world there was no room for that kind of sentiment. She sometimes found herself wishing there was a little corner where she could entertain such pleasures as true love. But like wealth, it was a luxury reserved for a very few, and much more difficult to attain. And there was no time for such conversations.

"Berf, we must talk of this, but not now. First we must obtain the ring and act quickly."

"That's really all you care about, isn't it? Getting the evidence for the FBI."

"No, I am worried for you. Strange found you because he can track the ring. He can track you here."

Jake's eyes darted toward the door in alarm, but Berf just stared at her. "Why don't we just call the FBI and let them take care of it?"

Rita was about to answer, but her phone rang. Fernando. "Yes?"

Fernando spoke quietly and quickly. "They're gone, but they have Kate. We're going to hit the office and see if we can find the laptop."

"We'll be there as soon as we can." She hung up. "They took Kate."

Jake jumped up as if he wanted to do something but didn't know what. The whole bar watched. "Where did they take her?"

Rita stood. "I don't know. But if we want to help her, we have to protect the ring."

Jake turned to Berf. "It's up to you now, old man."

Berf leaned back in his chair. "It's not like I can flip a switch and—" Suddenly panic washed across his face.

Rita checked the front door. No one had entered. She scanned the room. "What's wrong?"

Berf stood and clutched at her arm. "Which way is the bathroom?"

"Why don't we go back to the apartment?"

"I can try, but first tell me, are these your favorite jeans?"

"You can make it," Jake said.

"Have you seen *A Bridge Too Far*?"

"Come on." Jake led the charge.

Berf followed, taking quick, conservative steps, like a rookie on ice skates. Rita brought up the rear. It wouldn't be long now.

# CHAPTER FORTY-EIGHT

Pearl swore under his breath and watched the screen. If Sully hadn't screwed up, he wouldn't be walking the barrio streets in search of Tweedledumb and Tweedledumber, gun in one hand, GPS in the other. How hard could it be? Maybe Sully should consider retiring if he couldn't control a few unarmed nimrods. He should be out here on this snipe hunt and Pearl should be driving Kate and the boss back to the office.

The dot moved through the grid on the GPS, left, right, left, right, like it mattered how many turns they took. Let them wear themselves out. Pearl moved in the general direction of their flight, keeping an eye out for locals who displayed too much interest. It was too dark for anyone to see his gun unless he wanted them to, but if anyone bugged him, he wouldn't be shy about it, that's for sure.

The dot seemed to settle down. Pearl kept a steady pace, wondering when Strange would see the absurdity of Pearl reporting to a guy half his age. It wasn't right, but what could you do? This corporate mentality didn't care about tradition or seniority. It was all productivity and profits and no relationship building, all bright ideas and no wisdom.

This was the block. Must be in the bar across the street, a real dive. No telling what kind of hoods hung out in there. They'd be lucky to come out alive. Pearl smiled. Let the Mexicans do the dirty work.

Then he frowned. Unlike Sully, who obviously didn't think things through, Pearl had no interest in the messy job of cutting Wiggins open and digging through his intestines to get the ring. Or the equally unpleasant job of disposing of the remains. He'd rather keep the nimrod alive until he delivered a sparkling clean ring. If the Mexicans killed him, it was back to the messy job. But going in there after him might be even messier.

Pearl stood behind an oleander bush and pondered this conundrum. He wasn't sure how long he stood out front, but his problem was solved for him when Oakley came out, followed by Wiggins, walking with a sense of purpose. He consulted the GPS. Wiggins still had the ring, and judging by his stride, Pearl would have it soon.

A woman in a white motorcycle outfit came out of the bar and joined the nimrods. He recognized her as the local Wiggins had latched onto the first night they showed up. Pearl didn't like that. It complicated things. It was the way the universe tried to defeat civilization. Complications played into the Hindenburg Principle.

In the view of the old man, views which Pearl shared, simpler was better, which was why the old man always worked alone. Don't bring more people into the job than was absolutely necessary. Don't knock over two places just because the second was handy to the first. And that meant don't snatch three people when you came to snatch two and the third was in the way.

He'd have to think on this. He trailed them from a distance and was only mildly surprised to see them return to the same apartment building. Must be the girl's place. He stood on the street and waited until he saw a light come on. He checked again. It wasn't a window. It was a balcony with French doors.

Pearl was no parkour expert, but he could manage a balcony. He climbed on the patio railing of the apartment below, grabbed the balusters of the balcony, and pulled himself up. A minute later he was leaning against the wall, listening to the activity in the room.

Wiggins: "Holy crap!"

Oakley: "Here, take this coat hanger."

Wiggins: "Are you serious?"

Oakley: "You can hook the ring with it."

Wiggins: "No way, J-Bird!"

Oakley: "From the toilet bowl, when it comes out."

Wiggins: "Oh."

Oakley: "I'm going to make some coffee. You want some?"

Girl: "Sure."

Wiggins: "*¡Ay Chihuahua!*"

Girl: "Berf, honey, are you okay?"

Pearl peeked through the curtains. The girl stood outside the bathroom door. Her jacket was unzipped. Pearl caught a glimpse of a shoulder holster and a gun. Damnation. More complications. This was not good. He pulled back and leaned against the wall.

Wiggins: "Sunny beaches!"

Girl: "Berf?"

Then the sound of a toilet flush and of running water. Pearl peeked in the window. The bathroom door opened and Wiggins came out, holding up the ring. "It's a boy!"

Complications or not, it was time to make his move while he had the element of surprise. Since the girl was armed, he'd have to take her out first, then get the ring, then get the nimrods out of the building and call Sully.

# CHAPTER FORTY-NINE

Segundo fished a wad of pesos from his pocket, dropped them on the bar, nodded at Luis, slid off the stool, and shuffled to the door. He'd only get a few hours sleep before he had to get up to start the baking at the *panaderia* across the street from the cathedral. His cinnamon *buñuelos* were very popular.

He'd had a few extra drinks tonight. That always happened when he saw Rita. Funny thing those gringos coming in the bar, and even funnier Rita leaving with them. What did it mean?

She was a little *marimacha* in primary school, tough like a boy. She knocked him down once. It was the only time they had ever touched.

By secondary school, she seemed to be all girl. If you didn't know, you would think she was as sweet as a *buñuelo*. But Segundo knew. She might be all girl on the outside, but she hadn't become sweetness on the inside. Her mother had to buy a doll for her to give away at her *Quinceañera* because none of her dolls had survived her childhood. Not that he was invited to her *Quinceañera*, but he came. Well, he was nearby.

Segundo knew about Rita. He saw things. He heard things. He deduced things. He might be poor, but he wasn't slow. She wasn't satisfied to stay here. She wasn't satisfied to get some coyote to ferry her across the river and clean some gringo's house either. She had ideas.

He found his feet taking him past Rita's place, like they often did after he'd had a few extra. He'd stand there under the window, under the moon, under her spell. Then he'd go home and draw with charcoal until it was time to take a shower. It was foolishness and he knew it. But what else could he do? Destiny didn't ask permission. And Segundo couldn't say no to destiny. Who could?

Segundo rounded the last corner and walked silently, his thoughts his only companion. Someone exited the apartment complex and ran down the street, away from Segundo, toward the boulevard. Segundo neared Rita's window.

What was that stain on the wall by the balcony? No, a shadow. It moved. Not a shadow. A man. Who held his arm like he held a weapon. Who moved from the railing to the door.

Segundo searched for a weapon. He kicked a brick loose from a flower bed, hefted it to gauge its mass, and let it fly. Destiny never missed, and neither did Segundo.

# CHAPTER FIFTY

Kate sat at her desk in the back office of the SV building. They'd cleaned up the mess since yesterday. It was hard to believe it had only been twenty-four hours since she'd duct-taped Pearl to a chair and ran out the door into an insane kaleidoscope of emotions and events. Despite the drive from town to Hotel Row, her heart rate had not returned to normal. She wasn't used to having a gun jammed against her head and didn't think she ever would be.

Michael sat across the desk from Kate, no longer holding the gun on her, although it was handy in a shoulder holster. Sully was gone, back to the city to rendezvous with Pearl, who could evidently track Jake and Berf via the ring.

"I've reconsidered. I was too hasty in my judgment yesterday and too Draconian in my methods today. We're all professionals."

Kate listened to Michael's speech, staring at him without expression. She heard the words and understood them, but they didn't matter. She knew it was a sheer animal reaction, probably fueled by residual adrenaline, but at this point nothing Michael said made any difference. He might as well have been reciting the alphabet or reading the phone book. All she could see was the man who held a gun to her head and used her as leverage. To win.

"As you rightly pointed out, it was just a simple misunderstanding. While words have been spoken in anger, and perhaps rash actions have been taken, no irreversible harm has been done, and suitable compensation can be arranged for any inconvenience."

"Except for Mr. Summers."

Michael seemed startled to hear her speak. They were the first words she had spoken since they left the apartment.

"What?"

"Mr. Summers is dead."

"Oh. Right. That is unfortunate, and as you say, irreversible. That will have to be attended to, but I will make it my personal responsibility to do what can be done to set it right, insofar as it can."

Kate quit listening again. What would he do once he had the three of them together? She saw the wisdom of Jake and Berf escaping. Michael wasn't likely to take definitive measures until he cornered all three of them and recovered the ring, but she still felt a little resentment at the way they had abandoned her. Berf, well, that wasn't surprising, but Jake?

To be honest, if this had happened within the first day or two of their arrival, she would have expected him to run too. But he'd said some things in the past few days that had set her to wondering. And last night he was on the verge of saying something big. She'd felt it. Since then he'd not been so impressive, perhaps, but whose life prepares them to be captured and threatened with execution? He'd done what he could to get them out and had almost succeeded. Actually, he did succeed, and they would have escaped if Berf hadn't unwittingly brought along a homing beacon.

She tried to visualize Jake in Micronesia. It had been difficult last night, but after today's adventures, it seemed more possible. And seeing Jim's face when Jake showed up at the clinic, now that would be amusing. Jim would probably go all medical on them, flaunting bewildering terminology in a territorial display of exotic plumage.

Michael was talking about financial settlements and use of his personal jet to the destination of their choosing and other trivial details of things that didn't matter. They were the roaring of a monster. They had no meaning. They were just sounds.

# CHAPTER FIFTY-ONE

As the van pulled up to the SV office, Runyon moved to the back. Fernando crawled over the console, his pistol in his hand.

Runyon checked the Uzi. "Do we go in easy or hard?"

Fernando stared at him blankly.

"Cut the power and hit them with flashbangs, or go in covertly?"

Fernando's face gradually took on a panicked expression.

"Okay, look. We don't know the situation in there, so it'll be tough to go in hot. We could walk into a firefight. You cover the back. I'll slip in the front, do some reconnaissance, and form a plan."

Fernando nodded, evidently relieved, and pulled the side door open. He jumped out and padded around the corner of the building, keeping low and to the shadows. Not a leader, that one, but a damn fine follower. Runyon could use a guy like that.

Runyon sprinted to the front door. It was locked, but that was no more a barrier to him than it had been the time before. He was inside without a sound in twenty seconds. He remembered the layout from his previous visit. The front office was dark, but light came from the back office. He slipped across the room noiselessly, stood to one side of the door, and inched it open. No reaction. He peered around the edge of the door.

Kate sat at a desk facing him, a thousand-yard stare in her eyes. Strange sat across from her, his back to the door. Runyon pushed the door open a few more inches. Kate gradually noticed him. He held a finger to his lips and stepped into the room.

Kate stared at Strange, who was saying something about closing down the venture and going back to specialty vacations of the non-lethal variety. Good luck with that, buddy. "What about Jake?" she said.

"What about him?"

"Will he be free to go?" Good. She was distracting him. She was golden.

It was working. Strange was obviously annoyed. "Of course. I just said we would deliver him to the destination of his choice."

Runyon was halfway across the room.

"And Berf?"

"Yes, him too. Both of them. Wherever they want to go."

"Safe?"

"Safe as houses."

"And what will you do?"

Gotcha. Runyon thumped the barrel of his gun up to the back of Strange's head. "I think he'll raise his hands slowly."

Strange's head remained motionless. He raised his hands.

Runyon turned to Kate. "And the gun?" Kate reached across the desk and slipped the gun from Strange's holster. Runyon held out a hand and she passed the gun to him. He put it in his jacket. "Where are the others?"

"They're after Jake and Berf."

"Did you find the laptop?"

Kate scanned the room, checked a few desk drawers, went in a supply closet, opened a safe, pulled out a laptop case, and returned.

"Good girl. Now we wait for the goons to come back with the ring."

# CHAPTER FIFTY-TWO

As Sully rounded the corner, the lights of the SUV flashed on the beat-up VW minibus. That would explain why the GPS led him here. But why would they come to the SV office? And were they armed? He pulled up behind the van, killed the engine, and jostled Pearl, who had nodded back off, drooling on the passenger window.

Pearl jerked awake. "Puppy biscuit." He shook his head. "What did she say?"

"They're here. You still got your gun, princess?"

Pearl shook his head, rubbed his eyes, then the back of his head, where a large knot was already visible.

Sully wasn't surprised, seeing as how the little weasel fell off the balcony. He was lucky his neck wasn't broke.

"Yeah, yeah, I got my gun."

"Okay. Just follow me and keep quiet. And don't shoot me."

Pearl followed him in, muttering.

Sully stopped. "Shut up. Not a sound." Pearl waved him forward with his gun.

Sully slipped through the front office and peered into the back room. Kate was on the left, holding a laptop case. Sully peered farther in. G.I. Joe held an Uzi on Strange, who was sitting in a chair with his hands on the back of his neck. He didn't see the rest of them. Not good.

G.I. Joe said, "Good girl. Now we wait for the goons to come back with the ring."

Sully pulled back into the front room. They were still waiting for Wiggins and Oakley to show up with the ring? A puzzling situation that didn't fit the facts as he understood them. According to the GPS, the ring was already here.

The first step was to regain control of the situation. Strange was fast on the uptake and Sully could turn these amateur's tricks against them and see how they liked it. He whispered to Pearl.

"I'm going to flip off the light." Pearl nodded his head. "I'll rush in. When I fire a single shot, you flip the light back on." He was counting on Strange to dive the moment he realized the lights were out. Pearl kept nodding, even after Sully stopped. Sully jostled him. "You got that?"

"Yeah. Light. Rush. Shot. Light."

"Don't screw it up or you'll have more to worry about than losing your dental plan."

And so it happened. Light. Rush. Pistol stock against G.I. Joe's head. Kick in the kidney. Knock him over the desk. Hear the Uzi clatter to the floor. Fire a shot into the ceiling. Light comes on as ceiling tiles rain down around him. His gun in G.I. Joe's face.

"How do you like *me* now, Percy?" Sully said.

Strange got up from the floor, dusted himself, straightened his creases, and shot his cuffs. "Good timing, Sully." He checked those present. "Where are Oakley and Wiggins?"

That changed Sully's tune. "They're not here?"

# CHAPTER FIFTY-THREE

Berf had to admit that Rita was a woman of uncommon sense. Every time he tried to bring her back to the most important point, she reminded him that Strange was tracking the ring and could catch up with them if they stayed in one place too long. First it was all rush back to the apartment, then it was impossible to talk about anything until they recovered the ring, then it was all "Where is Jake? He must have gone after Kate." Then it was a pulse-stopping nighttime trip through town on the back of her motorcycle where the wind caught every word he yelled and tossed it aside like a frayed bit of rawhide.

And that ring. He obviously hadn't been thinking of Chekhov and the gun on the mantelpiece when he set down that particular trail.

Berf had never shied away from doing his duty. After all, a man had to face a man's problems a man's way, and in the heat of the action he had choked down that ring like a goose swallowing a snail. But that was small potatoes compared to the excitement that awaited him back at the ranch.

In his worst moments, the nadir of his travail, he was almost moved to curse Strange for his inconsiderate ring size. Instead, there, alone in the crucible of that small room, he had faced his demons in stoic silence and pushed through to lay hold of the brass ring.

But the Berf who emerged from the *baño* in Rita's apartment was not the same Berf who went in. He was a changed man, a man with a broader view of life, no longer vexatious over every little bur under his saddle. And in addition he now possessed increased sympathy for chickens and other unfortunates that regularly expelled large objects through small orifices.

But despite his vow to avoid vexatiosity, if he could use that word, there was an 800-pound gorilla that had to be addressed.

As they approached the SV office, Fernando's van came into view, parked in a pool of light cast by the streetlight. There was a faint light visible through the front office window. Rita throttled up and blasted past down Kukulkan Drive. Berf watched the office recede, puzzled. Where was she going?

They passed a few hotels and veered down a service road. She pulled up to a loading dock and killed the engine. Berf dismounted as gingerly as possible while wearing skin-tight jeans, aware of the implications of every movement for the sphincter ani, both internus and externus. Rita got off the bike and pulled off her helmet, evidently unconcerned with the state of his sphincter.

Berf smoothed the ruffles on his shirt. "Why didn't you stop at the office?"

"Where's Strange's car? There are seven people. We don't know who's inside, who's in control, and who's waiting for us." Rita pulled a cell phone from a zippered pocket, dialed, waited, and hung up. "We must be very cautious, and from here on, you must be very quiet."

"Before we go . . ."

Rita already had her helmet on. She got back on the bike. Berf let out an economy-sized sigh and followed suit. They retraced their path, only much more slowly and quietly, coasting the last hundred yards.

It was a funny thing, really, when you thought about it. Up to now, as a drifter on the trail, Berf had been content to leave the unspoken unsaid. Too many times talking ruined things, scuffed off the shine of the moment and left it dull and lifeless.

But that was before he proposed.

Sure, he'd been engaged a half-dozen times or so, but he'd never actually proposed to anyone. In the usual case he would find himself in conversation with an agreeable woman of his acquaintance. A kind of "mind the music and the step and with the girls be handy" sort of thing. And then the next thing he knew she would wrap her arms around his neck and say, "Yes, Berf! I will!"

And then what was a man with a Code to do? Sure she had got ahold of the wrong end of the 'coon, but you didn't go breaking a woman's heart, cast her aside like a spent cartridge, just because she was momentarily confused.

Besides, Berf had learned that if you just gave her a little time, a woman would realize that you can't really tame a mustang without crushing the very thing that made it what it was. Then she would call it off on her own, without any assistance from him, and life would return to normal.

But what was normal anymore? A setting on a washing machine was what.

No doubt everyone in the room expected Berf to be relieved when Fernando revealed that they were working a case for the FBI, that the whole "marry my sister" thing was just part of their cover. Everyone including Rita, no doubt.

But what nobody seemed to realize was that, for the first time in more engagements than you could count on one hand, Berf had agreed to the marriage. Had actually given his word. And a man with a Code did not give his word lightly.

Yes, it was a monumental act of self-sacrifice, but they had not caught wind of the true monumentalness of it. Of what those ninety seconds of anguished silence in the minibus represented. Not capitulation to their scheme in an act of desperation. Far from it.

No, it was a man wrestling with his demons in the wilderness, asking himself whether this moment, here in this strange place, in this strange circumstance, in this strange way, could actually be his Ange Kerry moment. The point where a drifter who is always passing through, who has never dared to hope for more than a polite nod and tip of the hat, so to speak, finally discovers that Fate may have taken notice after all and tossed a diamond his way.

Rita was not your average bear. Unlike Berf's previous fiancées, she didn't seem intent on reforming him or molding him into her vision of what a husband should be. In fact, she could take a few smooths with a rough without missing a step and throw a curve ball or two of her own. And she seemed handy in a pinch, whether the knock on your door was from an ambassador or an assassin.

In short, for the first time in his life, he had found a woman who understood the Code.

Even though he had done the math a hundred times, Berf still couldn't believe that it had been a mere twenty-four hours since he had proposed. If you could call it that, and he certainly did. Since then things had happened too quickly to do much more than hang on for the ride, but that moment had been at the forefront of his mind for the better part of the last twenty-four hours, shaping his perception of everything that had transpired since.

Everyone else was preoccupied with other things. Berf understood that. But now it was just the two of them, and who knew what would happen next?

Rita stowed the bike in a patch of greenery fifty yards from the office and they proceeded on foot. A black SUV was now parked behind the VW minibus. Rita approached it slowly, checked inside, then went to the minibus. She dug around inside for a while, came out carrying an Uzi, and slipped Berf a handgun.

"Do you know how to use this?"

Berf nodded. You didn't survive the Wiggins household without learning to shoot out the eye of a gnat at fifty yards. But he'd never strapped one on, tied it down to his thigh with a strip of rawhide, and stepped out onto the main street at high noon, and he wasn't sure he wanted to start now.

Any Sackett knows that when a man straps on a gun, he'd better do it with the knowledge that he could end up on the receiving end of a hail of lead and the other guy could walk away. But he wasn't ready to shoot or be shot, and especially the latter. Not now. Not when so many questions remained unanswered.

Berf held the gun out to Rita, but she pushed it back to him. "Better to have it and not need it than the other way around. Stay by the front door. I'll go in and check."

Rita turned to go. Berf grasped her arm. She turned back, annoyed, but when she saw his face, her expression changed. To what, he couldn't be sure.

"Rita, I have to know."

She looked back at him the way he remembered, the way of his life before, back when he had only known theoretical death, death as a possibility, not a probability, back when the presumption of a tomorrow was implicit in the celebration of today.

She stroked his cheek with the back of her fingers. Her hand slid to the back of his head. She pulled him to her and kissed him. A luscious, giving kiss, full of promise. Her fingers clenched his hair in a fist and relaxed.

Then she pulled away, reluctantly it seemed to him, but it could have been his own heart he heard. He studied her, trying to hear her thoughts. Her long, straight black hair was pulled back into a ponytail and tucked into the collar of her leather jacket. Her bottomless eyes studied him back with an expression that could almost say anything he wanted it to.

His hand reached up to her face involuntarily. Her hand intercepted it and their fingers intertwined.

"No one knows what tomorrow holds," she whispered. "In the next minute, we might both be dead. But if not, then we will find out." She pulled her hand free.

Berf followed her as she slowly approached the building. He wanted to tell her, but there was no time. She was right. His question in the bar about the past was immaterial. It mattered not what he meant or what she meant but what she would do now that she knew.

The faint light visible through the front window went out. Rita stopped, flicking a restraining hand at Berf. Faint sounds of a struggle came through the glass, then a gunshot and the light came back on.

Rita entered the front door cautiously. As instructed, Berf stopped at the entrance. A crack of light came from an inner door. She slipped up to it, pulled something from her jacket, tossed it in the door, reached in, and flipped off the light.

A blinding light and a deafening concussion blasted through the crack in the door. Berf dropped the gun. Rita kicked the door open, flipped the light on, jerked somebody out of the room, and crashed in. The somebody stumbled over the receptionist's chair and collapsed on the floor. Berf scrambled to pick up the gun. He heard a burst of automatic fire.

Berf started for the inner door when something grabbed his shoulder and he shot a hole through the water cooler.

# Chapter Fifty-Four

When Jake heard that Strange had Kate, he kind of lost it for a second, but he quickly realized he had to make sure Berf made it back to Rita's place. She seemed capable of keeping him alive, so the first time she was distracted, he slipped out of the apartment, found a major intersection, and flagged down a taxi. Then he realized he had to give a destination.

Jake tried Strange's suite first. When he walked in, he remembered it was trashed out and they probably wouldn't be there. It was empty, but he found his clothes in the bedroom, sodden and heavy. He dug around in the mess and recovered wallets and passports and such. Then he ran to the SV office. As he approached, Jake heard an explosion and gunfire. He raced to the door and found Berf in the shadows.

If he had known Berf was packing, he probably would have said something instead of grabbing him. Jake considered himself lucky Berf shot just the water cooler.

"What's going on?" Jake hissed in Berf's ear.

Berf recoiled in horror, then gradually calmed as he recognized Jake. "Rita just went in there. I don't know who else is in there, but I heard shots."

Jake pushed past Berf, but Berf pulled him back.

"And somebody is behind that desk."

They crept forward and peered over the desk. A sliver of light fell across a body. It was Pearl, a large, painful-looking knot on the back of his head.

"One down," Jake whispered. He started forward when voices from the other room stopped him.

Rita: "Where's Strange?"

Kate: "He must have gone out the back."

Rita: "How is he?"

A pause. A groan. Cursing through clenched teeth. Sounded like Sully.

Runyon: "This one? He'll live."

Kate: "Here's the laptop. I'm done."

Berf leaned over to Jake. "That's all of them. Pearl here. Strange out the back. I guess Rita shot Sully." He started toward the door.

Rita: "I'll take that."

Runyon: "I don't think so."

Berf paused. There was noise of a scuffle.

Kate: "Derek! What—"

Jake pulled Berf back.

Runyon: "Keep the bag. You're coming with me."

Rita: "That's not part of the deal."

Runyon: "Jack Heald wants Kate."

Rita: "Who is Jack?"

Kate: "Jack Heald?"

Runyon: "Remember the guy you killed for $200 million? His son wants his money back."

That rocked Jake back a step. Who was Jack Heald and did Kate really kill him? Perhaps she was here in Cancún hiding out from a murder back home. After all, she did work for Strange Vacations where people were killed all the time. It made complete sense. The wheels came off when Frank got killed by accident and she ran, knowing that when people started asking questions, the trail would lead back to Heald. How could he have been so stupid as to fall for that do-gooder routine? Nobody's that good.

Kate: "I never wanted the money. I was headed back home to straighten it all out when Mr. Summers died and all this happened."

Or maybe somebody was that good. After all, when Frank died, Kate didn't run. She came to the hotel to warn them. She even said she had some kind of plan to get them out.

Runyon: "Well, now you're going to get that chance."

Of course Kate didn't kill this Heald guy, whoever he was. He had to get her out of there. Jake saw the setup in the next room in his mind's eye. Kate with the laptop. Runyon, one arm around her neck, the other holding a Rambo gun to her head. Rita with a weapon but powerless to use it.

Jake wanted to grab the pistol from Berf and burst through the door, diving in slow motion with the gun held sideways, gangster style like in the movies, pumping slugs into Runyon, watching the tectonic shocks undulate through his body with each hit, blood spurting out like blown squibs, a ballet of poetic justice and death. But that was the movies. In this world, ballet was expensive and boring, justice was rarely poetic, and shootouts were won by those who spent hours at the firing range, not by the VP with the bonus check. For an exec to close a deal like this, he needed leverage.

Jake grabbed Berf's arm and dragged him out the front door to the minibus.

"What?" Berf rasped.

"Start it up," Jake answered, running to the door on the other side.

Berf scrambled into the driver seat, cranking the VW to life.

Jake jumped in the back, leaving the side door open. "Remember how you backed that boat into the country club?"

Berf turned in the seat, a hurt expression on his face. "J-Bird, you know I—"

"It was brilliant. Do it again. Put this van right next to that scumbag. But be careful of Kate."

"And Rita." Berf smiled wickedly and slammed the stick into first. He was all in.

Jake caught the gleam in his eye. "To the right of the door. That's the sweet spot."

Berf jerked the van forward. Jake grabbed the back of the passenger seat. Berf slammed on the brake, shoved it into reverse, revved the engine, and popped the clutch. The van rocketed back. It crashed through the front office, obliterated the water cooler, and slammed through the back wall in a shower of sheetrock.

A spray of automatic gunfire perforated the back doors and sliced through the roof. Berf stood on the brake. Jake held on. The van stopped, mostly in the next room, with its nose protruding into the front office. Jake could see Pearl, still unconscious behind the receptionist desk.

Jake jumped out the side door and rushed to the back of the van. Runyon swung an Uzi in his direction. Kate pulled away from Runyon and slammed a bag into his head. He staggered back. Rita took him down with a flying kick. The Uzi slid across the floor.

Jake held a hand out to Kate. "Come on!"

She ran to him. He pushed her into the back seat of the van, jumped in next to her, and slammed the door shut.

Jake slapped the back of Berf's headrest. "Go!"

Berf stared out the back window. Jake followed his gaze. Rita stood with one foot on Runyon's chest, the barrel of an Uzi shoved up his nostrils.

"Go!" Jake yelled.

Berf hesitated and turned to him with an expression Jake had never seen from Berf, a lens Jake had peered through only a few times in his life. The view of the first clod of dirt on his dad's coffin. The sight of China walking away through the wreckage of the country club. The face of loss.

"Berf, we have to get out of here," Jake said softly.

Berf took a deep breath, shoved the minibus into first, and rumbled through the rubble.

Kate braced herself. "How did you—"

Berf cut the wheel away from Kukulkan toward the service road.

Jake grabbed the seat to avoid flying across the van and smiled at Kate. "Sorry about the transportation. The BMW wasn't available."

Kate seemed to be in shock. "Michael. He—"

Jake rested a hand on her shoulder. "He's back there. And you're here, with me." Berf whipped around a corner. "With us."

Jake caught Berf's eye in the rearview, a black hole of resignation. Something had happened after Jake left the apartment. Something big, whatever it was. Jake squinted a frown at Berf, a silent question. Berf looked away.

"You got the laptop," Jake said.

Kate responded like it counted for nothing. "Yeah. But what about the ring?"

Berf spoke from his funk. "I have the ring."

Jake slid his arm around Kate and wrapped his fingers around her shoulder. "And I have a plan. Putting a few thousand miles between you and Rambo."

Kate watched the palm trees flit past. "I guess I was wrong about him. And about you." She started. "Hey. Look."

Fernando stood under a streetlight on the sidewalk. He had Strange at gunpoint. Berf slowed.

"Keep going," Jake yelled.

"But that's Fernando," Berf said.

"I know. Look."

Fernando held a laptop case. They rolled past him, eyes on the case.

"Is that . . .?" Kate zipped the bag in her lap open. It was full of cash. Lots of cash. More than enough cash.

Berf glanced over his shoulder. "Hello, nurse!"

Jake watched the forms of Fernando and Michael fading into the distance. "I think we have just enough here to buy a flower. A desert flower."

# CHAPTER FIFTY-FIVE

It was Gus's favorite time of day, the first few hours of the night when the tourist frenzy went into temporary stasis, a lull between their daytime frolics and their nighttime revelries.

He sat in the dark, listened to the waters of the Nichupte Lagoon lap against the side of the *Desert Flower*, and enjoyed a snifter of brandy. VSOP. The only improvement would be if he were a hundred miles out, safe from the intrusions of the occasional drunk college girl trying to make her boyfriend jealous.

Gus felt restless. It was time for a change, but not another two-year circuit of the Caribbean. Something more. Something different. Maybe shoot the Horn and do the Pacific for a while. He could make a killing in Tahiti.

No, that wasn't it. The idea didn't excite him anymore. It was time for something completely different.

It came to him slowly as the satellite image in his mind swept over the surface of the globe. The Andes. The longest mountain range in the world, over 4,000 miles.

Twice as long as the Appalachian Trail. Had anybody ever hiked it end-to-end, from the top of Venezuela to the bottom of Chile?

Spider would know, might have even done it himself, but Gus hadn't seen Spider for a while. One night he's sharing a $400 bottle of tequila and talking philosophy, the next day he's gone. He'd turn up somewhere though. He always did.

Gus's thoughts were interrupted by footsteps on the pier. He rolled to his feet and stepped to the railing. Three people. Two of them stopped a ways back and one approached, carrying a briefcase. He passed under a security light.

Gus smiled. He liked this guy the first time he saw him, but after he came back from the dead towing a shark the size of Rhode Island, Gus loved him. He was of the brotherhood of ancient souls, a fellow traveler on the journey to enlightenment.

"Evening, Mr. Oakley." Gus held out a hand. "Care for a snifter?"

Jake took his hand. "I'm in the market for a boat."

# Chapter Fifty-Six

Berf watched as Jake disappeared into the cabin of the boat. That boy always did have a head on his shoulders, even if sometimes he forgot to use it. But he was on the right track this time. With a boat, you could pretty much disappear, leaving no tracks for the posse to follow.

No matter what happened, if Strange went to jail or went free, they'd be out of it. It was the perfect solution. So why did he feel like he'd swallowed a truckload of sand?

He stared across the lagoon at the lights of Cancún.

"Is it Rita?"

Berf glanced at Kate, startled out of his pensiveness, but didn't speak.

"She's an opportunist."

"I know."

"She's playing Fernando."

"I know."

"She'll play you if you stay."

"I know."

"You know all this."

Berf nodded.

"But it doesn't matter, does it?"

Berf knew it didn't make sense. He'd be the first to stage an intervention if Jake went off the rails like this. Any man with even a half-ounce of self-preservation would get on that boat. Go back home to his studio. Live the dream.

It was like Tell Sackett packing Kid Newton over the mountain in a blizzard. Almost dying to save the very man who tried to kill him about ninety pages earlier. Just plain inexplicable.

So why was it that the more he thought about going back to Austin, the more it felt like a life sentence?

Gus climbed out of the cabin and off the boat, carrying a large backpack, the kind you take when you're going to be gone a long time. Jake followed him, no longer carrying the case.

Gus walked past them. "Hey, Kate."

"Thanks, Gus."

Gus turned his gaze on Berf like he was about to say something, but he didn't.

Berf wished he had time to engage in conversation with this fellow traveler. He could tell they had much in common, were kindred spirits, men of the trail, used to the lonely places in this world, the far flung mountains, the vast deserts of the oceans.

But it was not to be. Perhaps in another life. Instead Berf just nodded solemnly.

Gus raised an eyebrow and was gone.

Berf pondered on that expression for a spell but decided it was probably the clothes. Not everyone could appreciate a man in ruffled blouse and jeans that fit like a second skin. Sometimes not even a kindred spirit.

# CHAPTER FIFTY-SEVEN

Jake gestured to the sailboat that they now owned free and clear. "All aboard, partners."

Kate stepped on deck. "Are you sure about this?"

Jake followed her onboard. "Absolutely. I know the Pacific Seacraft from stem to stern. No problem."

Kate stared at the boat like she'd never seen it before. Well, she hadn't, if you thought about it. Before it was just a boat you got on to do an excursion. Now she was part owner. Now it was her boat. That changed how you saw things.

In the moonlight, in Rita's dress, with that gleam in her eye . . . Jake took a deep breath. It was best to quit thinking and get to doing.

"No, I mean the clinic," Kate said. "The kids. It's nothing like your old life."

"I'm sick of my old life."

"It's primitive."

"I can do primitive. If I get tired of it, I can always live on the boat."

Jake turned to cast off and realized Berf was still on the pier.

"Berf, let's go."

Berf held up the ring. "Rita has the laptop. If she's going to get paid by the FBI, she'll need this too." He peered through the gloom back down Hotel Row. "Plus we're engaged. I think."

Jake stepped onto the pier. "Berf, a wise philosopher once told me to think before I talk."

Berf studied him. "And did that stop you?"

"Come to think of it, no." If it had, he wouldn't be here now with Kate, about to disappear into the seventy percent of the surface of the planet that was water.

Jake didn't know what Berf was up to. After all, it was Berf. Nobody knew what went on in the fun-house-mirror maze Berf called his brain. Jake dug into his pocket and pulled out the wedding ring that he had rescued from the clothes in Michael's room.

"Then you better take this too."

Berf reached for the ring. Jake grabbed his hand. "Berf, thanks for . . . for . . ." He couldn't finish the sentence. There was too much.

"No need for words, J-Bird. Not between us."

Berf always knew what to say. And what not to say. It was hard to leave him behind, but a man had to make his own choices and then live with them. Jake hugged Berf, a long, tight man hug, and stepped back. Maybe they'd cross paths again one day. He hoped so.

Jake got back on board. Berf cast off the lines, waved, and walked back to the minibus.

Jake cranked the auxiliary engine, pulled away from the pier, and headed toward the channel to the open water. They passed the SV office as the minibus skidded to a stop and Berf jumped out, the ruffles on his blouse waving as he ran to the door.

Strange, Sully, Pearl, and Runyon filed out of the building with their hands on their heads, followed by Fernando and Rita with Uzis.

Jake and Kate powered to the open sea without talking. He cut the engine, set the sails, and the silence settled in, the quietness of wind and water and his own thoughts. He stared into the shimmering trail on the water that led to the moon.

Kate put her hand on his shoulder. "Think he'll be okay?"

Jake wasn't sure. "The old Berf? No question. But now . . ."

Nothing could touch the old Berf. That Berf could survive anything. But this new Berf—who knew? Rita could make him or destroy him. He would come through it either way, but what would he be on the other side?

"It's a good thing," Kate said with conviction.

"I hope so. It's up to Rita now."

"No, it's still up to him. But probably for the first time in his life, he's playing for keeps."

Jake looked into Kate's eyes. "He's not the only one."

Kate looked back with an expression that could mean everything or nothing.

Jake heard Roger's voice in his head, felt Roger's finger on his chest. *Marge, the jury is still out on that boy.* Boom, boom, boom, boom.

Kate's eyes narrowed and she took a breath. Jake thought she was going to answer. Instead, she said, "So, does this mean we're partners on this boat, a two-way split?"

"Three way. Berf has sweat equity in it. Big time."
Kate frowned. "The ring," Jake said. Kate considered and
then nodded.

Jake reached for the rigging. "You ever sailed before?"

"No."

It was crazy. After a ten-year detour, after being seduced by the system, burying himself in a mountain
of stuff, and marrying the wrong woman. After almost
getting killed by fight-chair, Scuba-Doo, shark, skydive,
fire, and Uzi. It was like waking from a nightmare into a
dream life.

Jake smiled and shook his head. "Today is the tomorrow you dreamed about yesterday," he said to himself.

"What?"

What was it that Runyon said just before Jake de-
feated his evil plot? "So who is this Heald guy?"

"Which one?"

"Pick one."

"Dyke Heald was my last patient. He died at age
ninety-four."

"Did he really leave you $200 million?"

"Yes, but it's in the Netherlands."

Jake spun the wheel to the left. "Change of heading.
North by northeast. Next stop Amsterdam."

"Where Jack Heald is."

"Who's Jack Heald?"

"He's the guy who hired Derek to kidnap me, take
me back to the Netherlands, and put me on trial for the
murder of his father so he could invalidate the will."

Jake spun the wheel to the right.

"Change of heading. South by southeast. Next stop
Borneo."

"Micronesia."

"You heard me, woman! Like I said, next stop Micronesia."

Kate smiled and looked out to sea.

# Brad
# Whittington

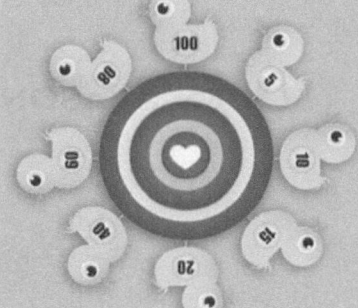

# OPEN
# SEASON

## A JAKE AND BERF STORY

# OPEN SEASON

# CHAPTER ONE

"When I was a mere tadpole, knee high to a grasshopper, my grandpa Wiggins gave me a Monopoly game. No surprise there. But my grandpa Berford gave me three gifts: a set of watercolors, a print by Remington, and a little book called *Sackett* by Louis L'Amour. Not much, you might say, Tom."

The cabbie said no such thing. Instead he turned east off Exposition Boulevard directly into the rising sun as it peeked above the tree line over Austin.

Berford Oswald Wiggins, riding shotgun as usual, flipped down the visor and continued.

"You may well think of it as not much. You might as well say the same thing about Einstein's first slide rule or Lincoln's first whisker or Stalin's first manic episode. Seemingly inconsequential at the time but monumental in retrospect. It changed the course of my life. Right then, right there."

Berf gestured. "Take a left here. Of course Dad didn't think much of it. Couldn't see how to turn it into money. Plus it came from his father-in-law, so he would have spurned it even if it had been the original plates from Fort Knox."

Tom raised an unkempt eyebrow as they slid through the dawn shadows pooling under the oaks in Tarrytown but otherwise declined to interrupt the story.

"Grandpa didn't know it, but when he handed me that box, he threw me a lifeline. Or maybe he did know. After all, he had a TV, just like every bully in my junior high. He saw the commercials. He must have guessed what I was going through. Pull up right here."

As they coasted to the curb, Berf cracked open the door and set one foot on the street. He handed Tom a scrap of paper and a Franklin. "Here you go, Tom. That's my cell number."

Tom crammed the cash and the note into his shirt pocket, which was already bulging with random scraps of paper and a crumpled pack of Marlboros. "Gotcha."

"Half now, half when you find it." Berf slid out of the taxi. Before he closed the door, he stuck his head back in. "Vintage 1966 Jaguar XKE. Silver with black interior."

"Got it all right here." Tom winked and tapped his forehead with the two fingers that held his cigarette, ashes dropping onto the ledge of his eyebrows.

"Thanks." Berf closed the door, knocked on the roof twice, and watched the cab disappear around the corner. Seemed like a nice guy, even if he did have an unfortunate resemblance to Kid Newton, especially that time in New Mexico when the Kid called out Tell Sackett. It was the eyes. Too close together. Squinty, you might say.

But that wasn't Tom's fault. As Berf had discovered in his twenty-nine years out here in the old west, a feller didn't get to choose his face, only his fate. And his wardrobe.

Confident that he had put his best man on the job, Berf turned toward his rambling, multi-level house nestled under an oak canopy. He breathed in the cool morning air and sighed with the anticipation of a quick breakfast and a solid day's sleep.

Then he caught sight of Jake in the bay window of the breakfast nook and remembered that he wasn't home alone. They locked eyes for a second before Jake slowly lifted the business section of *The Statesman* to block him out.

Berf preferred the sound of "Berf, party of one" when he returned to his Tarrytown fortress following a night of revelry. But when Jake showed up on his doorstep last month after disappearing into the jungles of Borneo for a year or so, Berf saw his duty and stepped forward.

It had been years since he had shared his campfire with a fellow drifter, and they were still working out the kinks. Jake was of the "early to bed, early to rise" school of thought, and this difference had caused a bit of domestic tension. Berf could appreciate Jake's philosophy, at least on a theoretical basis, but sometimes a feller had to bust loose from the traces and raise a little sand.

Berf checked his watch. Friday, 7:47 a.m. Just over an hour before Jake had to be at the salon. Well, Berf could manage a few minutes of awkward conversation, especially if supplied with a stiff cup of coffee. He sampled the breeze. And a slab of bacon, if he wasn't mistaken. You could always rely on Jake to scratch up a little grub in your hour of need.

He moseyed up the sidewalk to the front steps, across the sitting porch, and into the foyer. His reflection in the hall mirror pulled him up short.

His face was smudged, as if he had been shoveling coal in a locomotive, and his normally sleek black hair looked more like two mangy coons fighting. The ruffle on his shirt hung as limp as a haberdasher's handshake, and his bow tie circled his head like Willie Nelson's bandana. Not bad, considering.

These days Berf's bag of undomesticated oats was half empty. On any given evening he was more likely to be at home sitting by the fire with an improving book than out on the tiles running rampant and pilfering traffic signs.

But despite his sedentary and reflective nature, he did feel a certain obligation to set an example for the younger generation. After all, things should be done a certain way, and if a guy was going to paint the town red, tradition dictated that he at least get the hue right.

Berf glanced at the framed 1965 first-edition cover of *The Sackett Brand* hanging in the foyer and pushed open the swinging door to the kitchen as if daring Kid Newton to draw on him.

The only evidence of Jake's presence was a set of fingers curled around the wall of newspaper that hid his face. Berf let the door swing shut and dropped onto the chair opposite Jake. He draped an elbow over the back of the chair and snagged a slice of bacon. "Coffee?"

A hand slid a teapot from behind the newspaper. "Oolong tea."

Berf stared at the teapot as he would at a rattlesnake with a chip on its shoulder. He munched the bacon while considering whether to expend the effort to grind beans or to just cash in his chips and head off to the bunkhouse.

Jake's voice floated from behind the paper. "What happened to the Jag?"

"In the course of the evening festivities, I somehow became separated from my trusty steed."

"You must be heartbroken."

"I figure it was somewhere along the trail of the pub crawl that broke up at the Scoot Inn. But fear not. I have deputized a reliable confederate to locate the little filly and repatriate her to the Wiggins corral."

As Berf delivered this bit of information, a jingle and a few clicks sounded from under the table and a Jack Russell terrier sprang into the third chair.

Berf frowned at the dog and studied his back trail, paying particular attention to the driveway. "How does Hank come to be here?"

"Roger dropped him off."

Berf half rose from the chair. "Dad? Is he still here?"

"Gone to take Trixie to see the Great Wall of China."

Berf settled back in the chair and regarded Hank the Jack Russell with the reservation that a cowpoke fresh off the trail from Durango might regard a bottle of rotgut whiskey. Both offered certain entertainments, but the chances of an unwelcome ending were practically inescapable.

"Do me a kindness, then. Mark the date of Dad's return on the calendar so I can make arrangements to be in Tucumcari for the week."

Wherever Hank the Jack Russell was, Dad would eventually turn up, and through the years, Berf had taken strong measures to place as many miles of dead air as possible between himself and his father without having to forgo the sybaritic pleasures the greater Austin metropolitan area offered.

To say nothing of Trixie, Dad's new wife. Berf shuddered and scratched the dog behind the ears. "Is Hank *persona non grata* in the People's Republic?"

"Roger was afraid he would become an entrée." Jake folded the paper. "You know how them Chinese are," Jake said in a surprisingly good impression of Roger. "They'll cook anything,"

Berf gave the wiry dog an appraising glance. "More like an appetizer."

Jake set the paper aside and slid a stack of twenties across the table.

"What's that?" Berf asked after wrapping himself around another slice of bacon.

Hank the Jack Russell probed the air with a quivering nostril, but remained silent.

"Rent," Jake said.

Berf made no move to take it. "That's a lot of hairdos."

The money lay next to the jelly in the no-man's-land between them, silently reproaching Berf. He drew another bacon slice from the plate and poked the cash back toward Jake.

"Jackson's the accountant. Give it to him." Berf nibbled the bacon. "I'm the silent partner. Very silent. Think of me as Tell Sackett, riding beside you on the cattle drive from Laredo to Dodge City without saying a word. Wrapped in a Navajo rug, staring into the—"

"Not for the salon. For the room."

"Oh." Berf glanced at the pile of cash with even less enthusiasm. "Has it been a month already?"

Jake nodded at the newspaper. "November first."

Berf glanced at the paper and back to Jake, but his head snapped around for a closer look. Under the headline "Halloween Gala Is Scary Good," a large photograph featured Berf on one knee before a bevy of luscious debutantes, microphone in one hand, the other outstretched in song.

"'I Did It My Way?'" Jake asked.

Berf shook his head. "Probably 'Crazy.'" He pushed the paper aside with the bacon slice and gestured at the twenties. "You're going to need a deposit to get your own place." He bit off a chunk of bacon. "Plus it's mostly my fault. I introduced you to her. Although, in my defense, I was drunk at the time and—"

"There's plenty of blame to go around."

"Yes, but she's my sister. I knew better. Shoot, half of Austin knew better."

"And now I know better."

"That cinches it." Berf shoved the cash back to Jake's side of the table. After everything that had happened in Cancún, he owed Jake a lot more than one month's rent.

Jake picked up the twenties and fanned through them, pulled a brochure from the bottom of the stack, and set it on the table. "Or we could use it to drown our sorrows in Aruba for the weekend."

Berf snorted. "Aruba's great. If you want to go missing and end up with your driver's license photo in the tabloids."

"That lady disappeared almost ten years ago."

Berf shook his head. "Only one of many. You obviously haven't been keeping up with your tabloid reading."

The doorbell rang. Hank the Jack Russell leapt from the chair with a single yap and dashed to the swinging door, where he awaited a doorman to do the honors.

Berf picked up the brochure, glanced at the idyllic tropical scenes. "What next? Cancún again? Umbrella drinks?"

The bell rang again, this time in an urgent staccato that indicated a lack of good breeding. Berf tossed the brochure aside and looked at Jake. "You expecting someone?" Unlike many of the modern generation, Berf didn't allow bad manners to instill a sense of urgency. Let them ring was Berf's motto.

Jake shoved the money into his pocket. "I'll get it."

Berf glanced over his shoulder at Jake's retreating back and slurped down half the tea in Jake's cup. He took another look at the newspaper photo. He didn't have a recollection of that moment in the evening, or many other moments, for those keeping score at home, but providing amusement for the masses was just one of the many services he offered.

He turned the paper around to see it straight on. Not that he was the type of man to expect others to take notice, but he had to admit the photographer had captured something of his essence. Maybe he would clip it for his scrapbook.

Jake's overly loud voice interrupted his reflections. "Amelia! What a surprise!"

Despite the bolt of electricity that sizzled through Berf's nervous system, he had to smile. Setting aside Jake's questionable views on circadian rhythms, he was a good 'un and could be relied upon to give a feller a heads-up regarding an impending crisis.

In less time than it took Tell Sackett to snatch that kid from the wigwam in the Sierra Madres, Berf shot up from his chair, turned toward the door, hesitated, and then grabbed the last few slices of bacon before lighting a shuck to the safety of his bedroom suite.

Amelia was a jewel, practical and sympathetic, if a bit horsey around the face. The flower of good old pioneer stock, always ready to rescue a stray or do a good turn to those in need. But the unvarnished truth was that on such a morning as this, what a feller wanted was fewer Amelia Barkers and more closed shades and warm blankets pulled up to his chin as a vintage requiem on the iPod lulled him to the shores of Lethe.

But the hesitation for bacon had cost him. When he pushed through the swinging door, he ran into Amelia.

"Oh!" Amelia staggered back.

Jake, who was right behind, steadied her. Hank the Jack Russell sprang out of the way without a sound and stood by with wagging tail for further instructions.

"Well, Amelia Barker," Berf exclaimed. "If that don't beat all. We were just wondering what you were up to these days. Why, just a second ago I said to Jake, 'I wonder what Amelia Barker is up to these days.' Didn't I, Jake?"

Then he realized she was staring at the bacon strips in his hand. He held them out to her. "Bacon?"

Amelia selected a slice cautiously, as if expecting a trick, and held it in front of her like a candle at a memorial service. Her gaze wandered to his forehead.

Ah! The bow tie! He snatched it off his head and tossed it into the umbrella stand. Then he toasted her with a bacon strip and took a bite. Crunchy, yet chewy, just the way he liked them.

"So, Amelia, what brings you to Chateau Berf at this unlikely, if not ungodly, hour?"

She stood before him in the gloom of the hallway, a rangy woman with reddish-brownish hair and the expression of an assayer inspecting an unconvincing sample of iron pyrite. "You invited me to breakfast."

# Chapter Two

"Breakfast," Berf said. "Of course."

He ignored the exasperation emanating from the general vicinity of where Jake stood. It was entirely possible that Berf had invited Amelia to breakfast at some point in the past. She was a reliable trail hand and he had no reason to doubt her word. "What I meant was that we were wondering when you would get here. Right, Jake?"

He backed through the swinging door and held it open. "We're fresh out of cornflakes. How about flapjacks and cowboy coffee?"

Amelia hesitated. Hank the Jack Russell darted through the door and assumed his former position in the chair that backed to the bay window. Amelia took the seat facing the door.

"Come along, Jake, let's rustle up some grub for our guest."

"I have to get to the shop," Jake whispered.

"Where are your manners, pardner? Besides, we both know that place runs on autopilot and Suzie never schedules your appointments before noon."

Berf gestured him in. Jake snorted a sigh like an annoyed bull and pushed past him into the kitchen. Berf let the door swing closed.

"Amelia, you remember my ex-brother-in-law, Jake?"

"I was China's maid of honor," Amelia said. "As the best man, you escorted me down the aisle at their wedding."

"Of course I did." Berf had done his best to smooth out that little wrinkle in his hippocampus, with spotty results. He stepped to the pantry and rifled through the packages. "What are you in the mood for? Cheese toast and baked kale? Vienna sausage and biscuits? Sautéed asparagus with capers and salsa?"

Jake pulled Berf out of the pantry and extracted an onion from a net bag. "I'll make a Denver scramble."

"Say what you will about Jake, but he can sure put the groceries together. I'll whip up some coffee." Berf put on a kettle and poured beans into the hopper of a burr grinder.

He had to admit that seeing Amelia here, fresh as a mountain meadow and soft as a morning sunrise, unsettled him no little bit. They had a history, and though he had no desire to restore her to most favored nation status, he was not indifferent to her finer qualities. A sentiment that had landed him in her web when he was young and had not yet learned the value of caution when dealing with the gentler sex.

"I was just wondering when was the last time I saw you," Berf shouted over the grinder. "I said to Jake not ten minutes ago, 'Jake, when was the last time we saw Amelia?' Right, Jake?"

Jake declined to answer.

Amelia gazed at Berf with an expression that filled him with a vague sense of unease, like Tell Sackett noticing a broken branch on a trail where no branch should have been broken. An ambiguous expression, like she couldn't choose between annoyed and amused.

"It was last night. When you invited me to breakfast."

Berf masked his faux pas by dumping the grounds into the French press. "Ah, yes, at Justine's."

"At the gala." She glanced at the paper. "Just before you sang that song."

"Of course!" Berf poured the water over the grounds and set the timer. Then he looked for tasks that would save him from sitting down across the table from Amelia and looking into her eyes. He retrieved a carton of half-and-half from the fridge, set it on the table, and cleared away Jake's breakfast dishes.

"Are you still painting?" Amelia asked. "I loved the ones you did back in college. What was it? Space aliens sitting around a card table?"

"Mutants," Berf said.

A lot of people had liked those paintings. He'd paid cash for this Tarrytown house from the prints he'd sold on eBay. In the past few years he had moved on from photo unrealism, as he liked to call the genre he had invented. The new stuff didn't have the broad appeal of mutants playing poker, but had attracted the attention of galleries and collectors. In the words of the great philosopher Anatole, Berf could take a few smooths with a rough.

Amelia turned the newspaper so she could see the photo. "I always loved that song."

Berf moved the travel brochures to the buffet and tried to remember which song he had sung. "It's a good 'un."

Amelia smoothed the crease and hummed a melody. She sang a few lines softly. "When I'm alone with my fancies, I'll be with you, weaving romances and making believe they're true."

Ah, that was it. Berf suppressed a smile. Old Satchmo and "Kiss to Build a Dream On." That song used to reel them in by the dozens back in the day. In fact, Amelia was the first he had reeled in. Or was it the other way around?

Amelia glanced over at the stove where Jake sautéed onions, bell pepper, and ham, and lowered her voice. "I didn't realize Jake would be here. I mean, when you came back from Cancún you said he ran off to Bali or Java or somewhere with some nurse—"

"Borneo. He showed up on my doorstep last month."

"No wonder he's back," Amelia breathed. "It was too soon after your sister and he . . . well, they say you should give it a good year after a breakup before you try again."

"Very wise." Berf stepped to the counter and pushed the filter down on the French press. He poured three cups of coffee, left one for Jake, and took the chair opposite Amelia.

Rather than talk, he took a long, slow sip. Even black, like any good trail hand preferred, it was darkly rich without a hint of bitterness. He watched Amelia doctor hers until it looked more like hot chocolate.

Such was ever the way of the gentler sex, smoothing the rough edges, soothing the troubled waters, taming the wild things, blunting the red tooth and claw of nature.

It warmed the heart when you thought about it, this civilizing force in the world. After all, what was the point of man blazing trails through uncharted lands, carving out a patch in the wild places, if not for woman to come along behind and transform the wilderness into a paradise?

But that kind of civilizing took a special kind of woman. Someone who was about more than picking curtains and planting window boxes and keeping sensible hours. Someone who could flourish inside a paradox, who could see both sides of the coin without feeling the need to call heads or tails, who could embrace the tension of the philosopher-warrior.

A woman who could break a wild stallion without breaking his spirit.

Berf had found a woman like that once. Or thought he had, but in the end he came back to Austin without her.

"Just like old times," Amelia said.

Berf blinked at her, startled from his ruminations by the sentiment in her voice. He had let himself relax, like staring into the campfire until you lose your night vision and become unaware of the threats lurking in the shadows.

Amelia sat with her elbows on the table, the "Don't Mess with Texas" mug cradled in her two expertly manicured hands, and gazed at him through the steam.

"You and I," she said. "Together. Sipping coffee at sunrise."

He took another sip, reminded of one particular sunrise they had shared over breakfast. She had pulled an all-nighter studying for her finals in library science. He had stumbled into the diner after a dusk-to-dawn painting session fueled by martinis. It was the morning when he had . . .

"You put a quarter in the jukebox and played that song," Amelia whispered.

That song. The one he sang last night, if she was right, and she usually was.

Amelia's eyes flared. "And when it finished, you said—"

"Ah, yes." He remembered what he had done. Hit her with the one-two punch of Satchmo and Browning.

*Grow old along with me! The best is yet to be, the last of life, for which the first was made.*

And the next thing he had known, he was engaged to Amelia Barker, although he didn't remember actually saying the words. It just sort of happened. And not for the first time. There was the time when they were freshmen, just after they had watched *Big Fish* in the theater. It was a life lesson. Be wary of Tim Burton movies.

"And now here we are again," Amelia said. "Three's a charm." She reached across the table and took Berf's hand, the one that wasn't holding the coffee. "The best is yet to be."

This sounded disturbingly familiar. "Ah, well," Berf said. "Twenty-nine is hardly the last of life. More like the first, I should have thought."

"And it will only get better," Amelia said.

Berf studied her. Perhaps he was wrong about Amelia. Could she be that rare woman, the one in a gazillion? Maybe the first two times around he had been too young, too raw to recognize her mettle. One thing was for sure, she wasn't short of perseverance.

"I knew what you were thinking last night as soon as you started that song. The time has come." Amelia squeezed his hand.

"It has?" Berf glanced at the clock. "Oh, is that the time?" He jumped to his feet, pulling his hand from hers. He needed space to think. A lot of space. "I hate to cut this short, but I have a . . . thing. I was just headed out when you arrived."

Although the possibilities might be boiling around in his brain, he was not prepared to pull the trigger over a Denver scramble.

To Berf's surprise, Amelia smiled. "Oh, Berf, you haven't changed a bit after all these years. Too shy to show your true feelings. But I want you to know the answer is yes."

Berf stared at her, his mind racing for some way to unask a question that hadn't been asked. Was this how it had happened the first two times? "Well, the experts say one shouldn't rush into these things. Give it a year, you know."

Amelia stood just as Jake arrived at the table with a skillet full of breakfast goodness. "That looks wonderful! Since Berf has to go, could I take a doggie bag?"

Jake looked from her to Berf.

"Me too," Berf said. "I have this thing, but just roll it up in a tortilla and I'll have it on the way."

Jake shrugged, set the skillet on the stove, and pulled out some plastic containers.

Berf turned to Amelia. "Sorry, have to change. For this thing." He indicated the one-sleeved tux jacket. "But I'll catch up with you later."

"I'll come by this evening," Amelia said. "We can get drinks at Annie's and dinner at Bess Bistro."

Berf heard the last bit faintly because he was already through the swinging door and halfway down the hallway.

On the way up the stairs and down the hall, he discarded the amputee tux jacket, the tired ruffled shirt, the scuffed shoes, and the wrinkled pants in a sartorial trail that led to his bedroom.

She would be back in twelve hours. Could be ten. Either way, it was hardly enough time for him to process this notion, the possibility that what he had been looking for had been in his own backyard all along.

This type of thing was best pondered on the trail, wandering among the lonely places, maybe with a laconic partner off whom he could bounce the odd thought or conjecture. At any rate, the operative phrase for this moment was "somewhere else."

Berf barely looked up when Jake entered and held out a Denver scramble taco. "One for the road."

"Make one for yourself too."

Hank the Jack Russell scampered in and immediately began chasing Berf around the room as he dashed about in his undershirt, boxers, and socks, cramming clothes into a suitcase.

Jake leaned against the door and took a bite of the taco. "It's only Amelia."

"Only? You've met her, right?" He made room for a bottle of Bulleit bourbon. "It's only the slippery slope, the nose in the camel's tent, the gentle boiling of the frog. She has this way, this . . . thing where you think you have her just where you want her, and the next thing you know, it's the other way around and you're buying rings. And maybe . . ."

He stood and faced Jake. He couldn't explain, not here, not now, not even to himself. He'd deal with that when the time came. First the logistics. "You got those flight times for Aruba?"

Jake froze in mid-bite. His eyebrows flickered a good centimeter. "Don't toy with me, Berf."

"Someone can cover for you at the shop, right?"

"I can make some calls." Jake finished off the taco in two bites and stepped to the phone by the bed. As he reached for it, it rang.

Berf convulsed like he'd been jacked into the mains, scattering underwear around the room. "If it's Amelia—"

Jake calmly swallowed and picked up the phone. "Yes?" He glanced at Berf. "Hold on. He's right here." He held out the phone. "It's for you."

Berf took the phone and held it to his head like it was a gun. "Hello?"

"Berfman!" a voice blared from the receiver.

Berf pulled the phone away, shook his head, and then held the receiver somewhere in the proximity of his ear. "Chipster, are you vertical?"

"How's the head?" Chip asked.

Berf put his hand over the mouthpiece and turned to Jake. "No worries. It's just Chip."

Jake looked back with a weary stare. "I—"

"Since when do you care about my head?" Berf said into the phone and resumed his packing one-handed.

"You were feeling no pain last night. That's why I waited so late to call."

"Late? It's barely nine a.m."

"I'm already in the second hour of my tai chi routine. Look, I need a favor."

Berf hated to disappoint an old fraternity brother, but this was a clear case of every man for himself and devil take the hindmost. "Can it wait until next month? I have a flight to catch."

"I'd do it myself, but Zoe rushed me out right after your karaoke act. By the way, you still got the old special sauce."

"I aim to please."

"When are you going to lasso a filly of your own and settle down? You could have had your pick last night."

This comment hit a little too close to home for Berf's liking. "Don't start. Besides, when you snagged Zoe, you got the pick of the litter."

"That's why I'm calling." Chip's voice suddenly dropped to a whisper. "Can you pick up a ring at Langstrom's? I'm popping the question tonight."

"Chip, you old horse rustler! Congrats." Berf wasn't too surprised that things had come to this despite the fact that Chip and Zoe had been back together for maybe three months at most. Chip was known throughout the territories as a fast worker.

"It's a big decision, Chipmeister, but you won't regret it. Zoe Payne is a fine woman. Good old prairie stock, that one." And Berf was one to know. He'd been engaged to her three times himself.

"Thanks. Now about that ring."

"Any ring of yours is a ring of mine."

"Can you pick it up?"

"Why can't you get it? I'm in desperate straits. I can't go changing horses in the spur of a hat."

"I'm down at Payne's ranch."

"El Rancho del Bolero?" Berf straightened up in mid-pack, a stray sock dangling from his right hand. The tumblers realigned in his mind, unlocking a better exit strategy. A Hill Country retreat. Long western vistas. A well-stocked bar.

"I know it's a three-hour drive," Chip said. "But you wouldn't abandon a Sigma Chi on the big day, would you?"

A three-hour drive was three times better than a ten-hour flight, and a lot cheaper. And unlike Aruba, at the Payne ranch, Berf faced considerably less risk of becoming a record in the FBI missing-persons database. Plus if things really got desperate, it was halfway to Laredo and the border.

"How long will you be there?" Berf glanced at Jake, who regarded him with narrowed eyes as he leaned against the door.

"A week or two," Chip said.

Berf smiled. "Your legendary luck is sprouting in spades. I'm in the market for a remote getaway. How are you fixed for spare rooms?"

Jake pushed away from the door and took a step toward Berf.

"Got a house full of them," Chip replied.

That was all Berf needed to hear. "Where did you say this ring was?"

Jake waved his hands and mouthed an emphatic "No!"

"Langstrom's on San Jacinto. Paid for. An obscenely large diamond."

"One obscenely large diamond coming faster than you can say 'obscenely large diamond.' Book two rooms for the duration. Jake will ride shotgun to safeguard the cargo."

Jake threw up his hands and turned away, shaking his head.

Berf hung up the phone and tossed it on the bed. "Before Amelia can say 'prenup,' we'll be sipping Mexican martinis poolside in Bolero."

Jake spun around, pulled the cash out of his pocket, and waved it at Berf with such force that Hank began barking. "I said Aruba. Bolero is nothing like Aruba."

"True. For one thing, you can save all that cash for a bottle of premium tequila, because the rooms and meals are provided courtesy of Dr. Payne, proctologist to the stars. And the sunsets are spectacular."

Jake shoved the money back in his pocket and picked up Hank. "This doesn't solve anything. Amelia will still be here when you get back."

"If I get back," Berf said as he resumed packing. After all, he didn't yet know what fruit his cogitations would yield. "Remember my motto: take life one disaster at a time." He redistributed the boxers in rows rather than piles. "Also we'll have to take your Volvo. I'm short one car at the moment."

Jake turned without a word and walked out.

"Another bonus," Berf called after him. "Payne's ranch is on the southwest corner of the Hill Country. You'll feel like you just walked into a Sackett novel."

# CHAPTER THREE

It seemed like every other day JL Martinez boasted about being a self-made man. And Yvonne thought it was decent of him to take all the blame instead of trying to shift it onto someone else.

She squinted into the sunset and filed her nails as JL drove the Lexus LX 570 west on US 90. With the Friday rush hour traffic, it had taken over an hour to get out of San Antonio as far as Hondo.

The boys sat silently in the back, absorbed in their electronics, and JL was about to get on her last nerve with his lectures about how she should behave in respectable company.

"And no stories about your Uncle Thibodaux and growing up on the bayou. It may look like we're headed out to the middle of nowhere, but we're spending the weekend on a seventy-thousand acre ranch, not in a trailer park."

Yvonne smoothed out a jagged spot on her pinkie nail. "Maybe I should just wait in the car with the AC running."

JL slapped the steering wheel. "That's just the kind of smart aleck comment I don't need this weekend, Yvonne. The important thing is to stay positive. Upbeat! Grease the wheels and close the deal. We aren't driving all the way to Bolero so you can spend the weekend boring everyone with your personal problems."

Of course not. JL never wanted to talk about problems, personal or otherwise, in company or alone. He built his own business from the ground up, starting when he was still an undergrad at UTSA, tackling problems left and right, but ask him to talk to the boys about a problem at school and prepare to have your head taken off.

Yvonne opened a bottle of nail polish, Pole Dance Red, and pulled the brush out. Only half a bottle left. She made a mental note to buy more. "What exactly am I here for anyway?"

"God bless America, Yuh-vonne!"

She hated it when he called her that—the pronunciation she had left behind when she left the bayous for Texas. It meant he thought she had done something stupid.

JL rolled down all the windows at once with the push of a button, turning the car into a wind tunnel that undid two hours at the hair salon in two seconds. "Are you trying to gas us all?"

Yvonne cut her eyes over at JL. Built like an oil drum with a crew cut, forest green polo pullover, and khakis, what did he know about the effort required to put your best foot forward after two kids and a lifetime of pleasing everyone except yourself?

Sometimes she thought that if it wasn't for the kids, she'd just beat a trail back to Louisiana and let JL see how long he could last without her. That would fix his wagon right good. Wouldn't be forty-eight hours before he'd be on the phone begging her to come back.

The only reason she didn't was because she knew it wouldn't be twenty-four hours before she'd be clawing the screen off the door of her parent's house to escape. That was the reason she'd hooked up with JL in the first place. Back when he was thinner and nicer.

She screwed the top back on the polish, tossed it in her purse, and threw it to the floor. "Tell me again why you dragged me out here. I don't know the first thing about cows."

"It's a bull. Champion line."

Yvonne rolled up the one window she had control over. "Good for him. Why couldn't you just drive up by yourself and pick him up?"

"It's how these old-timers do business. Bring in the family, wine, dine, soften them up for the negotiation. Plus the boys could use some good country air. Right, Zachary?"

Of course he would try to get the kids to gang up against her, but she knew it wouldn't work. "Sure, if you can peel them away from their toys for half a second," Yvonne said.

Zachary glanced up from a Will Ferrell movie long enough to deliver a wordless sneer.

"Payne's got thousands of acres to explore. Canyons, arroyos, mesas, buttes. Sounds fun, right, Josiah?'

Josiah just grunted without missing a lick in the game he was playing.

"The trick is to play along, keep Payne happy, thinking his tactics are softening us up, and then at the end, you close in for the kill. That's the secret. Create the climate for success. Negotiation skills."

"Sure, José. Like that deal on the emus?"

She saw him wince but knew he wouldn't say anything. He hated being called José as much as she hated being called Yuh-vonne.

"What? I got a good deal on those emus. Fifty-percent of market value."

"Market? What market?"

"Who knew the emu market would tank?"

"Duh, I dunno. Maybe the guy who dumped them on you right before it tanked."

"Never mind that. The beef market has been stable for centuries. Tiny is a grand champion from excellent breeding stock. All we have to do is get him down on the price."

"Just what we need, a bull to frolic about with our emus."

"It's a no-brainer."

"Then you're the right man for the job."

Zachary snorted, which amused and surprised Yvonne. Who knew he was actually listening? She tossed a small smirk at him and he returned it.

JL took the turn north up TX 127 practically on two wheels, which was just plain crazy even if he wasn't pulling a cattle trailer. "That's just the kind of—"

"The kind of comment you don't need." Yvonne grabbed the armrest for support. "Tell you what. If I promise to behave, will you promise not to kill us all before we get there?"

# Acknowledgements

Thanks to the Austin Writer's Workshop for enduring countless drafts of the screenplay, Deanna for believing in the story from the beginning, and novel critique groups NIP and El Gee for picking up the torch.

Thanks to Rebecca Leach and Charlene Good for making the inside gooder and Hilary Combs for making the outside rock. It should be noted that both of them noted that "glintzy" is not a word, but when Berf decides to use a word, there's not much we can do about it.

Thanks to Bill for the nautical advice and Jackie for turning me on to Buckley, Jr.

— BRAD WHITTINGTON —

Sign up for the newsletter to get other sneak peeks and freebies.

BradWhittington.com

# About the Author

Brad Whittington was born in Fort Worth, Texas, on James Taylor's eighth birthday and Jack Kerouac's thirty-fourth birthday and is old enough to know better. He lives in Austin, Texas with The Woman. Previously he has been known to inhabit Hawaii, Ohio, South Carolina, Arizona, and Colorado, annoying people as a janitor, math teacher, field hand, computer programmer, brickyard worker, editor, resident Gentile in a Conservative synagogue, IT director, weed-cutter, and in a number of influential positions in other less notable professions. He is greatly loved and admired by all right-thinking citizens and enjoys a complete absence of cats and dogs at home.

BradWhittington.com